PASSAGES

THE DOORS ARE OPEN

LAZARUS SPIRAL II

T. KULP

ISBN: 978-1-956612-36-3 (Paperback)

ISBN: 978-1-956612-35-6 (eBook)

This novel is entirely a work of fiction. The names, characters and incidents portrayed in it are the work of the author's imagination. Any resemblance to actual persons, living or dead, events or localities is entirely coincidental.

T. Kulp asserts the moral right to be identified as the author of this work.

Making Adventure Publishing

16944 York Rd, Suite 63

Monkton, MD 21111

to eveyln,
may all doors open
to where you wish

OTHER BOOKS BY T. KULP

BLOTS

[dis]connection

Library of Lessons & Lies

Shadows, Stains, & Secrets

16

Early Birds Pay Double

Life Changing Yard Sale

Passages

Origins

BY TIM'S PEN NAME CY BORGMYN

Trial of Mirror Mountain

Treasure of Crumbling Cavern

The Light of Enki

Monsters Dance to Twilight

"When one door closes, another opens."
Alexander Graham Bell

"Don't ever take a fence down until
you know why it was put up."
Robert Frost

"The enemy of my enemy is my enemy's enemy.
No more. No less."
Howard Taylor

INTRODUCTION

Welcome to book two.

No, you don't need to read book one before you start here. Yes, it will provide some context and clarity, but you should be able to enjoy this read without it. Yes, this series is a collection of novellas that are all connected. Yes, I plan on sticking to that formula for the rest of the series.

These are the most common questions I've been asked, so I'll start with their answers here. The last common question, *Why is the series called* Lazarus Spiral? Well, you'll find that out in this book.

In book one, *Life Changing Yard Sale*, we discovered that toy collector Neil had died and his collection of haunted toys was sold off at yard sale. Of the four stories in that book, two happen before the yard sale and two after. This book's five stories follow the same design, with three being before the yard sale, and two after. While *Life Changing Yard Sale* introduced you to the world of Neil and his strange collection, this book, *Passages,* takes you deeper into his obsession, along with some familiar faces. Lucy, Nadia, and Trudy from the last book are back to understand the horrible events that unfolded after the yard sale. We'll also meet some new faces in this book that will be friends, and foes, in our journey through the series.

To be clear, when I began writing "29," the first story I wrote in *Life Changing Yard Sale*, I didn't fathom that it would be a series. It was just a fun short story that became a novella. By the end, I had so many questions that I wanted to explore, I just kept writing. Some of the stories I wrote appear in this book, some appear in the next, and others will be in future books. I had written most of this book before I fully completed *Life Changing Yard Sale* and was already neck deep into the third book's content. While I have planned out the series somewhat, you never know where your creative brain will take you, and so while there is a plan, that plan can change.

The *Lazarus Spiral* is deep with many doors, and there's always somebody willing to open them. I hope you enjoy this world and these toys as much as I have.

Now join me as we go deeper into the spiral and begin with the death of our main character, Neil Lessman.

Sincerely,

Tim

December 31, 2023

42

ONE

This was it. The last toy Neil needed. He could feel the finality of tonight's transaction, the last transaction, the trade he'd been waiting 30 years to make was going to finally happen; he was going to get his brother back. After so many deals, so many dark deeds done, Neil was finally going to help his brother how he should have helped him years ago.

And that moment was the first time he had thought about the last transaction with Bracker. "I was surprised to get your call," Neil said as he followed Bracker into the man's basement. "After our last trade, I didn't think I'd hear from you."

The coffin-width stairs made Neil's voice boom. Dark wood-paneled sides hugged Neil's large frame. He'd been making too many stops at Burger Boi and not enough stops at the gym. But these past few weeks hadn't made time for anything more than driving. Each wooden stair creaked under his heavy steps.

"Shit happens in this business." Bracker, a ghastly gaunt man, waved away the idea. The stairs didn't creak under his skeletal frame. His lumberjack wardrobe didn't match his frail body. Living this far out in the woods, Neil expected Bracker to have grown some weight from chopping firewood or whatever was necessary this far from any big box store. "Accidents happen."

The trade was no accident. Neil was aware that the toy was worthless, a piece of junk he was eager to eliminate from his collection. When Bracker agreed to the exchange, Neil forgot to mention the truth about the little matchbox car, which was as haunted as any ordinary piece of plastic could be. Neil swapped the car for Bracker's genie lamp, a coveted addition to his collection. Once the lamp was his, Neil's guilt over deceiving Bracker quickly vanished.

Now he followed the little man into his basement. Bracker was nervous. His call was stressed, almost pleading for Neil to come over for a special trade. According to Bracker, it had to be tonight, and so Neil drove a few hours to Bracker's cabin in the woods. When Neil arrived, Bracker was right to business. No offer for conversation, no sharing stories about their trades, just direct to the task at hand. Neil had seen this kind of behavior before, usually from someone who didn't know the world of haunted toys, but from someone like Bracker, someone deep in this world, the behavior was odd.

"Right over here." Bracker stepped off the stairs and turned the corner into his basement.

Neil followed.

The basement walls were the same dark wood of the stairs. Two exposed bulbs lit the area with harsh white light and razor-sharp shadows. Once, this place was a museum of possessed playthings; now it was an empty mausoleum. Neil was struck by the barren shelves. Not long ago this room was filled with toys. The heat of spiritual energy had radiated in this basement as if it were filled with space heaters. But now, all energy came from a single place, and it pulsed in the hot breath of a dragon ready to melt Neil.

"What happened…" Neil turned to the source of the dry hot breath and staggered back when he saw her.

"She did," Bracker said nervously. "Now we're done, right?" He turned to the doll on his workbench. "I did what you said." His words slurred in drunken panic. He motioned to Neil, an offering, a sacrifice to this doll.

On a plain white worktable, a three-foot Baby-B-Real doll, the toddler edition, sat staring at Neil. Her blue marble eyes were wide and unblinking under chaotic strands of black hair. She wore a mildew-coated pink shirt with blue jean overalls. Splotches and splashes stained the overalls in dark browns that could have been mud, blood, or both. Bare feet were caked with black muck, as were her fingernails. A general dirt crust dusted her vampiric pale plastic skin.

Neil nodded. Payback was a bitch. He recognized this toy, nicknamed *the Death Doll*. He'd heard about her online. Collectors slung tales of woe from their encounters with her. The world of haunted toys was filled with games and rules. This doll had one game, and that game had a time limit. Neil took out his smart phone and started a timer for 24 hours. All his life's work, shattered by a mistake from his past: one lie, one bad deal, that now led to everything falling apart. He'd failed. He'd failed his brother.

"She's not done with you until we've done our business." Neil cited one of the rules guiding the haunted toy trade. He'd never questioned the rules, only followed them. "I'm assuming you can't take a toy. How's a dollar?"

Bracker nodded quickly and held his quivering hand out to Neil. The gaunt man's eyes pleaded for Neil to make this quick, to free him of this burden. How close was Bracker to the 24-hour limit?

"Was I the first one you thought of?" Neil took the dollar from his pocket. He stared into the doll's blue marble eyes, searching for any sign of life.

Bracker nodded again. "You screwed me. I didn't want to do this to anyone else." He didn't apologize or try to explain, only shook with the pleading of a homeless man begging to be seen, to be helped.

Neil slapped the dollar in his hand. The trade complete, she was his problem now, but Neil knew that was the case from the moment she saw him. This doll wasn't like the other haunted toys. He never heard about its Resolution, the process of spiritual decoupling from the toy. Her rules were different, and he needed to discover them fast in order to survive the night. Thirty years of work depended on it.

"I'll get a case," Neil said and backed away from the doll, keeping his eyes firmly on hers.

"No need." The doll's mouth dropped open with a mechanical click. It didn't form words, only opened like a black pit and released the voice of a middle-aged woman, sharp and battle worn. "I can walk."

"We're done?" Bracker again motioned to Neil with the dollar crumpled in his hand.

"For now," she answered. "Don't make me come back." She didn't look at Bracker as she waddled, stiff knees and ankles, past the old man.

Neil felt the power, the heat, boiling off her like a fever. His mind spun to why he came here tonight. The final trade. She was it. With this much energy burning off her, she was the last thing he needed for his collection. Maybe the trade would be able to happen after all. And maybe she'd give him a break. If he explained to the doll what was happening, why he was doing this, would she cut him a deal? Neil laughed quietly at the thought. She wouldn't care. Dead things, haunted things, are not known for their empathy. He wanted to kill Bracker for this, for damning his brother, but that was the last line Neil hadn't crossed. He'd done so many horrible things, but never murder.

Ideas filled Neil's head as he started to piece together a plan for how to survive the night. He turned to the stairs and waved for the doll to follow. Blanketing himself with the confidence that he would find a way—with the knowledge that he always did—he asked the doll with a tone bordering bravado, "Ready to go?"

TWO

She paused at that, looked at him with those empty eyes, and slowly nodded. Her plastic head screeched against her plastic neck.

Before going upstairs, he looked at her little knee-less legs and asked, "Need any help with the stairs?"

Again, she paused and studied him. Now her empty eyes narrowed, but the plastic face didn't betray curiosity or insult. "No. I can navigate obstacles."

Neil wanted to see how she did this, but instead focused on his own ascent. His knees were bad, his heart worse. At the top of the stairs, he took a moment to catch his breath and checked on the doll. She was directly behind him. No sound, no effort, as if she teleported up the stairs. Neil staggered forward, keeping his hands from her, knowing that she couldn't touch him, but she could make it so *he'd* touch her. The touch, that would spark Resolution, and Neil didn't want to know what that meant for a doll rumored to kill on sight.

Neil remembered the lesson from his mentor Sister Wendy. She had once described Resolution as a spiritual entanglement, a concept that Neil found himself wrestling with now more than ever. He could still hear her voice, echoing in the back of his mind, explaining how the touch of human skin against a haunted object could bind their spirits together until certain obscure rules, called Resolution, were satisfied.

The rules of Resolution varied with each haunted toy, and while part of him yearned to uncover the doll's mysteries, his will to save his brother was stronger. Discussions on a haunted toy subreddit, where whispers of the Death Doll circulated, said this doll didn't have a conventional Resolution. Merely being seen by it was enough to forge a bond. Neil was skeptical, yet he didn't want to test the theory. The risk of entanglement, of becoming irrevocably bound to the doll, was a gamble Neil wasn't willing to take.

"Car's outside," Neil said.

They left Bracker's house without the host saying goodbye. Like a gentleman, Neil opened the door for the doll. She wobbled like a duck to the passenger side of Neil's station wagon and climbed in. Neil got in and started the car with a throaty hacking cough from the engine. For a moment, the car quaked and jittered as it decided if it wanted to start or not, then gave in, wheezing a quiet submission. Neil tried again to start the car, this time the engine only revved.

"Do you know how this works?" The doll asked.

"Yeah, usually it turns over on the third try," Neil answered and showed a smile.

"Not the car." Her tone sharpened as if scolding a child.

That made Neil smile on the inside. "Oh, you meant," he motioned between himself and her as he turned the car over again, and this time it choked to life with a vibrating hum. "You're like other toys," he said, leaning into the dismissiveness.

"I am nothing like *anything* you have ever encountered." The doll's eyes angled in her plastic face, defying the hard plastic's limitations. To her it was skin, and it moved like skin yet shined in the moonlight like dulled, dirty plastic. "You have 24 hours to disperse your collection or I will kill you and disperse it for you. There will be no negotiations. Don't bother begging. I don't sway," she said with a hint of pride.

Neil began forming a profile of the doll in his mind just as he did for all those he dealt with in this business. Pride and arrogance were tools he could use. She also assumed he knew nothing, and assumptions were always fatal.

"I don't beg." Neil put the car in reverse and rolled out of Bracker's driveway.

"Everyone begs," she said.

Neil opened his window to let some fresh air in. The heat baking off her was making his head spin. An early fall wind blew in to cool him. They rode down the well-maintained dirt road for a few moments as Neil wiped away the sweat pooling on his forehead. A county road met them quickly, and Neil sat at the stop sign for a moment.

What if she wasn't enough? Once he went home, he'd be done. No other chance. If she wasn't enough to make the trade for his brother, he'd be screwed. Tonight was his last chance to keep his promise, to save his brother, and there was no room for error.

He took out his phone and loaded the haunted toy subreddit.

"You got a name?" Neil asked as he tapped out a message to see if there were any collectors near him that would make a trade tonight.

He still had the toy originally meant for Bracker in his trunk. No sense going home if he could squeeze in another trade.

"Viola," the doll answered.

"Just Viola? Like Madonna, or Prince?"

"Their names were stage names. Mine is too complex for your language, and so I simplified it for you," Viola said with a dismissive sigh.

"A haunted doll that knows 80s pop. That's unexpected." Neil chuckled as he got a message from a trader. "Fan of the music?"

She shrugged, her joints squealing as they ground together. "Why do you care?"

"I like to know my killers."

"Killers? Plural?" She snapped back around too quickly for her joints to protest the motion.

Neil returned her shrug with his own joints popping. "I'm a popular guy." He settled the details of the trade with the collector online. "We've got a stop to make before we go home." The collector was an hour from Bracker's house, and that would still leave Neil 19 hours to deal with Viola's game if the trade for his brother wasn't enough. Neil put his phone on the magnetic charger in his car, the only thing modern about his car, and started Prince's *Purple Rain*.

Viola didn't protest.

As Prince screamed "Let's Go Crazy," Neil turned right and disappeared into the early evening traffic heading toward West Virginia.

THREE

"Why is there a 24-hour rule?" Neil asked after "When Doves Cry" ended.

"You must be given the opportunity to change." Viola's jaw opened and the words came out as before. When she was done speaking, her mouth closed, and she sat staring out the windshield into the empty road and the blackness beyond the headlights. Her marble eyes jittered as she watched the darkness. He didn't see anything, but she did. In quick glances, he could see her eyes tracking things in the dark. Deer and other woodland critters were common on empty highways like this span of I-68.

"But that isn't real change," Neil said. "That's a Scrooge change."

"Scrooge change?"

"Yeah, like, Scrooge changed on Christmas, but how long you think it was until he went back to being a bastard? People don't get shocked into being a new person." But as Neil said it, he didn't believe it. Isn't that what happened when Drew was taken? What he saw in the basement of his grandparents' house changed his life forever. Changed *him* forever.

Viola made a noise that might have been a breathless laugh.

"Scrooge change. Yes. Most people like you don't really change. They adjust to the moment and then fall back to their ways when they think I'm no longer watching."

"But you're always watching," Neil said, then paused. That sounded too knowing. He watched for any change in her, any sign that she saw more than he meant to show.

"Always," Viola answered. "Where are we going?"

Neil, thankful the comment went unnoticed, guarded his next words to ensure he didn't convey the worry he felt. "Graveyard." Neil shrugged. "Since I'm about to die, I figure I'd get one more toy before I do." He laughed and turned his voice dull to fulfill her perception of him being a dullard. "You know what they say, the man with the most toys in the end wins." He chuckled.

But trading in a graveyard was foolish. Haunted things attracted the attention of haunted things, and trading in a place like a graveyard was just courting disaster. This trader was new. Neil could tell by the arrogance displayed in the messages. Statements like, *I don't care what people say about you,* and, *We're doing this my way,* told Neil all he needed to know. This guy was new and didn't know he was stepping into a hornet's nest.

"How many do you have?" Viola asked. "Toys?" She didn't let on that the graveyard bothered her, but Neil thought he saw a shift in her demeanor.

"You are 42."

"I'm not part of your collection," Viola hissed.

"According to the rules, you are. I traded for you. The parties agreed on a fair transfer. You're mine," Neil pressed, seeing her face twitch. "When we get back, for the next," he glanced at his watch, "22 hours, you'll be in my collection—that is, if I don't get rid of it all like you asked."

Viola stiffened. "I do not belong to anyone. I'm not one of your *toys*." Her blue marble eyes quivered in the streetlights flashing above Neil's car. This was the closest he'd gotten to a violent reaction from her.

"Look like a toy to me." Neil kept focused, his mind zeroing in on what he wanted to know. "If you're not a toy, then what are you?"

Viola shook hard, her eyes narrowing, nostrils flaring, face creaking with the strain of stretching plastic. She lowered her head, blinked hard, and took a deep breath. She turned back to face forward. Neil had been caught in his plan, or she caught herself from saying more than she meant to.

Trying to recover his position, Neil asked, "So, you are a toy?"

But she answered his question with her own. "How much farther?"

"We're almost there." Neil kept the disappointment out of his voice and tried to get his positioning again. "We'll get the other toy tonight and head home. Two in one night. You and what I'm told is a marble with a galaxy in it." He watched for a reaction.

Nothing.

Pivoting, he tried to press with the same question in a different way. "Who was your first owner?"

"Why?"

"I love the history of toys like you," Neil said. "I jot it down in my journals at home."

She was silent for a moment. Neil assumed she was calculating what this information would give away. Then she answered, "Ely Adams."

"Ely Adams...?" It was Neil's turn to calculate, to recall a familiar name he couldn't place. "I don't think—" But then it clicked. Ely Adams was a toy collector everyone feared. The few people who traded with him did so only once and always at his home. They never went back after one interaction and often disappeared from the world of haunted toys altogether. "I think I've heard of him. He lived in West Virginia, near that haunted rail trail?" Something about old train tracks converted to hiking trails was always creepy to Neil, but this one had stories of ghosts, monsters, and murderers lurking around every bend.

Viola didn't move. Her jaw was already open. "The same."

"Didn't he die in a fire?" The news stories came back to Neil clearly now, with pictures showing the mammoth Adams estate gutted, a charred skeleton of what it once was. "He was a collector too."

Ely was, supposedly, dabbling in other worlds, forces that bound the spirits to the toys. Dark things that stained the soul worse than theft, blackmail, bribery, or even ignoring the crimes of a child killer. All things Neil had done, sometimes too often.

The choices that led to tonight could have been different. It wasn't just one bad trade, it was all the trades that led to it. The deals with child killers. The turning a blind eye to the origin of some of these toys. Going further back, it was his grandpa's heart attack that took him out of the house. It was what Drew did while Neil was at the hospital. It was Drew's choices that led to the heart attack. To their parents' death. But none of those choices foretold tonight and the ultimate end Neil knew was inevitable.

Neil shivered. Grandpa used to say *someone stepped over his grave* when he shivered like that. Was Viola the person stepping? Was Drew?

"Did you set the fire?" Neil asked.

Viola's mouth fell open. "He kept his collection." She shut her mouth.

"Who did he get you from?" Neil asked.

"He didn't."

"You found him?" Neil nodded knowingly, but Viola shook her head slowly, denying his assumptions.

"No. He found me." Viola turned to her window and watched the highway road signs pass. "How much farther?"

Choices led to tonight, and now a new choice formed in Neil's mind. Another stop could be the opportunity he needed to break free from Viola. She didn't want to talk about her past, being owned, she thought Neil a fool and less than her. But Ely Adams' house was little more than an hour away. Perhaps there he could find some answers. Maybe there he could find a way to finish his life's work, survive, and rid the world of the Death Doll.

They pulled off the highway outside of Morgantown and took the backroads to the graveyard suggested by the polite voice on the GPS.

"Stay in the car. I'll keep it running," Neil said. "I don't want to scare this guy off."

"He'll see me eventually," Viola said, disinterested. "Might as well be now. While he can change his ways."

Neil turned into the graveyard parking lot. A man in a jean jacket and white pants leaned against a sleek red sports car. Aviator sunglasses covered his sharp cheek bones. A single streetlight lit the small gravel parking lot. Fog gathered over the graveyard diffusing the light into an orange haze. As Neil stopped, his headlights caught the glint of a knife in the man's hand. He had it tucked tight in his folded arms.

The knife didn't bother Neil. He easily had 100 pounds and a foot or more on this guy. It was what Neil saw behind the man that gave him pause. Things more dangerous than a knife. He looked to Viola. She saw what he saw with those darting blue marble eyes.

"Stay in the car," Neil said and got out.

FOUR

This graveyard was old. Beyond the orange glow of the parking lot light were angled ruins of an old church. No moon tonight, no stars, just a cloud-riddled sky beyond the cornfields surrounding the graveyard. The night air tasted like a winter frost, but Neil knew that had nothing to do with the weather. Gravestones slashed through the brown grass and black mud smeared over the ground. Creeping around the tombs were hazy phantoms glaring hungrily at the man in the jean jacket.

Neil wasn't surprised to see ghosts lingering here. It's an old graveyard. Old graveyards have deep histories and deeper emotional resonance. Neil didn't know how a spirit got trapped in a toy, or why the dead couldn't move on, but he knew powerful emotions were the key. That's why toys were such a good thing to collect that spiritual energy: kids have the strongest emotions of all. Here, the spirits were hungry; this far from any main road, they must not see the living often. And lonely spirits are hungry. Everything in existence has to eat something, and from what Neil knew, the dead ate the living.

"Drawing attention?" Neil gestured towards the graves. The spirits, unafraid, moved closer, revealing bodies ravaged as if by a tempest of sharp blades, and heads devoid of features. Their arms, unnaturally elongated, ended in fingers that bent like the limbs of insects, sharp and menacing. Necks twisted grotesquely, allowing their heads to roll in aimless circles, their mouths agape in a macabre imitation of hunger, as if gasping for air in a futile attempt to breathe life into their spectral forms. They skittered across the gravestones, drawn to the intrusion of strangers into their domain

The man didn't look where Neil motioned. "No attention out here." His bravado was not plastered on like Neil's. It was genuine, clueless, and full of self-importance.

An iron fence surrounded the graveyard, and that gave Neil some comfort. Spirits were allergic to iron; most supernatural things were. The fence's gate was slightly askew, but Neil didn't think one of the spirits could fit through it. He didn't want to find out.

"Heard you were some big shit," the man said and pushed off his car. "Boogieman-level shit." He scoffed. "Look more like beardless Santa Claus, Pops."

Is fifty that old? Neil guessed to this twenty-something—probably wealthy, probably given everything in life—a 50-year-old man who had to work for everything all his life looked old. Neil felt old and just laughed at the kid, knowing a hard reality laid ahead of this boy if he stayed in the business of haunted toys. These things weighed heavily on you in time. No collectors were young for long.

"You don't see them?" Neil pointed to the graveyard.

"Don't try your shit here." The man waved the knife. "I'm here to trade and go."

Neil nodded. "Then let's trade." The kid couldn't see the spirits. He was really new. All the collectors eventually saw spirits; Sister Wendy said when you see them, they see you. When you know of haunted toys, the world of haunted things knows you. "I got mine, but I ain't getting any closer to that graveyard." Neil went to his trunk and got the container in the back.

"Did you bring a kid?" The man scoffed.

"That ain't no kid." Neil came around his car. "Keep away from her and you'll be fine."

"Don't try spookin' me. I know you're supposed to be big shit and all, but to me you're just some punk. Y'all bleed the same."

The spirits now moved closer, drooling for the heat of bloodshed. Neil wondered how their senses worked. Was it like a person, where sight was the dominant sense? Neil thought not. Instead, he believed there was a scent, more like a dog's primary sense, that the dead were attracted to. The smell of fear. Of violence. Of the negative vitriol that leaked from most people.

"Let's get the trade done. No need for nothing more." Neil came out from behind his car carrying the long plastic case. Inside, clearly visible from the streetlight, was a baseball bat.

The other man stood with a white cardboard cube box, the size of a baseball, in his hand. It was worn and yellowed with time. Rips in the box made Neil cautious. He placed his plastic container on the ground and went back to the trunk for a pair of leather gloves. Slipping them on, his attention was caught by a spirit daring to challenge the gate. It pressed forward, a desperate attempt marred by a misjudged angle that left its shoulder snagged against the iron. A hissing sizzle punctuated the moment as the iron seared its ethereal flesh, forcing it to recoil. Yet, driven by a hunger that overpowered its agony, the spirit gathered itself for another charge. With a frenzied burst, it breached the barrier, wisps of smoke trailing from its singed form, a testament to its determination.

The spirit's hunger was palpable, its mouth agape in a grotesque mimicry of longing as it inched closer to the living. Its gaze, if it could be called that, fixed on the man in the jean jacket. The man, noting the approach, tensed, an instinctive understanding of the threat drawing near. The air thickened with anticipation as the spirit, undeterred by the barrier it had overcome, moved with a slow, deliberate malice towards him.

Neil picked up the plastic container with the bat. "Don't move," he said quietly to the man and moved around the car quickly. "A spirit is coming toward you."

The man's brow twisted in comic dismissal. "Nice try."

"He's not lying," Viola said. She stepped out of the car and waddled her knee-less walk up to Neil. "You were a fool to select such a location for your transaction." Heat baked off her in waves, a stark contrast to the chill from the graveyard spirits. The crawling ghost reached for the man with long spindly fingers, but froze at Viola's voice.

"What the hell is that?!" The man screeched, still unaware of the icy claws held at bay by the doll. "What. The hell. Is that?" He stepped away, closer to the spirit.

Neil was curious to see what happened if the spirit got the man. Would it devour the flesh? The soul? What do spirits eat? Neil knew they fed off the living, emotion and lifeforce. That's why they congregated in emotional places like graveyards. Such places were feeding grounds.

Viola raised her arm in a straight, elbow-less point at the spirit. The spirit recoiled from her, retreating farther from the man. Its ethereal form pressed against the cold iron gate. As it made contact, a faint sizzle whispered into the air, the sound of spectral energy melting on iron. Its visage, a haunting tableau of conflicting emotions, flipped between a desperate escape from the doll's gaze and an insatiable hunger, born from a long starvation.

"Come this way, away from the graveyard, and we'll complete our business." Neil presented the container with the baseball bat. "As promised, this is the Maroni baseball bat that was used to murder his mistress." Neil invited the man to come closer and see the bat, but he didn't move. Didn't step away from the spirit. He only stepped back away from Viola, again toward the spirit.

"You said you had something special? Something unique? What is it?" Neil said softly to change the direction of this situation. But it was too late.

The spirit's eyes jumped from Viola to the man, hunger winning. It reached its prey, leeching onto his ankle with an unhinged jaw. The man swayed, instantly exhausted as the spirit drank deep from his lifeforce. Neil closed his container and moved to catch the other man, but the spirit hissed at him to stay away. Neil stopped.

Viola took a wobbling step forward, her arm still held out. The man being eaten weakly screamed and tried to shield his face from her. A whip of lightning slashed out from Viola's fingertips and split the spirit from the shoulder down. It howled and evaporated in blue electrical smoke. Neil sprung back from Viola and stumbled to the ground.

The man's color instantly returned. "Yeah, you see her too?!" He pointed at the doll as she lowered her arm. Neil looked at him, then at Viola. The spirits in the graveyard cowered behind their tombs.

"You didn't see that?" Neil searched the man's face to understand what he saw. "The flash?"

"He cannot," Viola said and returned to her door. "Please complete this transaction. We have business elsewhere." She climbed into the car and closed the door.

Neil panted, recovering from whatever Viola did. What *did* she do? She sliced that spirit in half with her…what? Weapon? Energy? The air still sizzled where Viola's lightning cracked, lingering long after it struck. "Well, you heard her." Neil pushed the baseball bat to the man with his foot. It slid across the gravel. Both men stared at each other, waiting for their breath to return and for the situation to regain whatever normalcy could occur in such a business dealing.

The other man stood and picked his box back up. "I heard about you. Heard you were weird." The man looked at Viola through the windshield. "But I thought it was all bullshit. A fish story."

"Most people do." Neil recomposed himself. The newbie didn't see what he saw. No spirits. No lightning whip. Just a creepy doll standing there with her hand out as if for a handshake. "You're new to this."

The man nodded quickly.

"Word of advice: Stay out of graveyards. Don't do business about the dead around the dead. They don't like it. Neither do I." Neil pushed his container at the man. "We done here?" Neil's eyes flicked back to Viola. "'Cause she says we are."

"Yeah, man. Yeah. Whatever she says. Here."

The two exchanged boxes. Neil could feel the weight of this new item, heavier than a glass marble should be. The extra weight was that of a curse. Perfect for his collection.

"Much obliged." Neil nodded and felt the warmth from inside the box. It was the real deal.

"Aren't you going to check it?"

"Already did." Neil chuckled as he went back to his car. "How'd you get this?"

"Family heirloom," the man said quietly as his eyes drifted into memory and a shiver rattled his shoulders. "Done with that family now. Your problem now."

Neil nodded and accepted his newest problem. At least this problem wasn't a problem yet. He wanted more of the story, and there was more, a lot more. But no time to chat now. Not in this place. The spirits were already starting to come out from hiding, some even testing a few steps toward the men.

"Leave here. Quickly." Neil pointed to the graveyard. "They don't care if you can see them. They see you." He got in the car and put the box from the man behind Viola's seat. "Why'd you help him?"

Neil backed out of the graveyard parking lot. The man got in his car quickly and sped away in a streak of red taillights from his sports car.

"It's my purpose," Viola answered. Her voice was sad, distant.

Neil nodded. "Can't deny your life's work."

Viola looked at him. Her blue marble eyes blinked slowly as her mouth opened. "A sacred mission is not a life's work. You choose your life's work. A sacred mission is thrust on you, a weight, a purpose that cannot be denied. No matter how much you try." Disdain took over her tone as she closed her mouth and turned back to the darkness outside the window.

Neil returned to the highway. He couldn't leave the words "sacred mission" and remembered something he read in Sister Wendy's journal all those years ago. The journal his brother used to summon demons and ultimately cost him his life. There were more than ghosts and demons in that journal. And Viola's story was getting clear. As he reached the highway, he took the west exit instead of the east toward his house.

"I have somewhere else to stop," he said as he opened his GPS app. He searched for the address and found it quickly. Tapping on the location, the directions loaded for him and Viola to go to the Adams' mansion.

Viola looked at the address and sighed. "You seek death."

Neil shrugged as if unbothered by the statement. "I seek answers."

"Let go of your collection. Be done and I will leave you. Life can begin again." Viola kept her eyes out the window. She didn't look at Neil, didn't need to. She knew the answer.

Neil considered it. The choices had led him here like dominoes, but if only one of those dominoes were plucked away, a different decision made, the chain could have ended. The doll, the marble; these things were enough to trade, but they were only an hour away from the Adams' house. What else could be learned there? What dominoes could be changed with the knowledge in that place?

Could Viola be freed? Could Neil escape her ultimatum? What if he still didn't have enough and needed something else? For years he'd been collecting the toys to enable him to get his brother back, but now, the secrets of Ely Adams could be the path forward.

Neil drove west, adding another stop before going home.

FIVE

"I figure we got three paths forward," Neil answered. "You kill me. I kill you. Or I free you from whatever is holding you here."

"Your third option is based on a false assumption," Viola said. No comment on the obvious, unmentioned fourth option: get rid of his collection.

"And that is?"

"That I can be freed."

Neil wanted to follow up with more questions, but felt the time for silence had come. The time for him to think, see the pieces of her puzzle he'd been collecting all night, determine how they made the picture of him surviving and getting his brother back.

***

They arrived at Ely Adams' estate an hour later. Home was four hours in the other direction. That left Neil with 17 hours. Plenty of time to complete the trade and get his brother back, if Neil had enough. Dodslav, the one who took his brother, was clear that when Neil had enough, it would come to him. That was 30 years ago. Was he close? Had he come so far just to be ended now by Bracker's vengeance? Having 30 years of work stolen from him for one bad trade didn't seem right, but there was so much wrong in this business, would he have known right if it bit him?

These thoughts flooded his mind as he drove on the highway. The rhythmic pulsing of the highway lights stretched longer and longer as he went down I-79. As they turned off onto 50, the lights stopped and the dark roads began. Viola didn't talk. Neil's phone lost connection and the music stopped. Radio stations found nothing but static. He turned off the sound, rolled down his window, and let the constant wind be his only distraction.

No other cars were on the road. It was after midnight, and this sleepy area of West Virginia had closed hours ago. A few churches spotted the road, two 7-Elevens, but no gas stations. Neil checked his fuel and saw it was getting low. There was a gas station back on I-79, and he could get back to it, but it wasn't time for that now. GPS told him to turn right off 50 onto a dirt road. The golden *Dead End* sign flared in his headlights as he continued down the small road that quickly turned to gravel.

Off that road was another gravel path, a narrow lane leading to their destination, according to the polite GPS voice. Viola and Neil bounced down the tree-lined road. Neil hoped his suspension held out. This road didn't have potholes, it had pits that were eager to pop a tire or eat a whole car. He drove slowly. They were enclosed in hulking trees that held branches over the road, making a tunnel so dark not even the headlights could pierce it. Neil wondered if the trees were hiding something from the night. Their branches covered the road so densely, not a single silver slice of moonlight broke through.

Cool air from the window blew away Viola's heat. But the air grew still, stagnant, dense as he drove deeper into the woods. The

stench of stale water, brackish and immobile, filled the air. He closed
the window, pausing as he noticed another thing about outside: it
was silent. No chirping bugs, no croaking frogs, not even a rustling
branch; the world beyond the trees was black and quiet and might
not have even existed.

He closed the window and turned on the air conditioning. It
groaned to life with a burst of dust out of the vents.

"You should not have come here," Viola whispered.

"Why?"

Viola didn't answer. Her hands curled into fists. She stopped
looking outside and now fixed her eyes on the dashboard map that
began to glitch. The arrow signifying their car's location flickered
as if the signal was lost. With the thick tree cover, this made sense,
but Neil could feel the energy outside. It was shifting. The mundane
normalcy was fading. Normal was left on the road off Route 50 as
they bounced into the dark.

"Anything I need to know about this place before we get there?"
Neil asked.

"You should not be here," Viola answered.

As Neil's car emerged from the dense tunnel of trees, the house
loomed before him—a monolithic gray specter of ruin. The road
curled into a roundabout, revealing the full, imposing scale of the
estate, now slowly succumbing to the relentless embrace of nature.
The once majestic façade was pocked with decay like cavities
burrowing into its yellowed-gray exterior. Deep slashes of black char
coiled around the windows and crumbling walls were a testament
to the violent fire. Above, the third floor lay in ruins, a gaping maw

open to the indifferent night sky, while the second floor's skeletal remains bore witness to the tragedy. In Neil's mind, the house was once a grand colonial mansion, a symbol of wealth and pride. Now, it was nothing more than a hollowed-out carcass, its windows shattered. Rotted vines crawled over its surface in a futile search for life. But there was no life here—only the haunting echoes of destruction and the charred remnants of a forgotten eccentric.

"This is where you came from?" Neil asked.

"No," Viola said. "This is where I was turned into this." She slowly raised her arms to imply her doll body.

Neil's car was still running, his headlights bathing the house in their harsh white cones of light. Long shadows stood motionless over the façade waiting to see what happened next. The engine choked but kept running.

"Wait." Neil tapped the steering wheel as the question formed. "You were Bound?"

Viola looked at the front door hanging askew, only the bottom hinge keeping it up. She nodded.

"He intentionally Bound you? Like, put you in this body?" Neil asked. He'd never heard such a thing. He understood the toys became haunted somehow, but never on purpose. The closest thing he'd ever seen to an intentional binding was that guy in Tennessee who was killing kids and keeping their toys as trophies. That monster was a good supplier for many years, but even *he* didn't make the toys haunted intentionally. "How?"

"Dark forces," Viola said quickly. "You shouldn't be here. I shouldn't be here."

But Neil saw the path forward. The way to fix his problem. Ely Adams must have kept notes or something about how he stuck Viola in this form. Maybe if he could find that, he could release her and, more importantly, he could build the artifacts he needed to complete the deal to get his brother back. This twist of fate was the doorway to completing his life's work, the loophole. All rules have loopholes, all games have some level of flex in their regulations, and this could be just what he needed to accomplish everything.

"We're here now. The answers to your problem, and mine, are inside. Unless everything was destroyed in the fire?" Neil asked hopefully.

"No. Not everything was destroyed. Fire can't purify everything." Viola shook her head. "No matter how much they should be." She looked at Neil. Her blue marble eyes softening, pleading. "Go home. Destroy your collection. You don't have to keep going."

Neil smiled, resignation mixed with determination. "But I do. I have to. I've come too far to stop. I'm too close." He shut off the car and got out. "Coming?" From the trunk, he got out a flashlight and some emergency flares.

Viola got out of the car and shut her door. She kept quiet as she waddled over to him and then followed as they walked to the front door.

Trees circled the property. Their branches leaned away from the house, reaching to escape this place. Above Neil, the sky was devoid of stars, moon, or even the faintest wisp of clouds; it seemed unnaturally barren. The absence of the sky lent an eerie quality to the scene, as if the very heavens were cowering from the horrors that saturated the grounds below. This void in the sky felt intentional, a cosmic aversion to whatever lived in this house.

Neil gently pulled on the heavy oak door. It fell off the last hinge holding it to the frame. It didn't slam on the floor. A muffled *poof* blew up a cloud of ash that swirled in Neil's flashlight beam.

"Where to?" Neil asked. "Where was Ely's library? I'm assuming it was a library?" He coughed through the ash cloud and covered his mouth. He still wore his leather gloves.

"You are never too far to change direction," Viola said, staring into the darkness of the house.

"My grandpa used to say something like that. He'd say, '*You're never too far to reach back and help someone else.*'" Neil stepped across the door's threshold. He thought of his brother. The fear and terror in Drew's face when he was taken. How Neil reached for Drew, but it was too late. He couldn't reach Drew. Hadn't been able to reach him for years at that point. No one could. But now, he was close. So close to getting his brother. To saving his brother. That would make everything right. The stealing. The dealing. The blind eyes and willing accomplices. Every shit thing he'd done to get here. It would all be worth it.

He continued into the darkness.

Viola followed.

SIX

Coming here was meant to get Viola talking with a trip down memory lane. It might prompt her to share something that showed Neil a way out of his predicament. But he did not expect the curiosity to be so intoxicating. As he walked into Ely Adams' house, seeing the aftermath of Viola's destruction, he wondered if she did this to everyone or was particularly cruel to her captor. What did Ely do here? What could *he* do with Ely's knowledge? Years of collecting could have been cut down to months if he knew how to do the things Ely could do. And now, here he was. The chance to be more than he ever was.

The house was once opulent. Neil could see that through the heavy fuzz of ash covering everything. He could see the perfect woodwork and symmetry of this house through the collapsed flooring and crumbled walls. Stained and rotten paintings hung on the walls with cracked frames. One painting survived, charred but still clear. It was an old man sitting in a throne-like chair. He wore a black cloak over a fine suit. A monstrous wooden bead necklace, each bead the size of a large man's fist, draped over his shoulders, with a stone spiral resting on his chest. Three black dogs—perhaps they were once another color, but the fire had charred them—sat at his feet. The dogs had long ears, long snouts, and green eyes. The green paint used had lost none of its vibrance over the years as the eyes of those dogs burned from the canvas.

"Ely?" Neil pointed at the painting with the flashlight. It was over a fireplace made of exposed stone. Neil could have easily walked inside it along with three friends his size, if he had any friends.

Viola nodded.

"The dogs die in the fire?" Neil fixed his flashlight on the creatures at Ely's feet. "Were they part of your body count?"

"They're not dogs," Viola said and walked away. "Follow me."

Neil looked again at the painting. Now he saw the creatures looked more like foxes, hyenas maybe…but no, not dogs. Too feral to be dogs. Their green eyes watched Neil as he moved throughout the room. He checked the corners of the room, those shadowy masses, to see if anyone else was there. Neil knew the feeling of being watched. It ran over his skin now, pulling up every hair on his arms as the eyes traced over him. No one was in the shadows. The green eyes in the painting hadn't moved.

Keeping an eye on the painting, he followed Viola out of the foyer into a large room. The door was broken, cast aside long before they arrived.

"The library," Viola said as she went to a collapsed desk at the far end of the room. "He spent most of his time here."

Neil followed her to the desk, scanning the room with his flashlight. A chill drifted over the air. He thought it was the night breeze, but knew better than to discount such a thing in a place like this.

Once the crown jewel of this mansion, the library now stood as a scarred relic of its past self. Its tall, ornate bookshelves reached toward the high ceiling, a stark contrast to the charred wood and peeling paint, testaments to the fire's intensity. The air was thick with the smell of burnt paper and damp rot, while ash covered surfaces and dulled the vibrant spines of books. Bitter flavors wafted through the air like dry flakes of burnt flesh and moist chunks of spoiled milk. Neil wasn't sure whether to hold his mouth, nose, or stomach to keep what little dinner he had eaten in his body.

"He wasn't a toy collector, was he?" Neil asked as he saw the books on the shelves. There were volumes he recognized—*Cryptic Symbols and Sigils* by Isabella Wraithwood, *The Shadowed Key* by Victor DeLacroix, *The Necronomicon* by Abdul Alhazred—but then he came to shelves of tomes he did not recognize. These books had their spines broken and pages worn around the edges from frequent use. *Grimoire of the Abyss* by Elias Blacktyrn, *The Dark Art of Interdimensional Travel* by Dr. Sebastian Elderthorn, *Codex Infestato* by Lorenzo Malatesta. He plucked the last one from the shelf. A thick crush of ash fell off, revealing the book's emerald leather cover with gold gilding. Neil opened it with a long, loud creak as the spine breathed for the first time in many years.

"What are you doing?" Viola whispered.

"Looking for answers," Neil answered, no whisper, as he flipped through the pages. Inside the book were diagrams similar to what he had seen in Sister Wendy's journal. He couldn't read them in her journal; they were in another language, like math was to English. Here the diagrams were clear, their purpose written in that same equation-oriented language.

Another cold breeze drifted through the house. Neil looked to Viola. "Do we need to be worried about that?"

"Die here. Die at home. Why are you worried? Your conclusion is becoming fixed every moment you waste."

There were hundreds, perhaps thousands of books in this library. Finding the one with the answers would take longer than Neil had. And if they all looked like these equations and diagrams, would he even know if he found the answer?

"Do you remember any of these books?" He asked. "Or, can you read this?" He showed her the pages.

Viola shook her head without looking. "No." She was lying.

"Did it happen in here?" Neil closed the book with a dusty pop. The sound bounced back to them from somewhere deep in the house, and with the echo came another cool breeze.

Viola shook her head. Her eyes were focused outside the library. They were looking down a hallway into a murky shadow.

"Where did it happen?"

"In the basement," Viola said and, as if on cue, another frozen gust blew over them. Neil saw Viola's hair sway. "I am not going down there."

This was not the first haunted house Neil had found. It wasn't even the first house filled with ancient evil tomes. His reputation for doing whatever it took to get the most horrible toys was well-earned, and a dark basement would never hold him back from his goals.

"Just point me in the right direction." A note on Ely's desk caught Neil's eye. He read it.

Descending the Lazarus Spiral leads only to one door. The door of dreams.

Neil pulled the note out to see what else was written, but there were only thick, black spirals drawn in deep scars on the paper. At the top of the page, written in stately font: *From the Desk of Ely Adams.* The spirals swirled into spirals of spirals. A casual observer would have thought the illustrator to be mad, but Neil knew better. He saw the pattern. The spiral of spirals rotating counterclockwise, or as the old-timers called it, withershins. No madness here, only the careful diagram of what Neil knew was the Lazarus Spiral.

"Where's the basement?" He asked as he pushed the paper back under the books.

Viola waddled out of the library toward the shadows she was watching. Her legs shook as if straining to bend them, but the grinding sound didn't break loose whatever was keeping her legs stiff. More grinding from her arms as they tried to flex, but nothing gave. Her plastic feet moved along the wooden floor with a rhythmic patting. Neil could hear the frustration in her steps as she marched toward an open doorframe that led to a lightless basement.

From the inky black, Neil felt slow pulses of cold wind blowing up. Viola stared down with him. He wondered if Viola knew what lurked in the basement, the thing that didn't die in the fire. Whatever it was, it was down there. It was cold. And it was hungry. A voracious thirst filled the house. Neil put a hand on the doorframe and descended further into the secrets of Ely Adams.

SEVEN

True to her word, Viola stayed at the top of the stairs. Neil went down alone.

His flashlight cast a narrow beam, revealing stairs dusted with ash and shrouded in darkness beyond. The stairs strained under Neil's heavy weight. Each step whined louder as he descended. Their cries echoed through the open space below and came back to him. He checked each stair but moved faster than he should have, eager to find answers down there, free himself of Viola, and leave.

The second-to-bottom stair snapped under his weight. Splinters leapt up in a cloud of thick bitter ash. Neil yelped as he fell through the stairs for a short drop to the concrete floor below. His heart raced, his breath lost to the shock. Dust and ash drifted down on him through a sparkling cloud caught by his flashlight beam.

Viola didn't call down after him.

"I'm fine," he groaned through tight ribs and aching joints. "I'm fine." He flashed the light up to Viola. She stood impassive at the doorway. She didn't care if he was fine. Neil nodded, shrugged, and scanned the basement.

As he stood, Neil found himself in a cavernous space. Charred wood bookshelves, towering and seemingly endless, lined the walls. Their burnt tang mixed with the smell of melted plastic in a pungent choking odor. The dim beam of light cast an otherworldly glow through the cloud that was still settling around him. To his left, the mundane world collided with the surreal—a cluster of house utilities huddled together in a very normal basement scene. They were rusted and broken but seemed out of place in this ancient home. It was a reminder that Ely Adams wasn't an ancient figure from long ago; he was recent. People were talking about him within the last few years, and this ancient carcass of a house had only recently turned decrepit.

To Neil's right, the basement stretched on, its vastness unknowable in this dark. His footsteps crunched in the ash like walking in a frozen snow. The sound echoed back to him on heavy air charged with the cold that signaled a winter storm. He walked to the first bookshelf he saw and scanned the shelves.

Melted toys dripped over the shelves in solidified plastic. He attempted to lift one, but it was inseparably bonded to the wooden storage unit. Most of the toys were unrecognizable, just puddles of once brightly colored plastic. The fire would have purged whatever spirits were contained within if the spirits were weak. Neil only knew two ways to destroy a haunted toy: Resolution and fire. Running water would paralyze the haunting, like flicking water on a spider, but once removed from the water, the spirit would still be bound to the toy. Fire, burning hot enough, could break whatever bound a spirit to this world if the spirit was weak.

Neil continued deeper into the basement.

The cool breeze caught him again. He froze and scanned the basement. His flashlight couldn't penetrate the murky expanse. The stairs were getting farther away, and now he could see that the second stair was broken, and the first stair was cracked from where he fell on it. To get back up the stairs he'd have to jump. That was going to make a quick exit difficult. Neil shook his head, pushing away the burrowing feeling that something was down here. He was being watched, and when it was time to leave, he'd be doing it in a hurry. This didn't stop him from pushing deeper into the basement's dark.

The stairs were out of the flashlight's range and had been for a few minutes. He checked his smart phone to see the time, but it didn't come on. After charging it all night, he nodded and knew an electromagnetic energy was coming from something down here, disrupting his electronics. Another thing that wasn't new for Neil but confirmed his suspicions: not all toys were destroyed in the fire. Something powerful was down here. Could it be the final thing to add to his collection? How many times did he think he had the final thing just to find yet another thing? His collection kept building.

Neil scanned the basement with his failing flashlight and found something other than bookshelves. Toward the center of the basement was a stone altar. It was once polished marble, now cracked and decayed, a rotten bone sticking out from the blistered concrete floor. He hadn't noticed until now how warped the floor was, how it rolled and bulged. The fire must have been as hot as an infernal blaze to reshape concrete.

Neil went to the altar and brushed the shelf of ash from the surface. A finely carved spiral on the altar. He noticed as he approached that his feet didn't crunch in the ash any longer. Pointing the flashlight to the ground, he was standing on a massive stone slab. Where ash should have been were streaks as if someone had swept. His flashlight couldn't find the edges of the slab, but when he spotted a deep curved ridge in the floor, he followed it.

Quickly, Neil understood he was walking in a spiral, tightening as he walked toward the center. A cold wind blew through the room again. He kept going, kept following the spiral to the center, and there he found what was breathing the cold air. In the center of the stone slab, at the center of the spiral, was a hole in the floor. A thatched bamboo ladder descended into the hole. He did not shine his light into it. He knew better and kept away from the edges.

In the world of haunted things, Neil had three mentors. One of them, the man who called himself Mr. Dream, told him clearly and early, *Never bring light into a place that's meant to be dark*. Neil had never seen a place this dark. No light could penetrate the basement, much less whatever was down there. He wondered if Ely Adams had done rituals down here, if light had ever touched this pit. He thought not. But the breathing continued. And breathing was the right word. Deep exhales of frostbitten air blew up from the hole in rhythmic gusts. Rational explanations flooded Neil's mind. There was an underground tunnel. The gusts were winds outside. An old well was down there, and some river somewhere was creating the drafts. But the stream of reasonable ideas was shoved aside by the manic, horrid reality, that wind doesn't make a wheezing noise as if breathed through a broken nose. Wind wasn't erratic in the gusts or rattles through phlegmy throats. Something was down there.

Neil backed away from the pit but paused. What if the answer he needed was down there? He edged his light closer to the pit, took a step closer, and stopped. This floor was a Lazarus Spiral, a model of one at least. Nothing good came from these. No answers. Drew sought answers here, and all he found was pain.

Neil turned away and followed the spiral pattern in the floor back away from the hole, from the ladder. He turned to his left where he thought the bookshelves were and walked straight ahead. The marble altar was at the edge of his flashlight after a few moments. On top of the altar was a book. Neil quickly scanned with his flashlight to see who put the book there. He checked the floor for footprints in the ash, but there were none. Did Viola follow him down? Neil moved to the altar. His flashlight darted around to see who was here with him. The light didn't break through the darkness around him.

The book's title was in a language Neil couldn't read. The words were pictograms, like hieroglyphics or kanji, but nothing like what he had seen before. A brass lock kept the brown book shut. Neil searched the altar for a key but found none. He looked again for who left the book, but saw no one, and so took the book.

Remembering where the shelves were in relation to the altar, Neil made his way back to them and then back to the staircase. He clenched the book tight to his chest and walked softly through the crunching ash. Behind him, a loud crack echoed through the basement. It was a falling broom, he knew it. That sound could be nothing else.

The icy breath of the thing in the pit hitched, choked, then stopped. Neil froze and listened. He focused on his own breathing, calming his heart, calming his mind to absorb what was happening in the dark around him. A quiet hollow tapping echoed behind him. The faint sound of bamboo tapping against stone. Neil moved quickly toward the staircase, now visible at the edge of his flashlight's glow. He held the book tight. This must be it. This must have the answer he was looking for. Questions on how it appeared on the altar, who put it there, who knocked over the broom, all fled his mind as he focused on the possibilities this tome could unlock.

Snarls broke through the darkness behind him; phlegmy snarls of something waking up, something angry its den was invaded. Neil gave up being quiet and ran to the stairs. Viola was standing on the fifth stair, reaching out to help him up. He reached for her, but she was too far.

He stepped up on the first stair to try and get to the third. One big step might do it, but the first stair crumbled under his weight. Bitter ash filled his nose and stung his eyes as the thing from the pit moved closer. It slid along the ashen floor with a wet sloshing sound, or a sharp clicking like a millipede sprinting toward him. Neil couldn't understand what he was hearing, but the primal danger sense within was screaming for him to escape. There were footsteps too, crunching through the ash. It was walking slowly, breathing in raspy sandpaper gasps.

"Give me your hand!" Viola reached down.

Neil reached up to her but couldn't get a grip.

"Jump!" She shouted. Her head flicked into the dark. Her eyes bulged. "Jump now!"

Neil dropped the book and jumped, reaching with both hands. She grabbed them with her own small plastic hands, holding him with unnatural strength. His right hand slipped out from the leather glove he was wearing, and he began to fall back. He reached up, Viola held out her hand, and he grabbed it. She flung him up the stairs and out the basement door. Viola followed, using her arms and legs to gallop up the stairs like a dog with all four legs in casts. She joined Neil in the foyer with a quick jittery motion.

"We have to go!" Viola shouted.

Whatever was slithering through the ash in the basement stopped at the stairs. The crunching footsteps stopped at the stairs too. A voice, decayed with rot and speaking through a raw, blistered throat, croaked, "Bring me the doll and the man."

Neil scrambled to his feet, picked up Viola, and ran for the front door. He glanced to the library as he left. The books, the knowledge in those books, they had the answers he needed all along, and now they were staying here as he ran away. Outside, he tossed Viola in the passenger seat and circled to the driver's door. Jumping in, he turned the key; it didn't start. He tried again: the headlights flickered on, but the car engine wheezed. The car's headlights illuminated the creature from the pit, it couldn't be anything else. It hung from the top of the door frame, dripping down in a wall of sludge as hundreds of spider legs stabbed out from the jelly-like body. Inside its body, the headlights twisted and glittered as the gelatinous form mounded on the doorstep.

Neil didn't need a better look; he turned the key again and the car sputtered to life. He threw it in reverse, whipped around, and hit high gear to get the hell out of there.

"Shit!" Neil screamed and slammed his hand on the steering wheel. "Shit! What the hell was that?! Shit!"

They raced down the rough road. The same potholes that threatened to devour the car earlier were throwing the car into the air, landing with metallic crunches, and Neil didn't slow down, he didn't let up; he pressed harder into the tunnel of trees. Branches clawed at the car with metallic screams, trying to hold them back, trying to give the monster whatever it wanted so it would leave them unscarred. Behind Neil, the creature from the pit was in the trees, its body searing the bark, snapping branches with its spindly legs as it tried to reach its prey.

"Shit! Is it following us?!" Neil looked back but couldn't see anything in the darkness without hitting his brakes, and that wasn't going to happen. The car roared as it hit a deep pothole, ripping off part of the front bumper as shrapnel flew away.

"You collect haunted toys. You see ghosts. And you are surprised to learn of creatures such as that?" Viola kept her eyes ahead.

"What was that? Who was that?" Neil thought about the book. The other person left the book. Did they leave it for him to find? "That book—"

"Are you ready to leave this world?" Viola asked. She turned to him. "Are you ready to destroy your collection and leave things like what you just saw behind forever?"

Neil finally noticed his missing glove. His sweaty hand slipped off the wheel as the car crunched over a deep pothole and went flying out onto the main road. Sparks flared up in front of the car as it bottomed out on the paved road. Neil gripped the steering wheel to straighten out; the tires screamed, but he didn't hit the brakes. He kept the accelerator down and his eyes forward. The haze of highway lights wasn't far. He knew he touched the doll, triggered her Resolution. Any escape now was impossible. His only hope was to complete the trade before she killed him. Another option, one he didn't want to consider, flashed in his mind. He pictured the item in his collection that could help him: Item 13. That might be his only option.

"Let's get home." Neil tapped the brakes to light up the road behind him a bloody red. At the edge of the tree tunnel was the blob of spider legs and a man standing beside it. The man wore a black cloak, charred and rotten. His face and hands were ancient, but Neil yelped when he saw the man's fingers. They were black, as if frost bitten but slick and dripping. Was it blood? A large wooden bead necklace hung around his neck with a spiral symbol in the center.

A question formed on Neil's tongue, but he didn't have the heart to let it go. The man in the cloak, the man in the basement, begged the question… Did Viola kill Ely Adams? Or did he find a way out? Could Neil?

They merged onto the highway and headed home.

EIGHT

Sunrise came and went as Neil drove in silence. The questions coiled and hissed in his mind. *Was that Ely Adams? How did he survive? Do I have enough to trade for my brother? What was in those books?*

Viola didn't talk. She stared into the passing darkness, and after sunrise, she watched the scenery race by as Neil drove home. They stopped once for gas and a snack. Viola didn't eat anything. Neil got the king-size Reese's bar. He'd never had one, but always wanted one and thought now was the time. He also got a Bavarian cream donut, a spicy chicken sandwich on a biscuit, and a bag of crab chips. All his favorites to make a last meal. The thought did occur to him with a chuckle that this food could lead to a heart attack while driving and that could be a way around Viola's attack, but that didn't happen.

He arrived at 1211 Gordon Avenue, his home, in the late morning.

Mrs. Morton was working in her garden. Her husband was barking commands about their azaleas and how he thought they looked terrible. She meekly responded how much she liked them, how pretty they were, but her arguments didn't sway him. Neil kept driving and gave a little wave that went unnoticed. He pulled into his garage and closed the door before getting out.

"Is there anyone else inside?" Viola asked.

Neil shook his head. "Just you and me."

She didn't wait for further clarity, simply stood at his door and waited for him to go in. Neil knew this was only a politeness. He'd touched her. Skin to plastic. She didn't need his permission to enter the house, to do whatever she wanted—he had touched her and, in doing so, activated Resolution. Time had run out. The 24-hour rule probably didn't apply anymore either, but he hoped to stall a bit longer.

"The collection is in the basement, but first," Neil opened the door, "could I show you my workshop and clean you up some?" He motioned inside like a gentleman.

"Why?" Viola went in.

"I pride myself on my collection, and if you are dirty, it's a reflection on my care." Neil pointed to her feet, her fingernails. "Let me do a quick scrub, then we'll go into the basement to discuss the collection."

Viola paused for a moment, calculating what Neil could be doing, and then nodded slowly, seeing only a delay. And that was indeed his angle. To delay, and hope that the creature he had to trade with came when it felt the presence of Viola and this final toy.

"This way." Neil closed the door and walked into his living room, leaving his shoes on the tile floor. He put the cubic box from the man in the graveyard on a small table along with his keys, wallet, and smart phone.

The living room was what you'd expect from a middle-aged bachelor. A recliner and a sofa, both facing the TV, with a small coffee table in between. Flanking the television, twin towering bookcases stretched from floor to ceiling, their shelves a dense mosaic of well-thumbed volumes bearing the scars of frequent use. Each shelf was tightly packed, with books not only aligned in orderly ranks but also piled atop one another, filling every space up to the shelf above. Not another book could fit on any of the shelves, and so there were towers rising from the shaggy carpet. The piles were well-ordered, with all spines facing out in the same direction for easy reading. Two books were on the coffee table, *Gulliver's Travels* and an old atlas of the Middle East.

He knelt and plucked a red journal from the bottom shelf. His hand wandered over the coffee table as he flipped pages, passed one titled *Inventory Note 41,* and came to a blank page. Finding a pen in the table's mess, he quickly scribbled on the page: *Inventory Note 42. Ely's Doll. Do not touch.* He flipped to the next page, then felt a faint breeze, cool and quick near the floor. It came from the hallway behind him, the hallway to the basement. No time to document the marble galaxy he got from the man in the graveyard. Neil put the journal back and tossed the pen back onto the table.

"Right this way." Neil turned down a hallway, flicking on lights as he went. All the lights were a lifeless white, more like a hospital than a home. The walls were a faint off-white, giving the hint of possible color but no clear personality to the blank, pictureless surfaces. He turned into a room and clicked on another white light. Viola followed.

This room was a workshop with pegboard walls holding tools of all shapes and sizes. Some tools were common to any workshop, such as hammers, screwdrivers, drills, and saws, but others signified the specific work done in this workshop: spools of thread, bolts of fabric, sewing needles, and containers filled with small parts. The containers were open-top plastic rectangular buckets on a shelving unit. Each had a label: *eyes, hands, wheels*, etc. On another wall were all the paints one could ever need to touch up any small object. There were spray paints, acrylic paints, brushes, drying racks.

"Do you consider yourself a craftsman?" Viola asked as she looked around the room.

Neil shrugged.

"My grandpa always said, if you're going to do something, do it right." Neil patted the workbench for Viola to climb onto. She did. "Go ahead and lay down and I'll get you fixed up. Just need to get something from the basement real quick before I get started."

She laid down. Neil wasn't sure if it was certainty on her part or curiosity to see what Neil would do next that led to her going along.

He left the room and went to the next door in the hallway. It opened silently with a cool chill gushing out. Neil knew that chill. His breath became fog in front of him as he walked down the stairs quickly. Each step was steel and silent as he reached the plush crimson carpet. The lights came on as he entered the basement, motion detectors awakening to his presence.

Red oak shelves lined the walls, filled with his collection. The toys were spaced like museum exhibits, each with a white paper tent in front of them showing a number in black ink. The blue big wheel bike, #6; the telephone with a creepy face, #7; a jack-in-the-box, #11; and the item he came down here for…a small white box labeled #13.

No matter why he came down here, he always went directly to the only toy not on a shelf. It was the dollhouse on a small table in the center of the basement. He reached out to it with his bare hand and felt the cool air, turning cold, drifting from the house. A spiral was carved into the basement of the dollhouse, and that was the source of the wind. This microcosm of the Adams' house made Neil wonder if Drew knew about Ely Adams. If his brother knew about how Ely carved a Lazarus Spiral, just like this, into his own basement. After 30 years of nothing, the spiral was coming to life. Neil was right. The Death Doll and the other toy was enough to summon the demon who took his brother. This was the cold of that night. When Drew was taken, and again when Neil summoned the demon to negotiate.

Time was running faster than he thought. The cold wasn't in puffs or weak wisps, but a solid stream making condensation on the walls, crystallizing the mists to ice.

Neil hurried to item 13 and pulled it out of the box. He didn't worry about gloves, he needed to wake the toy up. He needed to be ready for whatever happened next.

Item 13 was a small wire figure dressed in a Hawaiian shirt and flowery shorts. It was in T-pose waiting to be formed into a position. Neil held it in his hand and nodded. This item was a worry person, a shaved pipe cleaner twisted into a human form with two arms, two legs, and a wooden bead for a head. The myth of worry people was that you could tell them your worries and they'd think about them at night so you could have pleasant dreams. Neil knew this worry person did much more than worry for you; it could hold your consciousness like a safe.

From the center of the spiral, a faint blue light brightened. The light traced the spiral as the demon within navigated from its home in that dollhouse into the real world.

Neil hurried back upstairs to get the other toy, the marble he got from the man in the graveyard. But Viola was standing at the top of the stairs. She glared down, disapproving but resigned.

"Did you summon it?" She asked.

Neil shook his head. "It was waiting for me." He shrugged. "Waiting for my collection to be ready."

Viola hopped down the stairs slowly, mechanically taking each step with her knee-less hobble. "You never collected toys. You are not like the others." She was calm and slow as she descended the stairs, her demeanor switching from confident predator to cautious hunter. "Did it begin with the toys? Was it ever about the toys?"

Neil shook his head. "It began with my brother. I just want him back." Neil stepped away from the stairs, staying between her and his collection. "If I could get enough, I could trade it for him."

"Enough?" Viola asked.

The cold thickened and brought with it the convulsive chattering of an arctic night. "Spiritual energy. There's lots of words for it, but whatever the energy is that makes you more than just a doll."

"You did this intentionally?" Viola asked. Confusion overtook her. "Why? Why would you?" She quickly moved to the dollhouse. The spiral was filling with blue light. "You wanted this to happen? You wanted them to come?" She looked for an explanation in Neil's eyes. "Who's coming? Do you know?"

"I want my brother back." Neil pointed to the floor, anger curdling inside him. "Drew didn't know what he was doing. He shouldn't have to pay for that forever. It was a mistake! He needs me to get him out of there."

"I thought you were just a fool. A meddler in things you didn't understand." Viola shook her head. "But you are so much worse. Just like Ely. Do you know what they do with this energy?" She motioned to the collection. "Do you know—"

"I don't care!" Neil barked. "I've worked my entire life to get Drew back, to get Drew out of his mess! And now we're here! We're going to make this work!"

"Your life?" Viola scoffed. "Your life is a speck in time. My life!" She stomped toward him. "My life has been ages of trying to stop them! Trying to curb their machinations! And your kind just keeps handing them opportunities to poison this world! Poison all worlds!" Viola thrust her fingers at Neil's stomach, her arm reaching no higher. She would have pushed him in the chest if she could have reached. "You collectors are just farmers for them. You farm the crop they use to kill you. Kill all of us. But you don't care because you need to have your fill."

"I'm doing this for my brother!"

"No! You're doing it for you!" Viola said. "Your brother made his choice. You are doing this because you want to do this. You want to be who you've become, what you've done!"

Black smoke billowed out of the spiral. The blue light was now devoured in darkness as the cold intensified and thickened, suffocating and oppressive.

Neil shoved his hand into his pocket with item 13. He grabbed it and squeezed it tightly, letting the wire body puncture his palm. It was time. The demon who took Drew was here. The demon who called itself Dodslav. The trade, Neil's life work, was almost complete.

Viola scanned the room, her eyes seeing more than the toys, seeing the energy around them.

"Choose," she said. "Your time is up."

"It hasn't been 24 hours!" Neil said.

"When you activated Resolution, you lost that time." Viola would have spit on him if she had saliva. "And I see you will never release your collection willingly."

"Not true." Neil pointed to the black smoke solidifying behind her. "I'm about to release it right now."

Viola turned to face the onyx-black body stepping out from the envelope of smoke. The white mask it wore had two narrow slits for eyes and three sharp slashes up from the chin to where a nose should be but the black spiral in the forehead told her who this was.

"Dodslav!" Viola hissed.

"Little Viola?" Dodslav chuckled. "I wondered what he had that brought me. What smelled so delicious that I came running." His voice was thick and intoxicating. The creature smiled under the mask as glee radiated from the darkness around Dodslav. He was all the things you'd expect in a tempter, and Neil thought that to be the creature's true nature. But Neil hadn't a clue to the truth of this monster who was worse than a tempter, worse than a demon.

Neil wanted to ask how they knew each other. The tension between them was a dense weight in the air. Neil wanted to know the story, to understand how fate brought the three of them together in this moment. But after 30 years, he had only one thing to say to his brother's captor.

"I want my brother back, Dodslav."

NINE

Viola stepped between the two. She was tiny, sandwiched between Dodslav's long, lithe, muscular body and Neil's chunky frame, but both stepped back as she raised her stiff arms and shouted.

"Dodslav!" Viola waddled closer to him. "I've been looking forward to this." She shook, trying to bend her arms and legs. Every ounce of her quaked and screeched as the dirt and grime mucking up her joints flaked out from her clothes.

Seeing her move, Dodslav's body tensed, but after a moment, braying laughter erupted from him. "How the mighty have fallen." His laugh echoed in the room, blowing the black smoke drifting around him into a swirl. "Whom did you wrong for such a prison? So much less than your better half, and even less than your worst! Your human half would be a welcome improvement."

"The trade!" Neil shouted over them. "You're here for the deal!"

Dodslav stepped away from Viola. He kept laughing but his eyes, behind the mask, never left hers. "I can feel what you've gathered, but her presence skews the energy. How much is her? How much is your collection?"

"She's part of my collection." Neil stepped toward Dodslav. "I traded for her."

The basement's cold turned Neil's knees brittle. They popped and snapped as he moved. Frozen mist blew from his mouth as he shouted, but Dodslav didn't look at him.

A white whip of light slowly dropped from Viola's hand. She closed her mouth and eyes, jittered in concentration, and then her arms cracked and squeaked as her elbows bent. Her knees did the same as she worked her joints to have full range of motion. As she straightened her arms to stretch, dust fell from her sleeves. The whip coiled in the dust and sizzled as it touched the floor.

"No one owns me. I serve no one!" Viola said.

Dodslav relaxed for a moment, stiffening again when Viola tensed to strike. "No one since our first encounter?" He chuckled. "Did you come to the brother of Drew willingly?"

"She was traded! I paid a dollar for her," Neil said. "She's part of my collection."

Dodslav erupted in laughter. He threw his head back as the mask shifted to reveal a sharp jaw. "A dollar!? Oh dear Little Viola your worth has fallen."

Viola stepped out from between Dodslav and Neil. She kept both of them in front of her. "Neil, you have a choice. You've always had a choice. Don't continue on this path."

"Neil?" Dodslav crooned. "Oh, Neil. So long without a name, and now we know each other."

"I told you," Neil said to Viola, "I'm not turning back!" Neil's face burned even in this cold. He'd done all he could to keep his name from Dodslav, and now Viola had said it. She gave away something he strove to protect without regard for what it could mean.

Dodslav stepped toward Viola, turning his face in profile to Neil. Behind the mask, Neil could see cheeks building up in a smile.

"You are part of the collection?" Dodslav said with drooling satisfaction. "Little Viola. Sweet little thing. Failed guardian--"

"Shut up!" Viola screamed. The cold thickened, squeezing the breath out of Neil. He grabbed his chest to stop his shivering. "Neil, stop this. It doesn't have to be like this."

"I need to save my brother," Neil said. He clenched item 13 in his pocket.

Dodslav looked around the room, nodding. "This will do."

Viola's blue marble eyes fixed on Neil. He knew this was the last time she'd ask. The last moment to change course. She wasn't the first person to tell him to leave Drew to his fate. Hell, everyone told him that; Grandma, Grandpa, Mr. Dream, Sister Wendy, even Dodslav. Were they all right? It had been so long, would Drew even be able to come back? Would he want to?

On the table behind Dodslav was the dollhouse. The last thing Neil did with his grandpa before he died, before Drew was taken, before the collection began. In the dollhouse kitchen, Neil's eyes locked on a tiny sign that mimicked a real sign Neil's grandma had. In swooping calligraphy, it read: *Other things change, but we start and end with family.*

He mouthed the words and sighed through the dense cold. He turned to Viola, but she didn't wait for words. His face told her what she needed to know.

Her wrist snapped and the whip of white light lanced through Neil's chest. "Heart attack." Her command had no force, no want, only resignation.

Neil collapsed to the plush red carpet. He didn't feel the impact, only the fire in his chest. Drew's first overdose came to mind as Neil twitched on the floor. It was just like this. Neil gave Drew mouth-to-mouth and revived his brother, who cried and asked him why he did that. The image flipped as his chest squeezed, and now his parents were giving him a hug because he got an A on his science project. But Neil didn't smile; he had cheated on the assignment and the teacher was going to figure it out. Then Neil was at Mr. Dream's office, and the enigmatic preacher man told Neil he was proud of him. Drew wouldn't ever be free. Then Sister Wendy was dissecting a demon in front of him, bored and exhausted from his questions. His first toy, the cap gun, came to mind then the taste of spicy orange chicken and sweet tea filled his mouth. Cynthia and Aaron smiled at him as he ate another plate at their dinner table.

Neil tried to say all the things he wanted to say about his life, scream them, but only a yelp came out. The cold vanished as heat lanced through him in a crushing shockwave from his shoulder to his fingertips. Screams couldn't get through the rubble of his chest as he rolled into a fetal position on his side.

Dodslav and Viola rushed to him. Both leaning down.

"Make the trade!" Dodslav commanded. "Say the words!" The demon's gaze jumped from Neil to Viola. "Say it! I want it!" He screamed the last words while looking at Viola.

But Neil was saying something else. His chest constricted; his breath pushed out of him, but his left hand stayed firm in his pocket. Neil knew he wanted her more than his collection. The time for trade had passed. It was time for the next game with new rules, and Neil struggled to say the words he needed to say to escape this death.

Dodslav reached down to his face, lifted it up with the care of a child snapping up a rag doll. "Say it!"

"Too late," Viola said as she watched Neil. She saw his mouth moving, but no sound came from him other than a wheezing moan, a sharp grunt, as the heart attack clenched his body. His face turned red, then purple.

"You can't lose now!" Dodslav screamed. Pleading weaseled into his harsh voice. "You've done it! You've built the collection for me! Now give it to me!"

Neil's eyes rolled back as his mouth kept working, kept saying whatever it was he wanted as his last words.

Dodslav dropped him to the floor with a flat *splat*. "You failure." The demon snapped its long fingers in a sharp crack. A twisted sculpture appeared in Neil's line of sight. The form was abstract, perhaps once human but strained and stretched, knotted and gnarled by dull tools and a vicious craftsman. There were eyes in the wretched form: terrified eyes, pleading eyes that recognized the kid buried deep in Neil's dying face. "You failed your brother and now he stays like this forever, but you can still free him. Just say it. Give me all your collection! He's free. You die, but he's free. Put back how he was, returned to bury you."

Drew's eyes begged Neil to make the hurt stop. Neil had seen that expression when Drew begged him to go downtown and get his drugs. Or when Drew begged Neil to give him money. And finally, when Drew begged Neil to save him. A tear slipped out of Neil's eye and crystallized as it dripped to the icy carpet. It hit the floor with a faint shatter.

Viola knelt, pressing her ear closer to Neil's mouth, but the words were indiscernible. His final words—not about his brother, but an incantation. She didn't recognize it and perhaps mistook a babbling death knell for something else.

"He chose death over serving you," Viola said as she watched Neil strain a final word, a final breath, and go still.

"We both know what he chose," Dodslav spit at her. He snapped again, and the mutilated statue that was Neil's brother Drew, twisted and tormented spirit and flesh, vanished. "You took the choice away!"

Viola turned to face Dodslav, to begin the confrontation she'd waited so long for. The silence in the room stretched thin. In a blur of motion, Neil's hand snapped out, a vice grip on her ankle. His face, a mottled shade of purple, was contorted in a silent scream for salvation. Foam flecked his lips, bubbling from his nostrils as his bloodshot eyes, wild and wide, found hers. Viola's world shrank to the horror in those eyes—a silent plea for her attention, a final defiance against death.

"Wen…dy…" he groaned. "Help…"

He fell. Dead. Dropping his grip from Viola's leg.

"Our business is complete." Dodslav walked back into his cloud of smoke and shadow.

"We're not done." Viola flexed her knees and elbows, finding her body able to move again. She knew this form had its limitations and was ill-suited to the task of destroying one such as Dodslav, but she couldn't let the opportunity pass. Tonight was the monster's parade of her nemeses. Adams, now Dodslav, those who took so much from her, and what could she do but see them walk by. This body was frail, unable to fulfill her promises, her duty. The sacred duty she'd waited so long to perform. Vengeance.

"We are. You are…" Dodslav found the word easily but let the thought linger. "Pathetic." He dismissively flicked her away as if telling a child to run along. That's how he saw her now. Not as the warrior she was, nor the princess that could have been, but as the child she was imprisoned within. "There are always others. And what will you do? What can you do in this body?" He laughed. "You've lost. You just haven't caught on yet."

"I'll kill you," Viola said. "You'll pay for everyone you've taken from me. I'll kill you!"

"Not here. You can't here. Nor I you. Perhaps your prison is your haven?" Dodslav laughed. "Perhaps you chose this to hide. To atone for your failures?" His laughter intensified into a roar.

Viola didn't answer. Her eyes narrowed, the blue marbles no longer lifeless. Now they were filled with rage. "I'll find a way. I'll put your head in that box." She motioned to Item 11, a decorative wooden box with a crank handle on the side.

Dodslav waved away the comment. "Yes, yes. I'm sure you'll get right on that after your next toy collector. Boys and their toys making you a busy, busy little missy chasing their foolish blunders. Keeping you distracted, trapped." His laughter echoed, a chilling sound that seemed to linger even as he dissolved into his cloak of smoke, a sinister wraith in the dim light. The room's chill dissipated with him; a tangible absence left hanging in the air. The smoky tendrils, now a stream of dark vapor, twisted and writhed with a dancer's grace, funneling into the dollhouse's Lazarus Spiral. It was as if the structure itself inhaled, drawing him in, the smoke spiraling down with a hungry pull.

If it contained him, Viola would have destroyed it, but it was just a door. All Lazarus Spirals were just doors. Doorways to doorways. Destroying one wouldn't matter. Perhaps this door could be a weapon for her one day, but that was not today.

She closed her eyes and wondered when that day would come. A day when she wasn't stuck in this plastic body. Small. Immobile. Lifeless and cold.

Viola wobbled back to Neil, checking for any breath. There was none. She nodded, silently congratulating him on keeping his word. No begging or pleading. Instead, he used his last words for what? He wasn't asking for help, was he? Was he telling her where to find help?

Around her, the toys, their energy, watched. What did they think of their owner's passing? Few collectors had chosen death, and fewer had done so in the presence of their collection. For centuries she had stopped what almost happened tonight. Prevented those who sought power from obtaining it. Dodslav was getting bold coming for a collection.

This could only mean he was ready. He was hungry to get the final components. The last bits of energy he needed to fulfill his vision. And what was that? She didn't know for sure, but he was an artist. A sculptor of flesh and spirit who delighted in torment. One such as he opening the Lazarus Spiral, one who sought power and god-like control over others… Who knows his ends. Does even he?

TEN

Viola carried Neil upstairs and put him in his recliner. She closed his eyes, placed the book from his table, *Gulliver's Travels*, on his lap. Viola wondered what the story was about and why the spine was strained, worn to threads.

She pulled his hand out of his pocket and placed it on the book. It was clenched in a tight fist with blood trickling out between his knuckles. Her hand's lack of finger joints didn't allow her to open Neil's hand, and so she left it closed around whatever he held in his pocket. A tingle in her mind told her it was another toy, or some kind of artifact, but she didn't have time to waste. An ancient creature she might be, but she knew modern medicine would detect discrepancies in time of death if she didn't call for help soon.

She found Neil's phone in the kitchen and dialed 911, then left the phone on the counter. A voice was talking through the speaker as she went to the couch beside Neil's recliner. She crawled into it and sat staring at the bookshelf.

The basement could have been a museum. Everything was untouched. Ordered. Pristine. Here, on his bookshelf, was chaos. If everything had its place and all things were in their place downstairs, here on the bookshelf nothing knew where it belonged. Disorder ruled. The books were used. The toys were not. The books loved. The toys collected.

"He could have chosen life over his brother," she said as she stared at the ceiling. "He is free from obligation now."

But her mind couldn't leave the name he mentioned. Wendy. He mentioned her before. Someone with answers? Someone who could help? Those questions were usurped by thoughts of Dodslav. He saw her tonight as weak and broken. That was his mistake. And now, after the trip to Ely Adams' house, she knew her maker was still alive. She would make him unmake her and finish the work she set to long ago: kill Dodslav. But how? Who could help her? Wendy?

From the kitchen, the voice was louder now. Asking questions. Repeatedly saying help was on the way. Viola waited to see who would come. Would it be a collector? A curious innocent? Perhaps someone would take her to Wendy…but hope was not the province of her kind, only duty. With a deep sigh, Viola relinquished hope and waited patiently.

INVENTORY NOTE: 42

Ely's Doll

Do not touch.

ONE

"You gave Ray Walker $18 for this?" Lee picked up the toy phone. It dinged in protest to the rough handling. "Come on, bud, even I know the other kids call him Ripoff Ray. There's no way this is what you think it is."

Lee put the phone down a little harder than he meant to. It dinged again. The blue wheels clicked a faint whine as it crept along the kitchen counter. The eyes bounced on the once-white phone face. One of the eyes, a sticker, was half picked off, making the phone look like it was smiling and winking as if sharing a secret. It didn't know Ray never shared any secrets. A yellow string came out of the back and connected into a red handset.

"I'm telling you, Dad, it works." Bobby reached for the phone, but his dad pushed it back. The tires clicked quickly like a zipper pulled too roughly while the black string on the front squiggled backward like a retreating snake. "I thought, you know, you could figure it out."

"Figure out why you'd waste your money?"

"Ray said it calls ghosts." Bobby pointed to the phone. "Just try it. Dial 1. You'll see."

Lee shook his head and picked up the hollow plastic receiver.

He stuck his finger in the rotary dial for 1 and held it there. In his career, he'd seen his share of unusual things, but a phone that calls ghosts was absurd. He'd seen what others would call monsters, mostly science experiments gone wrong, and once he saw a person who really thought they were a vampire, but ghosts were one step too far. He flicked the one and let the dial run backward with a rusty chitter.

A dial tone began but was quickly interrupted by a series of fast busy beeps. They were different sounds as if dialing a number, but dialing so quickly that the tones were indistinguishable. There was a sing-song quality to them that muddled Lee's thoughts. He shook his head to regain his senses and picked up the phone, looking for a battery pack. His inspection stopped as a voice came through the receiver clearly.

"The Librarian refused my audience." The speaker was raspy with a high nasal voice. It grated on Lee's nerves, raising his arm hairs in annoyance.

"Did she now?" Another speaker said. His voice dripped with confidence and swagger. A boss if Lee ever heard one. "And your response was to cower?"

"Is there another way?"

"You fear her more than me?"

Lee pulled the phone away from his ear and shook the receiver, expecting to hear some speaker components inside, but heard nothing. He placed his ear back to the receiver as he flipped the phone over, carefully searching for a way to the mechanisms inside, but none were visible.

"That answer is not reinforced through your actions," the boss scolded. "Fortunately, I have others searching who are not so frail of spirit." A deep hissing came from the nasal speaker. The boss continued, "Now, Nujen, is that a proper apology?"

Lee slammed the receiver down on the white phone body. It shouted an angry ding. He examined the phone again, searching for the batteries.

"A recording," Lee said. "Clearly, you got ripped off. It's a recording."

"No. Dial again. You'll see—"

Lee held up his hand in the universal *Stop arguing with me* sign.

"Why are you wasting your money on this junk? You know Ray's just stealing this stuff. He's a shoplifter and resells the crap with a fantastic story to gullible people."

Bobby bristled and would have fought back on being called gullible, but took a different route to argue with his dad. "How do you know he stole it?"

"He's got multiple shoplifting charges against him."

"How do you know?!" But Bobby knew. He wanted his dad to say it.

"When a criminal is hanging around my kids, I make sure I know."

"Your work?"

"You know I can't talk about it." Lee put his hand up again, but Bobby pushed. The rising redness on Lee's face told Bobby he hit the nerve he was looking for. The *We can't talk about anything in this house* nerve.

"Yeah, I know. I know. *You can't talk about work.*" Bobby grabbed the phone. "Spy on me with your secret work crap. You could just ask. I know Ray steals stuff, but he didn't steal this. He got it from some old guy. I checked 'cause I knew you'd freak out."

"I'm sorry I care!" Lee grabbed his temples to brace for this conversation again. "I care. You know my work is important. I'm helping people."

"Just not helping people in your family. We don't get help, only surveillance," Bobby screamed as he stomped upstairs and slammed his bedroom door.

Lee sighed, took a deep breath, and walked to the foyer. Bobby's "Go Away" sign clattered on his door. Across the hall upstairs was Lee's office. The door was also closed and locked. The third door upstairs, the bathroom, was also closed. Every room shut in isolation, keeping those within away from the world outside.

"Take a walk," Lee said to no one and went outside.

The mailbox was overstuffed from a few days without anyone getting it. People were milling about their yards as they do to busy themselves after work. Every mailbox was closed and neat, every yard to match. Lee's was the exception. An intentional standout that ensured he blended into the community all that much better, having one thing that made him stand out so no one looked for anything else.

The neighbors paid him no mind as he went to the mailbox. That wasn't unusual. He knew how to blend in, and that's what made the man watching him from up the street so concerning.

TWO

Lee's FBI training told him what a stakeout looked like. It wasn't hard to distinguish someone watching you from someone passing by. Normally in a stakeout you try to be invisible, but this old guy was standing in the open, blatantly staring at Lee's house, then at Lee.

He was in his 60s, about 6' 2", perhaps 130lbs. The black work shirt, black jeans, and dull black boots stood in stark contrast to the man's ghastly pale skin which stretched taut over his skeletal frame. There were two distinguishing features on the man, a scar and a watch. The watch was a cheap gold that tinted the man's wrist green. It was designed to draw attention and probably didn't work as a watch, but it did work as a distraction for the unobservant. The scar was a different matter. It was a deep gouge from high on his scalp down to the outside of his left eye and hooking angrily into the man's mouth. Whatever got him was trying to slice his face off.

Lee pretended not to notice him and went about his mail collection, but the man approached and called out.

"Good day." His gruff voice was commanding. Lee wasn't sure if the man was asking or demanding that it be a good day.

Lee nodded and waited for the man to keep walking past. But he didn't. The man in black stopped and stood angled to Lee on his left side. Lee noted he was just far enough away that he would need to step forward to reach the man with his right hand, while the man's right hand was close to Lee's left wrist. This was a common position to stop someone from turning to strike with their right side, often their stronger side. It could be coincidence, but Lee's gut knew it wasn't.

"Morning," Lee responded.

"I'm new to the neighborhood watch. Getting to know the streets a bit." The old man glanced around, but Lee knew the man never lost sight of him.

"Seen anything?" Lee asked as he stepped back with his left to put his right closer to the man.

The man stepped in sync. "Bout to ask you the same."

"Nothing but a full mailbox." Lee held up the mail and smiled his trained, *Everything's fine, I'm a normal citizen,* smile.

"Then I'll be along," the old man said and slowly walked by. Lee waited for him to turn or say something else, but the strange man simply left. No protest, no probing, he just left. That triggered Neil to action, his gut telling him something was off about this man.

Lee hurried into his house and grabbed the Polaroid camera he kept by his kitchen window for such occasions. The world was full of weirdos, and in his line of work, sometimes they followed you home. He snapped a picture of the man who kept glancing at his house. The image spit out and he snapped another. Both photos were still white, but colors were quickly bleeding to the surface. He shook the photos as he hustled upstairs to his office.

THREE

Bobby's door was still closed. Lee leaned into it but didn't hear anything. He fished in his pocket for the office keys, found what he needed, and left Bobby's door for his own.

"Kids need time to cool down," Lee told himself. He knew 13-year-olds didn't know if they were coming or going and sure as hell didn't make decisions with their future in mind. To kids like Bobby, being popular, being accepted, was more important than being smart. Lee hoped he raised Bobby better than that, but maybe that's what his mom would have helped with. She died before she could really help shape Bobby. Lee smiled thinking of how great of a mom she would have been and said the same thing he always said when he thought of his wife. "Love you. I miss you." Even after twelve years, he missed her every moment of every day.

Lee's office looked like a study with a large wooden desk in the center of the room. Most studies didn't have a fax machine or wired telephone anymore, but those were some of his study's unique features. The walls were covered with books about urban legends and local myths from all over the United States. Large windows let in the early-June afternoon. He left the door open while he was in there unless he was on a clearance-only call. His oak desk had a comfortable chair, but that was the only chair in the room. This wasn't a place for company, even for his son to linger long. While in here, he was working, and his work couldn't be disturbed.

He sat at his desk and opened the top right drawer. Beside his service revolver was a black dial tone phone with white number buttons. He pulled it out and placed it on his desktop. Picking up the handset, he waited for someone to answer. This phone only called one place, and only one person would possibly answer.

"Can I help you?" The woman on the other side of the call asked.

"Yes, I have a priority package to deliver. Can it be sent yesterday?" Lee asked.

"Yesterday delivery is ready to be received."

"Please hold." Lee put the phone down and went to the fax machine. He placed the polaroid photos in and sent them to the only number the fax machine connected to. He picked up the receiver again. "I need an ID on receipt."

"Confirmed. Yesterday delivery with ID on receipt. Anything else I can help you with?"

"That's all." Lee hung up as Bobby's door opened. The phone was returned to the drawer before his son noticed. When Lee looked up, he saw Bobby heading for the stairs with a backpack and shoes on. "Going somewhere?"

"I thought you were working." Bobby came back up the stairs and stopped outside the office. He knew not to come in. "Mikayla called me to come study."

"I didn't hear the phone," Lee said.

"She called on the cell phone." Bobby held up a little black rectangle that Lee still thought looked more like a toy than a real phone. Bobby was always playing that snake game on it, which reinforced the idea that it wasn't a real phone. "It's really quiet."

"Be back by supper," Lee said as he closed the desk drawer and sifted through his memories on where he had Mikayla's parents' phone number. In his work, he often used the mantra *Trust but verify,* and that worked in parenting as well. Bobby never liked it, but that's how trust was built. You do what you say you're going to do, and the only way to know was by checking up without Bobby knowing. That was always a benefit of his career, even if Bobby hated it. Lee knew how to be invisible even when watching his son.

"Okay." Bobby nodded, then added, "Mikayla's number is on the fridge." As if reading his dad's thoughts. The two stared at each other for a moment, neither wanting to blink.

Bobby was the first to break the silence. "I know you're going to want to check in. The number is on the fridge if you need it."

Lee nodded. "No need." He knew this game. His son was trying to show that Lee didn't need to check in because if Bobby made it easy to check in, then Bobby *must* be going where he said. Lee smiled. "Have a good time and call if you need a ride home."

Bobby shook his head. "Nah, the walk will do me good." He went downstairs.

"Love you!" Lee shouted, but the door closed before he got it out. He followed Bobby downstairs and watched him leave the front yard, turning right toward Mikayla's house.

On the refrigerator, a piece of blue notebook paper was held up with a watermelon magnet. There were a bunch of numbers scribbled on it, and Mikayla's was one of them. Lee was certain it was correct because Bobby knew not to forge a number. His son was smart, and that was part of the problem. He was *too* smart, always thinking multiple steps ahead of anyone, but his old man dealt with smart people every day, and their hubris was always their downfall.

Whether it was a scientist who pushed an experiment too far, a government agency trying to cover their tracks, or old religions assuming they were forgotten, smart people did stupid things when they assumed they were smarter than you.

Lee went up to Bobby's room and looked around. He didn't normally check his son's room like this, he'd never needed to before. It was just the past few months where the trust was breaking down. His son had secrets now. It started with whispers with his friends, then hanging out with Ripoff Ray, and now, lying about where he's going.

The toy phone sat on Bobby's bed. Its googly eyes stared up at Lee with the eternal sticker-smile. The black string coming out of the front was twisted up from Bobby coiling it around his fingers. Lee knew Bobby was listening to the phone. That's why he was so quiet earlier. But why would he listen to a recording?

Lee picked up the receiver and dialed 1 again. The tone started again and, again, it made his mind turn to mush. Waves of disorienting nausea crashed through him, sending his legs into quivers and his stomach tensing. Lee sat on Bobby's bed to regain his composure.

The voices returned as clear as before.

"Return quickly, Nujen. I tire of your failures." Lee recognized the voice of the boss from before.

"I will not fail you again," the nasally voice replied, stopping before addressing their boss. "Cast me not from your domain—" Static interrupted the call. "I shall do better."

"I would never waste such as you." The boss chuckled. "You would always have a place in my collection."

Nujen, the nasal voice, gasped in panic. "No need. I am valuable outside," he swallowed hard with an audible click, "outside of there." Nujen became distant as he left.

Lee hung up the phone, feeling another wave of nausea bulge in his throat. He ran to the bathroom to retch, but the feeling passed. Kneeling at the toilet, he wondered who made the recording in the phone. To what purpose? Perhaps it was a game? Where did Ray get it?

Lee regained his composure and went downstairs. The phone numbers on the refrigerator caught his attention. It had been long enough for Bobby to get to Mikayla's, and so he called her parents to check in.

The phone rang.

There was no answer.

FOUR

Lee knew there was a problem, but it might be explainable. Maybe people were busy and didn't get to the phone in time. A lot of phones now had built-in voicemail systems and so, perhaps, after it rang, the phone silently went to voicemail.

But something wasn't right.

He went up to his office and checked the fax for a response. Nothing. Connections started snapping together that weren't necessarily related, and that worried Lee the most.

The phone.

Bobby's lie about going to Mikayla's.

The old man outside.

Bobby saying Ray got the phone from some old man.

In the Academy, he had learned to listen to his feelings and trust his instincts if nothing else. The gun in his desk invited him to take it, to get ready for the worst. But this instinct was ignored as Lee went back down to the kitchen to call Mikayla's house again. It had been a few minutes. Enough time for someone to be near the phone in case it rang again. He assumed the phone was in the kitchen, like in most people's houses.

He called again. No answer.

Upstairs, his office door was open, and from his office he could put out an alert for Bobby, get the police to pick him up. Maybe teach him a lesson on lying, but that'd get messy quickly. Too much paperwork. Instead, he locked up his office and went to his car in the driveway. An inconspicuous sedan that no one would notice, but packed with enough surveillance gear to hear a pin drop in anyone's house on this street.

He pulled out of the driveway toward Mikayla's house. That's not where Bobby went. Buying stolen crap, lying about going to a friend's. Where does this stop?

Lee kept one eye out for his son as he drove and the other eye looking for the old man. Something felt connected, and he wasn't going to ignore that.

FIVE

No cars were at Mikayla's house. No one answered when Lee knocked. He didn't linger. Back in his car, he started driving street by street in the standard grid pattern he used to track suspects. Unlike some of his cases, he knew Bobby was human and that limited how he moved, how quickly, and how far.

One case Lee remembered was with a genetic experiment that broke out of a government lab. It was part human, part wolf, would have looked like a werewolf to anyone who saw it. The thing could run extremely fast and jump crazy high, but in the end, its wolf instincts made it easy to track. Everything fell back on instinct, and what was Bobby's instinct? Curiosity. He was looking for something. That boy was always figuring something out. Lee knew Bobby knew more about his job than he wanted his son to know. The boy could piece together puzzles, mysteries were his passion. Nothing more mysterious than a dad who can't talk about why he left the FBI, what he does for work now, and where he goes during the day. Lee's secrets have mounted up in the past year. They had a physical weight. Bobby felt it too. Both of them carried secret lives, and now those lives had spiraled out of control.

Down an alley, Lee saw his son climbing over a construction fence. The chain-links rattled quietly as Bobby moved away from it on the other side. He had a shovel and digging pick along with his backpack, but Lee could see the backpack was empty.

"Where are you going?" Lee whispered.

Bobby moved quickly into the summer evening. A few moments later, Lee parked at the fence and followed.

SIX

Lee stayed to the shadows. There weren't many in this construction site. Based on the steel pylons sticking out of the ground, Lee assumed this site would become an office building. The center of the site was a deep hole with a ladder down. Bobby had already climbed down and was digging on the far side of the pit. Last night's rain made the ground soft and splashy. Each shovel full made a sucking, *shoolping* sound as Bobby scooped up more mud.

Across the pit, which was at least 120 feet wide, was a construction trailer. It sat uncomfortably close to the edge of the pit. If a few rocks tumbled down or a sheet of mud gave way, the trailer would certainly follow. Lee wondered who decided to, literally, live on the edge.

There was no one else around. It was after 6 o'clock and Lee assumed most of the construction workers went home after a normal shift. Someone could have been in the trailer, but the lights were off, and the sun had moved to a section of the sky that put the trailer's interior in deep shadow.

"Looking for something?" Lee called down to Bobby.

The boy startled and froze. He didn't turn to look. The voice was clear and there was nothing really to say except the truth. "You wouldn't help, so I had to do it myself."

Lee made his way down, while Bobby continued to fling mud with strokes of his shovel. Each arc of mud flew closer, Lee couldn't shake the suspicion that Bobby was targeting him.

The pit was murkier than expected. The earth had taken on a dark brown tone that sucked the light from around them. It was cool and wet, with every step squishing along the way. Sounds from the street, many yards away now, didn't make it down here. All Lee could hear was the mud sucking his shoes, the shovels stabbing into the slush, and Bobby's panting breath.

As Lee reached for his son to stop him from shoveling, a wooden *THUNK* echoed through the pit. Both father and son stopped cold. Bobby smiled. Lee scanned the area again. Bobby scraped the shovel around the object in the mud and quickly lifted a cube from the globs of earth. He wiped it off with jittering hands. Lee wondered if the nerves were excitement or fear. Under the coat of mud was a dark wooded box. The latch was dull metal, impossible to tell what kind in the dark and mud. Bobby clicked the latch, unlocking it, before Lee could stop him. The box gasped as air flooded the sealed interior. Purple velvet held a snub-nosed brass key with a white geode embedded in the handle.

"What is it?" Bobby said. He reached inside the box, but Lee grabbed his hand.

"We don't touch things when we don't know where they came from." Lee closed the box quickly. "How'd you know this was here?"

"The two guys were talking about it on the phone. I told you to listen." Bobby let his dad take the box without protest. "They wanted the key, and it sounded like if they got it, something bad was going to happen."

"So you lied to me to play into Ripoff Ray's little game?"

"It's not a game, Dad." Bobby looked around to see if anyone was watching. "There's something really wrong with that phone, and that's why I came to you for help. But you didn't listen. You never listen. You don't talk. You don't listen. You just think I'm stupid or something."

Lee shook his head. "You aren't stupid. You're irresponsible. Coming here *was* stupid. You think you overhear people wanting this thing and so you thought you'd just get here first?" Lee shook the box. He wanted to shake Bobby. This was stupid and dangerous. What if he fell down that ladder? It would be easy enough with the mud on the brackets. And what if this was all an elaborate trick from Ray to do something even more insane than shoplifting. "You get here and the people who want this are here. Then what? If they showed up right now, then what?"

"You'd be screwed," a high-pitched nasally voice called down to them from atop the construction trailer. "So, so screwed."

SEVEN

Lee's hand jerked to where he carried his service pistol, but it wasn't there. His eyes darted to the source of the voice. In the evening daylight outside the pit, the guy was easy to see. Based on the voice, Lee assumed it was a guy. The body was lithe with onyx-painted skin. A dark green tunic hung around his torso, reaching midway down the guy's muscled legs. A faint white light glimmered on his chest where the tunic was open along the neckline. The man wore a white mask with black slanted arrow eyes and three more arrows coming up from the chin.

The hands were too long to be a person's. They weren't the perfect symmetry of intentional design or chaotic asymmetry of an accident. Lee had seen both these in the field. Laboratory accidents gone horribly wrong, deforming the subjects, or scientists infected with their own humanity-stealing concoctions. These monstrous aberrations were always either too perfect or too malformed, never a mix like this thing. It wasn't designed. It was grown with the imperfections only evolution can construct in life. It was natural.

"Get to the car," Lee whispered to Bobby and pressed the car keys into his son's hand. "We were just leaving," Lee called up to the thing on the trailer.

He stepped forward, flexing toes twice as long as his skeletal fingers. Popping metal sounds echoed down the pit as the man on the trailer's talons punctured the trailer's aluminum siding.

"No need," the thing said. Lee thought it was smiling under the mask. "No need." It, no longer he but now an *it* in Lee's mind, flashed a claw for Bobby to come back, but he was already on the ladder. "Let's keep this simple. We heard you breathing, but how'd you do it? How'd you connect to us?"

Lee thought of the phone but kept his mind focused on the task at hand. His hands flailed as he paced in the pit, creating a steady nervous motion that held the thing's attention. Lee didn't look to see where Bobby was, he listened for the end of metal ladder rungs and the start of splashy running through mud.

"We didn't think we heard anything real. Just a toy." Lee raised his vocal range to sound panicked. "I, I don't know."

The thing crouched down. Its muscular legs tensed, about to spring down into the pit with Lee. A fall like that would break human legs, but Lee had seen animals and things that weren't quite animals anymore make this jump.

The splashing run started. Bobby was off the ladder.

The thing jumped, but not into the pit—it sprang across the pit, jumping almost 100ft and landing on the ladder. Lee recovered faster than he should have. The realization that his son's life was in danger broke through the disbelief and set him to motion. He ran across the pit in a sprint and leapt up onto the ladder. The creature hopped up rungs, three at a time. Lee didn't shout to draw attention or distract the thing. He knew he needed every breath to fuel him in catching that thing before it caught Bobby.

The mud on his shoes made his foot slip off the rung. It caught his shin and sent a singing vibration through his guts. He climbed with just his arms, grabbing the side of the ladder like the creature above him. It scaled the ladder holding on the sides, wrapping its too-long fingers, too-long toes around the steel rails.

Lee focused on what he was doing, moving faster up the ladder.

The creature was out of the pit and jumped into the just-started building's metal skeleton. Lee got off the ladder a few moments later. He was winded but had no time to stop now. Bobby was still running. He was over the fence and almost to the car.

"The trunk!" Lee screamed. "Open the trunk!"

"Yes!" The raspy voice screamed down from somewhere up high. "Open the trunk! It won't help! Give me the key!" It echoed around him, bouncing off the steel beams above, giving the nasal voice a resonate thrum that set Lee's teeth on end.

Bobby opened the driver's door with the keys. Lee was close enough to hear the trunk pop. He scanned the skeletal structure above him for the creature but didn't see it.

"Use the radio! Pick it up and call for Sidney, Oscar, Sidney!" Lee shouted as Bobby moved to the trunk.

The masked creature jumped down from the building, over the fence at the car. Lee was at the fence and climbed it with a quick jump, step, and roll. He hit the ground and rolled to his feet, giving the creature a wide berth as he passed. From the trunk, Lee ripped out a shotgun, pumped it, and took aim at the creature.

"Back off!" Lee said as he approached the creature to get a full shot into the thing if it came any closer.

Behind Lee, Bobby kept yelling into the radio, and Lee heard the operator's voice shouting back, "Inbound! Inbound!"

The creature stepped closer. Lee squeezed off a shot, blasting the thing's chest into an explosion of black smoke. It staggered back, dramatically feigning pain, as the smoke solidified into flesh. "You ruined my favorite shirt," it said with a chuckle.

Lee pumped the gun again, but before he could fire, the creature rushed him, smacking him into the car's windshield. The glass cracked loud, and a halo of spiderweb fractures radiated from where Lee's head hit. Blackness shrank the world around him to a pinhole of light.

When the creature jumped on the car's hood, standing over Lee, the pinhole opened a little, letting Lee see the thing's mask. It pressed its face into Lee's; the thing's breath was rotten eggs and dry heat.

"The key?" The creature was talking over Bobby's shouting behind the car. "The key, or this one's life!"

Bobby stopped talking. Sirens were in the distance. Too far away to help.

Lee wanted to shout to Bobby, tell him not to do it, but his mouth wouldn't work. His body was limp, the world fading again. From the trunk, the woman on the radio was counting down, "Inbound 20! Inbound 19! Inbound 18!"

"Then it will be both your lives!" The creature raised a claw, but something caught its eye. It sucked in a deep quivering breath. Lee looked where it was looking. Leaning against the last lamppost on the street, as the sun went down behind the trailer on the other side of the pit, Lee saw the man in black.

The man watched what was happening with a detached ease. He could have been watching someone walk down the street or vultures picking at a deer carcass. But the creature stumbled back off the car hood. It fell on the ground, hissed at the man, and launched itself into the building's skeleton. The man in black spit, turned, and walked into the growing shadows as the police cars arrived, their blue and red lights turning twilight to bloody bright day.

"Dad!" Bobby came to Lee as the world faded to black.

EIGHT

A bolt of thick ammonia raced from Lee's nose to his brain. The shock woke him up in a surge of energy. He sprung to his feet from the ambulance tailgate where he was dozing. A moment ago, the world was murky; now it was all there, clear and intense.

"Calm down, sir. You're with the police." An old police officer held up one hand in surrender but kept the other close to his gun.

"Police?" Lee asked. He scanned the area, quickly regaining his senses and assessing his environment.

"We got a call to get here and help a man and a kid." The officer looked around. "I ain't never heard anyone jump as fast as we were told to ta' get our butts here."

Lee nodded, remembering Bobby calling the SOS protocol. Where was Bobby now? Lee spotted him quickly. A pair of officers were questioning him.

"Stop questioning that boy." Lee pointed to Bobby but didn't yell. "I assume you were told who I am?"

"Merkins, Yantz, bring that boy here!" The old officer called to where Bobby was being questioned. Talking to Lee again, this time in a lower tone, "No. They didn't tell me who you were, just that you were the commanding officer and to take you to the station. Hell, the governor called my chief to make this happen, so whoever pulls strings for you, they got 'em tight around people in high places."

Bobby came to Lee. "You okay, Dad?"

Lee nodded. "We're heading to the police station now. You still got your bag?"

Bobby pointed beside their car's front tire where the backpack was dropped. Lee saw the hood of the car. Long toe talons had clawed through the steel, or whatever cars were made of nowadays. There were too many toes: seven. He had thought it was a guy in a suit; now he wasn't so sure.

"Anything in that bag that shouldn't be in a police station?" The old officer asked.

Lee glared at him, wordlessly asking how dare he question what's in the bag, then answered, "No. Just an old box and an old key. Some digging gear." Lee shrugged. "Nothing you need to worry about."

"I'd feel a lot better if I looked," the old officer said with a nervous tremble.

"Bobby, go ahead and show him." Lee motioned to the officer with a sly smile.

Bobby opened the bag and showed the officer. Nothing but what Lee said.

"That's my car there. I'll drive unless you got other plans?" The officer said.

"That sounds good." Lee gave Bobby a hug. "You okay?" He whispered in his ear. Bobby nodded. "Did you see the old guy by the lamppost?" Lee kept his voice so low, only Bobby could hear. "Don't answer, just nod or shake your head."

Bobby shook his head.

"Okay. Let's get going then." Lee smiled to his son and then to the officer. "Is anyone waiting for us at the station?"

"Expecting visitors?" The officer asked.

"Yeah." Lee sighed. "At least one."

The three climbed into the police car. Lights and siren started, and the officer—Lee never caught his name—raced back to the station to deliver his quarry and wash his hands of all this.

Bobby took out the box and key from the book bag. He showed it to his dad and, with only his eyes, asked, *What do you think's going on?* Lee shrugged. He hoped his visitor would have some answers.

NINE

The instructions were clear. Bobby and Lee were to get an office. There were only three in the small police station, and all three were occupied when they arrived. The old officer took Lee to the police chief, who gave Lee his office.

"Any listening devices in here?" Lee asked.

"They've been removed. We were instructed," the chief replied. He was visibly shaken around Lee. "Would, uh…" the chief sweated thick beads, "would you like a drink?"

Lee thought this a strange question. Of all the orders this man received around Lee, the first question asked was if Lee wanted a drink? Not who was he nor who does he report to; no, the chief went to polite refreshments.

"A water would be nice. Thank you. Bobby?"

"Water?" Bobby said. "Thank you."

The chief went out to get them their drinks.

"Dad, who's the visitor?"

"Mr. Timmins." Lee sat in one of the chairs in the corner. He took a deep breath to organize his thoughts. "You met him at that picnic we had years ago."

"What picnic?"

"You know. The one…" Lee tried to remember how long ago that was. It was before Bobby started school. That was eight years ago now. Had it been that long? The picnic was the last work function where family was allowed. That's when their orders shifted, their new division was created, and there was no more talk about work or what Lee did between the hours of 8am and 6pm. "Well, I guess it's been a while."

Bobby nodded and looked at the pictures on the chief's walls. They were pictures of the police chief shaking hands with a bunch of people Bobby didn't recognize. A few frames held awards and recognitions. They were easier to look at than his dad.

"What was that, Dad?"

"I don't know," Lee answered.

Bobby turned at the unfamiliar sound of the truth. "Isn't that the kind of thing you work with? I mean, I hear your calls sometimes. Weird things."

Lee shook his head. "You shouldn't be listening in." He wasn't mad; more proud than anything that his son was able to hear through the thick walls and quiet talking. "But whatever that was, it wasn't anything I've seen before." Lee pressed his palms into his eyes to relieve the headache building from his concussion.

"How do you know?" Bobby sat beside his dad and spoke in whispers. "How do you know that wasn't like that thing you handled in West Virginia?"

"You know about that?"

"Yeah." Bobby shrugged and looked away. "I listened in on your call." Lee leaned back, but before he could protest, Bobby jumped in, "I was worried. You were all cut up and I was scared."

That diffused Lee. Of course his 13-year-old son was worried. Lee was all he had, and when his dad came home cut up and bleeding, his boy wanted to know what was going on.

"That was what I'm normally brought in to investigate, a science experiment gone wrong." Lee kept his voice low. "But we aren't having this conversation." He tilted his head to make sure Bobby understood. "Experiments gone wrong are all the same. There's chaos in them. No chaos in the thing that came for us tonight."

"It wanted the key."

Lee agreed. "How did you know where to look?"

"They were talking about it on the phone," Bobby said. "I think the one guy is the leader. The guy, or thing, we saw tonight is his lackey."

"Why do they want it?"

"It opens a door on," Bobby air-quoted, "the spiral."

"What spiral?"

"They didn't say. The guy from tonight, he didn't like talking about the spiral. The other guy wanted the key. I think—"

"I think you shouldn't have gotten involved," Lee interrupted. "I know you said you came to me for help, but, Bobby, this was just dangerous, and now we're in it."

Bobby slapped his legs and sprung up. "There it is! I made a problem for you! That's the problem. Not that we have a phone to hell in our house and the devil wants a key to do something horrible!"

"No! That isn't the problem!" Lee pointed to the backpack. "The problem is you are thirteen! You are a kid! You shouldn't be messing with this stuff!"

"Leave it to you? Just hand it over and forget about it?"

"Yes! Enjoy your life! Does that sound so bad?"

"What life?" Bobby scoffed. "All I do is wait for you to get home or to come out of your office. Can't talk to you about work. Can't talk to you about anything."

"That's not true," Lee said.

A knock interrupted their conversation. Lee looked to the glass door and saw Mr. Timmins standing on the other side. Three security team members were a few feet away from him. Lee knew this was serious. He waved Timmins in.

Larry Timmins wasn't the kind of man that commanded your respect on sight. You had to know of him. Whispers hinted at his work in the CIA, FBI, NSA, and government organizations that didn't exist on any org chart, but no one knew anything for certain. Some people in Lee's office said Timmins was just a paper pusher, but Lee knew that wasn't the case. People who had seen the worst in the world kept that darkness in their eyes, and Timmins' eyes were the darkest he'd ever seen. He wore a brown suit, white shirt, puke-yellow tie, and black freshly shined shoes. He had a thin manila folder in one hand.

"Sir." Lee stood stiff to greet his boss.

"Lee." Timmins nodded to him, showing a glare of bald spot. "This must be Robert?"

"Bobby, sir." Bobby put out his hand for a handshake. Timmins shook it.

"You used to only want to be called Robert. You said it was your name and no other name mattered." Timmins smiled.

Bobby remembered that from when he was very little. He always argued with his dad about being called Bobby. When did he start going by Bobby? He didn't remember, but he thought it might have been around when his dad took this new job and they moved to this town.

"How much does he know, Lee?" Timmins asked.

"More than I knew." Lee shook his head.

Timmins nodded. "Of course. You aren't raising no rube."

Bobby wasn't sure what a *rube* was or why he wasn't one, but knew a compliment when he heard one.

"Let's get to business." Timmins presented the folder to Lee. "There's your guy. I assume this is about him."

Lee opened the folder to see the picture of the man in black he faxed to the office. There was another picture of him in Tokyo; Lee recognized Mount Fuji in the background. One last picture showed him in the background of a tourist photograph at the Eiffel Tower.

"What's this?" Lee asked.

"That's the file on him," Timmins said.

Three photographs. Lee scoffed at the lack of information. Everyone had a trail. Everyone had a file. Even Bobby, even Lee, and the files were pages and pages long. No one had nothing.

"This is all we have?" Lee asked.

Timmins nodded again, slowly.

"What about international?" Lee closed the file and handed it back. "Can we get info from our intelligence partners around the world?"

"That is the international file," Timmins said. "This guy doesn't exist. No traffic camera footage. No direct photos except the one you took. We don't even have a name. He's just John Doe 2202441."

Lee waited for something more from Timmins, but nothing came.

"Tell me what happened tonight," Timmins said.

Lee did. Every detail was included except the toy phone. Bobby heard the retelling and thought this was an important detail to leave out of the story. He tried to chime in, but his dad waved him off.

When the story was complete, Lee paused and asked Timmins, "So, what do you think?"

"None of the usual reports." Timmins talked with his hands as he often did when thinking. "Wild animals or bigfoot creatures stalking about town. You think it was a man in a mask?"

Lee shrugged. "Didn't feel like that. It stank to high hell and if the hands and feet were prosthetics, they were damn convincing."

Timmins nodded thoughtfully. "Anything to add?"

Bobby met the older man's gaze and shook his head.

"What's next?" Lee pointed to the mostly empty folder. "I think he's at the center of this, but don't know how."

"We know we're not the only government organization that doesn't exist." Timmins tapped the folder in his hand. He went to the pictures Bobby was looking at earlier and glanced at them. "Maybe we're in something above even our pay grade." A thoughtful silence settled over them as Timmins paced the room. "Did you get the feeling from this guy that he's one of us?"

"In Sector 7?" Lee shook his head quickly. "No way. Too old. Too…" He wasn't sure the word to use. Calm? Focused? He considered himself and his colleagues the definition of focus, of persistence, but the man in black exuded more than focus, it was certainty. He knew the answer to every question before it was asked. The old man knew something was happening, the phone, before Lee did. Lee picked up his sentence, "Too different from us."

"We know there's others. Don't know all of them," Timmins said. That made Lee feel queasy, the idea that Timmins didn't know something. "But probably should get you relocated and out of whatever it is."

Bobby deflated at the idea of starting over again. He knew what relocation meant. It would be the third relocation in five years. Just enough time between relocations to let him believe that things would be different, like his dad said every time. Enough time to make friends and like the town he was in. Enough time to want to stay.

Lee nodded, knowing this was protocol. When your assignment was compromised, you must move on. Lingering would only put them in danger. But if all this was about the phone, the key, could he just leave them for whoever and stay? Would life go back to normal for them, such as it was, without those things? He could tell Timmins about the phone, but Timmins was a man of science and rationality.

A phone that called hell, like Bobby said, would not make sense to such a man. If anything, it would make Lee seem superstitious and easily spooked; both attributes would be a fast track to dismissal from Sector 7. So, he said nothing.

TEN

One of Timmins' guys gave Lee and Bobby a ride home. The drive was silent and tense. Bobby clung to his backpack with the key in it, while Lee stared out the window processing the evening's events.

The guy at the construction site, the one wearing the mask, how did he jump across the pit? He must have had some kind of jet pack, but Lee would have heard that. A springboard? Something that shot him from the roof across the pit? And what of the claws and feet? The black skin could have been thick grease paint. The white mask didn't have a strap. Nothing held it to the guy's face. And the voice… It was the voice of the lackey on the phone.

An idea cracked through the rationalization: What if the masked guy wasn't a guy at all? What if it was some kind of extra-dimensional being? Lee had encountered people who claimed to be aliens before, what if this was the real deal? That thing was something else, something Lee had never encountered before, but he knew, as long as they had the key, they would encounter it again.

When they arrived home, Bobby left the car quickly and raced into the house. Lee thanked the driver and followed his son. By the time Lee got inside, Bobby was up to his room and slammed the door. Lee maintained pursuit.

As he went upstairs, his eyes didn't leave Bobby's room as the "Go Away" sign banged against the door. With his attention solely on his son's door, he didn't notice his office door was open.

"Bobby?" Lee knocked hard and grabbed the handle. The door was unlocked. "Bobby?" He said as he went in.

Bobby was sitting on his bed, seething. Lee could almost see the steam radiating from his son's head.

"Relocating isn't the end of the world. It's a safety measure."

Bobby didn't answer. He stared at the wall across from his bed. There wasn't anything on the wall. There wasn't anything on any of his walls. A faint grinding sound filled the tension between them as Bobby bit down on all the screams he wanted to let out. His sweaty palms kneaded his legs, needing an outlet for all the frustration building in him.

"What's the problem? We haven't been here that long," Lee said.

"I'm staying," Bobby growled. "I'm not leaving my friends again."

"You'll make new friends." Lee wasn't sure who Bobby was talking about. Sure, Mikayla was up the street, but Bobby never mentioned anyone else. Never talked much about school or anything.

"No," Bobby answered. The frustration steamed off him. His shoulders sank, relaxed and resigned. "No. I'm not going."

Lee didn't bristle against this, he was too confused. "You don't really get a choice."

"But you do?" Bobby asked. "You can say we stay and we stay? Tell Mr. Timmins about the phone. Tell him about the key."

Bobby's desk was empty except for a small sketchbook and a few pens. Lee didn't know when Bobby took up drawing, but lately pens have been more common on the grocery list. On the sketchbook was a drawing of the trees outside Bobby's window. The sketch was exceptional.

"Why didn't you tell him?" Bobby asked.

"We don't know what it is. I'm still not convinced it's not just some prank from Ripoff Ray." Lee looked for the phone. It was on the desk when he left. Through Bobby's open door, he saw his office was open. "Did you move the phone?" But Lee didn't wait for an answer. He moved quickly to his office.

"No." Bobby looked to where he left it, but the desk was empty. His dad's shift to high alert got Bobby off the bed and he followed his dad to the office.

In the office, nothing was out of place. It was just as Lee had left it.

The air in the house shifted as if someone opened a door. Lee hurried to the foyer. Staying upstairs, he listened and heard the familiar whine of the basement door. He pressed his finger to his lips and pointed to his desk. Bobby went to the desk quickly. Lee followed. He pulled a pistol out of the drawer and handed the black emergency phone to Bobby.

"Call 0 for operator. Tell them we have an emergency pickup at our house. Immediate service requested."

Bobby nodded and picked up the receiver, but it was dead. No dial tone. He told his dad, but Lee didn't believe him. Lee pressed his ear to the phone and didn't hear the normal dial tone.

"That's not possible," Lee said into the phone.

"Oh, but it is." A growling voice laughed on the other end. It was the boss' voice from the toy phone. "It is." The laugh rose to an echoing cacophony that curdled Lee's guts. He dropped the phone. The laughing could be heard until Bobby picked up the receiver and hung it up.

Downstairs they heard the slow clicking of the toy phone's blue tires across the hardwood floor—*click, click, click*—as it was dragged behind tapping taloned feet. Each step ended with a scratching sound as the wood was gouged out of the floor. A maddening pattern of clicks and scratches came to the stairs and stopped. Lee wanted to see what it was, but he knew.

"I'm armed! Come up here and you're leaving in a body bag!" He shouted out his office door. Without delay, he closed the door and locked it. Lee motioned to Bobby to help with a chair to make a barricade against the door.

Each step up the stairs was a fleshy barefoot slap, scratch, then ding as the toy phone hit the step. It was slow, ascending at a leisurely pace as if there was nowhere to go, and now, for Bobby and Lee, there wasn't.

"The key." It was the masked thing from the construction site. Its high-pitched, nasally voice cut through the commotion and clatter as Lee and Bobby barricaded themselves into the office. "The key for me. Life for you. Simple." It knocked on the door. "I don't even need to come in. Just slide it under the door."

Bobby had his backpack. It was behind the desk where he had the black phone.

"I'll come in if you don't send it out." The creature cooed, too delighted for Lee's liking. He thought about how the thing jumped across the pit and threw him into the car. This barricade would not hold if it was as strong as Lee thought.

"New plan," he whispered to Bobby. "Get your bag." He pointed to the window.

Lee got his shotgun out from under one of the bookshelves where he kept it for such an occasion as a home invasion. Nothing had ever followed Lee home, but he was prepared. Under another bookshelf, he pulled a long dagger, and from another, a taser. Lee didn't hear the tapping talons retreat from the door as he collected his weapons.

"Climb down the lattice work. It should hold you," Lee said.

"What about you?" Bobby asked, remembering the lattice wasn't all that sturdy.

"I'll be right behind you." Lee grabbed a bag from another drawer in his desk. He opened it, checked for the rope, flashlight, and extra ammo he knew he'd need tonight.

A scurrying sound above them made Lee freeze and drew his eyes up to the ceiling. "It's on the roof." The movement stopped above them. Lee motioned for Bobby to come close. "It's going to try to come through the ceiling?" That didn't make sense to Lee. It could have broken down the door, even with the barricade, if it was able to come through the roof. "Let's go." He pointed to the window.

They both walked slowly across the room. Lee kept his eyes up, breathing steady and gun ready. Bobby walked gently, trying not to make a sound. Both readied their minds for anything the way one does while cranking a jack-in-the-box. They knew the jump was coming, the creature springing from its place, but they didn't know when. At least with a jack-in-the-box you knew where it was coming from. Here, Lee and Bobby knew the attack could come from anywhere.

When they reached the window, Bobby unlocked it as the white masked face dropped into view. Bobby stumbled back, falling over Lee, who kept his wits and relocked the window. He raised the shotgun but held fire to prevent breaking the window.

The thing had climbed down their house like a spider and was upside down, outside the window. It tapped on the glass, and Lee knew it was smiling under that white mask. With all five long fingers, the thing outside the window tapped rhythmically. Lee helped Bobby back up and they went to the door, clearing the barricade.

"New plan," Lee said as he panted from shoving the heavy furniture. "Get out through the basement. I'm going to hold this guy here. Call 911."

"I'll go to the Carsons'," Bobby said.

"Who?" Lee kept moving.

"Al Carson's parents. Our next-door neighbors." Bobby grunted as he shoved the last chair out of the way.

Shivers seized Lee's muscles as the creature used its long claws to cut a wide circle into the window glass. It tapped the inside of the circle, and the glass fell in and quietly broke on the carpeted floor.

"I didn't want to alert anyone to our transaction," the thing whispered into the window, and then reached in to undo the lock. "Last chance. Give me the key. I can't go back without it, so you're not leaving with it."

Lee opened the door and ushered Bobby out. The toy phone was at the top of the stairs and almost tripped Bobby. Instead, the boy kicked it toward his room and continued downstairs. The creature slid the window up and slithered inside. Lee ran out of the office and shut the door. Bobby was already at the basement door.

"Which neighbor?" Lee asked when he caught up.

Bobby shook his head. "When you're looking at the house, they're to the right. The mailbox says Carson. You don't know our neighbors?"

Lee had read the dossier on this neighborhood, but that was it. No socializing. No discussions. The encounter at his mailbox earlier today was the longest conversation he'd had with anyone on this street.

"Call 911." Lee nodded and closed the basement door behind Bobby as his son ran down the stairs to exit the back door.

Tapping talons came downstairs at the slow pace of an unbothered stalker. Lee wondered how the creature's boss would react if it knew its servant took this chore so lackadaisically.

Lee raised his gun, took a calming breath, and squeezed the trigger.

ELEVEN

Bullets ripped through the green tunic and black flesh underneath. Puffs of smoke billowed out from the creature, but then quickly reformed to flesh.

"That won't help you," the creature said too happily.

"What are you?"

"I just want the key."

"Where does that phone go?" Lee pointed upstairs. "Who are we listening to?"

"It is impolite to eavesdrop." The creature was at the bottom of the stairs now and turned slowly to face Lee. "My master did not appreciate your attention."

"He knew we were listening?"

The thing nodded.

Lee glanced to his front door, immediately regretting it. His look betrayed his next move. He could have made it, but now the creature was stepping sideways to block the way.

"He wanted us to find the key?" Lee asked, and worked to reformulate an escape plan.

The thing nodded.

"Why?"

"He is an artist. A creator. How are we to know his true intentions?" The creature held out its long-fingered black hand. "The key?"

"What does it open?" Lee stepped back into the kitchen. There was a back door, but its lock didn't always open easily. Sometimes it got stuck, and he knew this would be one of those times. He could dive out a window, but his gut told him to buy time. That's what Bobby needed, and Lee could keep this creature's leisurely attention, or at least he thought he could.

But time had run out. "Enough questions." The creature blurred and closed the distance on Lee before he could react. It easily knocked him through the air into the wall. Before feeling the crunch of bone on hard wood, Lee heard the crumble of drywall above him. He looked up and saw radiating cracks from where he hit the wall. "Key!" The creature demanded, all leisure now gone.

"It's upstairs." Lee gasped, trying to catch his air from hitting the floor.

"Liar!"

"It was in my son's backpack. In his room." Lee tried to cover the lie with a truth. The key was in his son's backpack, but not upstairs. "It's in his room."

The creature glanced upstairs. It took two deep inhalations, as if sucking the scent of the key toward it, then shook its head.

"It is not in this house. But it is close." The creature moved toward the basement door. "Your son took it."

"No!" Lee tried to get up, but his vision was too blurry to find something to hold onto, and his legs too wobbly to support his body. "It's upstairs."

The creature laughed and walked to the front door. It unlocked the deadbolt and held the handle. "If he gives me the key, he can live. But your kind are too greedy to give up power when they find it." It opened the door and hissed.

A concussive force blasted from the doorway, sending the masked creature flying through the house. Its head smashed into the upstairs railing while its body froze against the wall. An unseen hand held it tight.

"You gonna invite me in?" A gruff voice called from the front porch.

Lee crawled to see out the front door. It was the man in black, his hand held high, pressing the masked creature against the wall.

"Invite me in or your problem stays your problem."

"Come in," Lee said.

The man in black stepped into the house and held the door for Lee. "Your son is next door. He's safe. Go to him and I'll take care of this." He shoved his hand to the ground and the creature followed with a cracking *splat*.

Lee found strength in his legs and stumbled to the door. He fell down the front steps and rolled over to see the man in black shut the front door behind him.

TWELVE

When the police arrived, Lee told them they had a home invasion. He and his son had escaped, but they thought the assailant was still in the house. The officers suggested Bobby stay with the Carsons and keep drinking tea with them while the police went to check out the situation.

Lee suggested he come along, but the police refused. They were not alerted to his position in Sector 7, nor his rank, and the last thing they wanted was a civilian messing up their crime scene.

Bobby and Al, a kid Bobby's age, were talking in the other room about their art teacher. Lee didn't know a kid Bobby's age lived next door, much less that his son knew him. It was in the dossier when he moved here, but Lee thought Bobby knew better than to get close to anyone when a move was just a mission away.

"Your son's a good kid," Mr. Carson said. From the file Lee had read, Mr. Carson went by Rich, but he'd never been introduced as such and so Lee didn't address him as such.

"Yeah," Lee said.

"Al's terribly shy. Your boy took right to him. Helping him come out of his shell," Rich said. "And he's been helping Al with his artwork too. So talented."

"Al?"

"No, your boy." Rich laughed at the assumed joke. How could a father be oblivious to their son's artistic talents? The thought was preposterous, yet sadly true in this case. "He's a really good artist."

Lee nodded and wanted to play off the joke, but instead the truth slipped out. "I work a lot and don't get to see that side of him much."

Rich didn't say anything, but Lee was starting to understand where Bobby went after school. How his son filled the time between school and when Lee got home from work. Bobby had a life. Whether it was a good life, a safe life, or a path to problems, Lee had no idea. Who was Al? Who was Mikayla? Even Ripoff Ray, who was that kid other than what was in his file? Who were these people shaping his son?

"We should have you over for dinner sometime soon," Rich said. "Minnie makes a beast of a roast. Get it? Roast beast!?" A hearty laugh spilled from the man's ruddy cheeks and full belly. In a few years, Rich Carson would be a great Santa Claus at the mall. He'd only need a white beard and red coat.

"I'd like that," Lee said as Bobby and Al started sketching.

The police returned a few moments later.

"Mr…" The police looked at Lee. "We didn't catch your name."

"Lee," he answered. "I'm Lee. That's Bobby. Is our house all clear?"

The officer nodded, a hint of suspicion gathering in his furrowed brow. "Yes, sir. They did a number on your house though. Gonna wanna call insurance first thing. Probably best you come see before your boy."

"Yes," Lee agreed, and asked Rich if Bobby could stay for a little longer. Rich said he was always welcome. As Lee walked out the front door, he noticed Bobby's backpack in the kitchen. He grabbed it and followed the police back to his house.

When the front door opened, the police turned and started to walk away. Their eyes were glassy and blank as they walked, even paced and zombie-like, back to their squad car and drove away. Not a word was said.

"Officers—" But Lee stopped talking when he saw the man in black sitting on the living room couch, relaxed, with a glass of whiskey in his hand.

"We were done with them. Hope you don't mind." The man in black raised the glass. "I do enjoy a good rye. Poured you one too." Another glass sat on the table in front of the man.

Lee walked in and closed the front door.

THIRTEEN

Lee sat in a chair across from the couch.

"Your problem is in the basement. I've bound it up and will send it home after our business is through," the man said.

"Who are you?"

The man in black savored his last sip of whiskey and swallowed it. "Folks call me Calahan. No folks you know. You gonna drink that?"

Lee wanted his wits sharp. He shook his head, and Calahan scooped up the glass.

"Folks I know don't know you at all." Lee said.

"That's good." Calahan took a long gulp of whiskey. He finished it and stood as his face tensed. The burn in his throat was blown out in a deep exhale, followed by a smile. "And if not for the origination of your problem, neither would you after our business concludes. I usually ensure I'm not memorable, but I have a feeling we're not done." Calahan motioned for Lee to follow him to the basement.

"Who do you work for?" Lee followed.

"We all report to someone. Mine don't like to be talked about." Calahan laughed a coarse chuckle. "Think of my boss like Timmins.

He don't like to be talked about either, unless it's to make him sound impressive."

"You know Timmins?"

"No."

They walked down the basement stairs with careless steps that echoed heavy and thudding back to them.

"How do you know about Timmins?"

Calahan laughed. "You have so many questions. And that's good. Good for your line of work. Former FBI, recruited to Sector 7, boy, you must be a hard ass. But these things don't care how hard you think you are." Calahan pointed to the creature pinned to an exposed stud board in the basement. A thick nail held the creature's arm to the board, and the rest of its body just sagged in defeat. The mask was broken in pieces piled neatly beside the pathetic thing. It breathed ragged and gasping. The mask now made sense. It wasn't to hide, but to breathe. It couldn't handle the atmosphere.

"Alien?" Lee asked.

Calahan shook his head. "Alien means from space. This thing is from much farther away."

"Hell?" Lee tried again, sounding less sure this time.

That took Calahan by surprise, but the old man regained his composure quickly. "No. Some call them demons, but that's not right. They're from a place between this world and another. They're sadistic and cruel, but no, not demons."

"What do they want? Why's it here?"

Gasping, the creature answered Lee. "I told you." It looked up, exposing an all-too-human face with long ears and a sharp nose. The mouth didn't hide fangs or spiked teeth, but the omnivore mix Lee would have expected in any human. If not for the hate in the thing's eyes, Lee could have mistaken it for angelic in beauty and grace. "I need the key." Nujen said.

"Our friend here has been rambling about this key," Calahan said. "Do you have it?"

Lee nodded and produced the wooden box that contained the key from Bobby's backpack. Calahan took it. He didn't open the box to inspect it, only took a deep breath in when he accepted the box. The creature sighed, seeing its defeat was now final.

"I am going to send our friend back home now, but before I do, I wanted to offer you a chance to ask it a question. Any question. Just know that any question will beget more questions, and some will have no satisfying answers."

"Why?" Lee asked.

"Mr. Lee Potterman," Calahan said. This brought Lee to attention. His original last name wasn't general knowledge. His current identity was Lee Roberts, which Bobby hated. Before that it was Lee Walters. Before that, Lee couldn't remember anymore. "I sense that you are a man of many questions, and if I were to rob you of the chance to ask one, you'd seek it out in other ways. I do not wish you to do that. My superiors do not wish that either. We all want a conclusion to this business here and now."

"Understood." And that did make sense. How many investigations did he pursue beyond what others would for closure. Tying everything up in a nice neat bow was an investigator's dream. And maybe not just investigators, but everyone. To have a final outcome, a solution packaged nicely so you know what you have. Knowing what you have is the key. That's what Bobby wanted. And he'd found it with others. Now, Lee needed to find it with his son. Who was his son becoming? This mystery above all others needed to be solved.

"How do I get a hold of you, Calahan, if I need you?" Lee faced the old man in black.

"If something's going on, I'll know. One of my fellow Inquisitors might come by. We know these things. They call to us." Calahan nodded slowly. "Is there anything else?" His eyes drifted to the basement ceiling, and Lee wondered if he meant anything else on the second floor that should be gotten rid of.

"No." Lee shook his head. "That's it."

"Very well." Calahan turned his attention to the pathetic, mewling Nujen. The old man pressed two fingers against his own temple and the creature flickered out of existence. The large nail stayed driven into the stud. The broken mask was picked up by Calahan and carried on top of the box. Lee offered the backpack, but Calahan passed.

They went upstairs and Calahan went to the kitchen. He pulled down the bottle of rye whiskey, examined it, and nodded approvingly. "Good flavor."

"I don't really drink it. If you want it, take it," Lee offered, but Calahan shook his head.

"Nah, I best be leaving treats like this behind." Calahan moved to the front door. "Lee, I hope to not see you again, for your sake, but we'll be keeping an eye on things for a while." He glanced again to the second floor. "Are you certain there's nothing else?"

Lee opened the door for Calahan. "I would have said so the first time." He motioned for Calahan to leave, and the old man's legs robotically took him from the house.

"So be it."

Lee and Calahan parted ways in the front yard. The old man walked slowly, vanishing into the darkness of the night. Lee returned to the Carsons' to get his son and begin the work of fixing his house.

FOURTEEN

Neither slept that night. Both processed what happened while they patched the walls on the first floor.

"I'm going to call Timmins in the morning and notify him that the issue is resolved. No need to relocate," Lee said as he smeared spackle on the broken wall.

"Isn't he just going to make us move anyway?" Bobby said with a groan.

"No. No need. The problem is resolved." Lee kept working. "Let's get this stuff patched up so you can have some friends over later this week. We'll have a staying-put party." Lee smiled at the idea. A cookout would be good. As he thought of it, he realized how much he missed having them. Bobby's mom was always the social one, and she loved parties. Maybe Lee could rediscover that love too.

"Want me to make some coffee?" Bobby asked.

"You know how to make coffee? Do you drink coffee?"

"Helps me get to school on time."

Lee shook his head. "Yeah, make a pot. Long night ahead of us." He motioned to a chunk of wall that fell off the staircase. "I'll go make sure that's stable up there."

The toy phone sat outside of Bobby's room, still where Bobby had kicked it earlier in the night. Its inviting smile and bobbing eyes focused on Lee as he approached it. He picked up the phone, took it to his office, and put it in the drawer with his black emergency phone.

Before he closed the drawer, the eyes bobbed up and down. He knew it was from the motion of him putting it away, but the eyes locked onto his expectantly. The one eye, its picked sticker seeming to wink at Lee, told him what he was thinking was okay. Better than okay, it was the right thing to do.

Calahan was right. One question was never going to be enough, but he knew who could answer those questions. The eyes stopped moving. Lee listened for Bobby and heard him in the kitchen, getting the coffee out.

Lee picked up the red handset and asked, "Hello?"

Gravelly laughter answered. "I thought I would be hearing from you."

"Who are you?" Lee whispered.

"I can be a friend. But for now, just call me the Artist. We're going to create such great works together." It laughed again, deep and loud.

Lee wanted to hang up before anything more happened. Hang up and escape the fate of Nujen. This was how servitude started, with one party needing that which the other party had. In this case, Lee needed answers. Who was Calahan? What was Nujen? Was this a threat to America? To his family? What did the key unlock? And with each question, he'd have to give something for an answer until those somethings mounted up into a debt he couldn't possibly pay.

Lee thought of Bobby. Of all he didn't know about the events of the night, he knew even less about his son. The coffee pot bubbled to brew and Lee hung up the toy phone as the Artist kept laughing. Lee sighed in relief. He chose his son. He chose right.

The phone rang. It was the toy phone ringing a sharp trill as the eyes danced out of sync in a crazed bouncing. Lee picked it up before Bobby could hear.

"I'll call you when I need you, Lee. And you best answer, or I'll call little Bobby and he'll do anything I tell him to do. Like, digging in a construction site. Or lying to his father. He'd come to me if I offered answers, just like his dad," the Artist said, and loosed a belly laugh that turned Lee's knees to water.

The Artist had him.

INVENTORY NOTE: ITEM 7

Item Number: 7

Components:

- Toy phone that calls demons

Collection: Public

We all make bad trades. This one, I'm not proud of. As soon as I can flip it, I will. Supposedly this phone can call demons and had an interesting story behind it, but there's no way to verify it. Also, I don't feel anything special about this phone. It just seems like a hunk of plastic.

The guy I traded with to get it said that the phone could call demons. He said that he got it from a middle-aged guy who said he stole it. Unusual when someone says they stole something like this, they don't own the theft, but that was this guy's story. Apparently, the seller stole it from someone who bought it from the seller when they were kids. When asked why the seller stole it back, he said it was to help the guy who bought it from him when they were kids. Weird, but that's this world.

The person who I traded with said there wasn't a verifiable backstory because the toy belonged to a guy who worked for some secret government organization. The way the trader was explaining it reminded me of the *X-Files* without the aliens.

The phone has never rung for me. As with all these toys, I'm not tempted to use it, so I will wait for it to do something. But I just want to flip this thing. The trader said the original seller was named Raymond and I could track him down, but so far my research has been empty. The trader said Raymond lived in Nevada during the early 90s and that's where he met the guy he stole it from all those years ago.

Junk. But that's how this goes. I'm learning more and more about this world. That guy in Tennessee has another toy for me. I'll be heading down there soon to get it. I hate trading with him, but I can't wait. Trades for this kind of crap take forever, and after all that time, I end up with what? A plastic phone? Aaron says to be patient, that this is a business of patience, but I can't wait. It's been years now. Years, and I've only gotten 7 toys. At this rate, I'll be doing this until I'm 80.

Can Drew survive that long? Is he still alive?

I have to keep hoping. Keep hoping and keep going. He needs me, and this time, I'm going to be there for him.

23

ONE

William tried not to shake. If he shook, they'd give him the medicine, and the medicine made him sick. He didn't want to throw up before his time in what he called, *the floating chair*. He let his fingers twitch once and then grabbed the arm rests of the chair and let the nurses strap him in.

The chair was surgical steel with green leather-wrapped cushions for his arms, butt, and around the hole in the back of the chair. There was a headrest, but he never used it. Bending his neck back during treatment made the headaches come. William wondered why the straps were so cold as the nurse wrenched them tight. This wonder led to thoughts of the room being cold, then the air vents, and the pinprick holes that speckled over the ceiling tiles. He began counting the dots until the squeaking metal wheels of a medical cart reminded him where he was and why he was here.

"Ready, Willy?" Nurse Leslie asked. She was nice. Everyone was nice, they just weren't kind.

William didn't respond. He was too busy keeping still. Keeping the medicine away.

"We'll get this done as fast as we can." She patted his arm. Her hand was cold. Not like the straps; it was cold and wet. She just washed her hands. Or she knew this was wrong. It was a horrible *treatment* that didn't help anything.

The doctor came in. He didn't talk to William, only to the nurses, asking gruffly if everything was ready.

Another cold wet feeling pressed into the center of William's back. The sponge, or whatever it was, lifted, but the chilly liquid ran down the parting of his hospital gown.

"Let's get going," the doctor said.

William felt a hot spike pierce his back, wasting no time with flesh as it found bone. A quick wiggle and it pressed past the bone, then cooled quickly to match everything else in the room. That change always brought the first wave of pain. His back tried to straighten, stiffen, but the straps didn't give.

Then the headache came. It didn't grow, it compressed. Not gradually, not slowly, but how your lungs seize when someone knocks the wind out of you. The pressure made him want to scream, but if he screamed, he'd move. If he moved, the needle moved and scraped against his spine. He held still to keep everything in place but gripped the chair harder. White knuckles strained to rip through his hands like razors.

"We're about done," the doctor said from the counter where he took notes.

A quick shake is what William needed. Let the energy out. His body knew that was what he needed. But he couldn't. The straps saved him from the medicine. A whine breathlessly squeezed out of him, unintentional, but he couldn't control his thoughts now. They were suffocated by the pressure. Pressure in his head, pressure from his guts coming up.

Gritting his teeth, the vomit leaked out his lips. A nurse was ready and blotted his mouth. He didn't eat on these days to keep the chunks out of his mouth.

The heat sliced through his back again as the needle was removed. And now came the worst part.

"Position one," the doctor called, and a nurse cranked the chair forward, each gear grinding as William was turned face down. As with his other times in the floating chair, when he was face down, he counted the tiles on the floor. They were pale green to promote calm, but how could he be calm with such a headache and so many things to count. The tiles. Their cracks. The grout's imperfections. The clamp in his brain tried to juice the gray matter within. Another spout of vomit broke free, this time spraying in slush over the floor. A nurse was ready with a mop, as always.

"Position two," the doctor called, and the crank began again.

The puke continued as the chair flipped over with William's head to the floor now. Vomit trickled up his cheeks, around his eyes. He was thankful it didn't get in his eyes this time. That stung. He wanted to sleep, but the nurses never allowed that. He needed to be awake and sharp. That's why now, unlike most other times, he couldn't be sedated.

"Okay, let's wrap up." The doctor snapped off his gloves and grabbed a clipboard from the counter. "Nice job, Willy. We'll get you sorted out yet." Doctor whatever his name was moved to the door. "X-ray room four." He left as the nurse finished cranking William back to sitting upright.

"Okay, sweetie, let's get you to the x-ray room." Nurse Leslie got him out of the chair. He couldn't walk. Couldn't think. William settled into a wheelchair and was taken to the x-ray room.

He didn't want to move anymore.

He just wanted to sleep, and after the x-ray room, that's what he did. It was the last peaceful sleep he'd have for a very, very long time.

TWO

"You always look so bad when you have your treatments," Lloyd Junior said when William returned to their room.

Lloyd never looked great himself, his own treatments being equally brutal, but Lloyd never complained. His vampiric pale complexion never shifted with treatment, and he couldn't lose any more weight at this point unless a bone fell out of him. William's condition wasn't fatal, just something horrible to overcome. Lloyd, William knew, wasn't leaving this hospital alive. Lloyd knew it too.

William always smiled when he saw Lloyd because he looked like one of those aliens in the newspapers his mom would read sometimes. Their skin, like Lloyd's, was extremely pale, almost gray. Their eyes were big, but Lloyd just looked like he had big eyes with the dark sockets surrounding his pale blue eyes.

"Did you throw up?" Lloyd asked and reached for William's arm.

William nodded and didn't want to be touched, but he couldn't move his arm. It was strapped down to the bed. The doctors said the restraints would help his body understand what it meant to be still. William didn't think it was working. His body couldn't move, but his mind sped along twice as fast. He couldn't concentrate on anything, but that's what the sedatives were for. To slow his mind down. Nurse

Leslie gave him a shot before she dropped him off and he was already feeling the anchors on his thoughts.

"Yeah." William nodded. "I threw up."

"You don't smell like puke," Lloyd offered in condolence.

"Thanks." William smiled.

The headache still squeezed William's brain, as it often did after treatment. "I think I'm just going to go to sleep." His words were already taking on the dreamy quality of someone who needs to get away from the waking world. The sedatives and the exhaustion hooked their claws into his eyelids and dragged them down.

"Before you go to sleep." Lloyd ran back to his bed and returned. "I want to give you this. His name's Sergei and he helps me feel better when I have a," Lloyd looked away from William, "rough day." He handed William a stuffed elephant with one eye. It was an old, worn thing, but not from abuse; from many long nights of loving cuddles. It reminded William of the Velveteen Rabbit, which made his mind jump to scarlet fever, and then to leukemia. Lloyd was dying of leukemia, and maybe the elephant was infected.

As if reading his thoughts, Lloyd said, "Don't worry, I'm not contagious." He laughed. "You can't get what I have from an elephant."

William smiled and accepted the elephant. He was too old for stuffies like this, but he needed something to feel better. The medicine didn't help, his mom wasn't around to hug him – not that she ever came by on treatment days, so maybe he'd give the elephant a try. Lloyd talked to the elephant sometimes at night and, for a dying kid, Lloyd seemed pretty happy.

"Thanks," William said, and let his head relax back.

"Take care of him, Sergei." Lloyd smiled, settled the elephant beside William's hand, and went back to his bed. "Tell Sergei," Lloyd chuckled, "he'll be okay. He's in good hands." Lloyd's bed squeaked as he climbed into it.

Sleep came quickly for both of them.

***

Sedatives normally stole William's dreams, so waking up in a dungeon was unexpected. The walls were large gray stones covered in streaks of water. There was a gas lamp outside his cell's rusty bars. He stood up after realizing he was sitting on the cold concrete floor.

His clothes were so soft, a welcome change from the normally scratchy things his parents put him in and a massive improvement from the drafty hospital gown. He was wearing jeans and a blue velvet shirt with a dark brown leather vest over it. And he wasn't a kid. He was older. Bigger. Muscular like an athlete, but not like those muscle guys on TV.

"I know what it means."

William jumped at the thick voice in the cell with him. He scanned the room quickly and saw another man, a giant man, in the cell's shadowy corner. The man stayed on the floor, his voice choked with sorrow.

"I know what it means that you're here and not Lloyd, Son of Lloyd."

Shuffling feet echoed down the long hallway outside the cell. Someone was moving towards them but it sounded like they were wearing muddy shoes, or dragging a wet blanket behind them. Then William remembered the man sharing his cell, and fear tightened his stomach.

"Who are you?" William asked.

"Did he go peacefully?" The man asked as chains clinked around the shadow. "I knew he was ill."

"Lloyd's fine. I just talked to him." William looked around the dream again and wondered why he was dreaming about Lloyd. "Who are you?"

The shadows shifted as the man stood. He was easily eight feet tall and as wide as a car. As he stood, the chains clanked together and a strange form emerged into the lamp's orange light. It was long, serpentine, but strong and turning in a curious movement. It made a strange noise that took William a moment to recognize. It was sniffing. The long form was a trunk.

The man stepped forward, straining against the chains. He was a humanoid elephant. William didn't move. He just took in all the details as his mind often told him to do. Large floppy ears. Wide face with a long trunk protruding where its nose should be and a mouth under that. Intelligent eyes…well, eye. One eye had a brown leather eyepatch over it. He was dressed in jeans with a frilly white shirt like a swashbuckler from *Treasure Island*. It was the last movie William saw in the theater before the hospital.

William knew he was dreaming, but wasn't sure why he was dreaming about a one-eyed pirate elephant. His dreams were normally much less fantastical. Often, they were on whatever happened that day or recently. Since he'd been in the hospital, he'd not had any dreams, and so assumed this was just his mind catching up for lost time. The elephant made sense.

"You must be Sergei?" William asked.

Sergei nodded. "And you?"

"William." But after looking at his hands, considering how much older he was in the dream, he thought he could be anyone. He could go by a more grown-up name like Will or Bill, but he hated the name Bill. Teachers used to call him Wild Bill because of the cowboy and his tendency to get out of his seat. He couldn't help it. Sometimes he just needed to move. "Will."

"It is a pleasure to journey with you, Will." Sergei nodded deeply, almost bowing. "Lloyd mentioned you. He said you were brilliant."

William looked around. "Why are we here?"

While others might have questioned the situation or dismissed it as purely the workings of a dream, William took almost everything literally. He knew it was a dream, but that didn't mean he wanted to sit in a prison cell with Sergei for however long this dream would last.

"Lloyd and I were captured at the gates. I failed to be as stealthy as required."

William laughed at the idea of anything this big being stealthy.

"Why were you coming here?" William pressed his face to the bars. Rust flaked over his cheeks. Down the hall, he heard the shuffling steps again. Now they were closer, and each step ended with a wet slosh. Whatever was coming their way was around the corner at the end of the hall and moving slowly.

"We need to lock the doors in the cellar." Sergei pulled on the chains, struggling with a grunt. "The guards are coming. When they see you, they're going to wonder where Lloyd went."

Thick gauntlets circled Sergei's wrists and wrapped around his hands. They looked like bullets hung from chains as thick as William's wrists. Those chains didn't budge as Sergei jerked and tugged against where they connected to the wall. A small detail in the chain made William chuckle.

"Wait." He motioned for Sergei to stop pulling. "There's a crack in the chain. Just pull there." William pointed to a spot on the chain where the solder that bound it was misaligned from the joint. It was a minuscule detail. He looked for something to put in the chain to twist for torque and heard the sloshing steps stop. A man whined from where the steps were. There was dripping somewhere in the cell. William went to look for it.

"Lloyd said you could see things others couldn't. I guess he was true." Sergei smiled, nodded, then wrapped the chains around his thick arms.

"See what?" William found a trickle of water, but it wasn't what he was looking for. "Where's that dripping?" It grated on his nerves hearing the steady *plink, plink, plink* of water on stone.

Sergei grunted, choking it back to keep as quiet as possible. "You know..." The chain creaked and flexed like clay under the strain of Sergei's strength. "You are handling this very well. Lloyd didn't take it so in stride."

SNAP!

The chain broke.

"I'll wake up soon." William pressed his cheek to the wall to feel where the drips were coming from.

"Will you now?" Sergei looked at the steel capsules over his hands.

"Back to the hospital. At least here we can get out." William tapped on the wall. "This is hollow."

Sergei tapped the steel gauntlets together, letting a bright chime ring through the cell. "Stand back." He approached the wall.

"Wait." William held up a hand. "Where's the water coming from?"

"Does it matter?"

"Yes." William felt the wall, felt the water streaming down. It was cool. The connection between ceiling and wall was tight, but the water had to be coming from there.

"Why?" Sergei knocked on the wall, hearing the hollow thud. A scream pulled Sergei's attention from the wall. Someone in another cell was screaming, but the sound was choked off by greedy slurping. William didn't notice it or was unbothered as he searched for the origin of the water.

"Because. I need to know." William stopped as his fingers hit a crack in the wall. "Ah, here. Here's where it is. Probably goes up to the next floor."

"Okay." Sergei went to the bars and looked down the hall. The guard emerged from where it just ate a prisoner. Sergei had seen things like this before. It was a bulbous worm wrapped in a black, chalky hide. They slid through the halls of this tower and devoured anyone they didn't like. Sergei knew they wouldn't like Will because he wasn't Lloyd. The guard was heading their way.

"No time. We gotta go." Sergei hurried to the wall. "Stand back." After William did, Sergei slammed his fist into the wall. The metal gauntlet cracked on the impact. He punched again. The wall buckled. Another punch. The metal broke free of his thick fist.

"What's that?!" William was at the bars. A thick mucus trailed behind the worm coming his way. It was four feet tall, but William wasn't sure his measurements were right now that his size was so much larger. It filled the hallway. Five feet, maybe six across. The sound he'd heard earlier, the sloshing, was this thing moving through the hall. It was louder now. A constant wet splashing as the worm drooled its slime to move across the ground.

Sergei struck the wall harder and harder until the gauntlets fell away. The wall collapsed and revealed a hallway.

"Follow me!" Sergei called, and William didn't question. He turned and ran as the worm reached their cell bars. It rose up to them, resting against them. Sizzling, putrid acid filled the air behind William as he ran with Sergei into the hall. The hallway wasn't even, with stones sticking out of the walls. One rough rock caught William's hand.

"Ow!" William yelled, but kept running as the worm dissolved the bars and wiggled into the cell. "Wait! What's that sound? The chimes?"

Sergei slid on the floor and turned. "Chimes? You hear chimes?" He ran back to William and grabbed his arm.

"Yeah..." William's legs went weak and he fell. The fall felt like it went through the floor, all the way into infinity, ending in his hospital bed. He woke up. Still strapped down. Eyes open, seeing the nurses checking his blood pressure.

"Oh, you're awake," the nurse said. William didn't recognize her.

Sergei, the stuffed elephant, sat by his hand. William looked to Lloyd's bed, but it was empty. A man was there collecting the boy's things.

"Where's Lloyd?" William asked too frantically. He couldn't calm down. The worm was just chasing him. He was running. He was out of this bed running. "Where's Lloyd?"

"I'm sorry, sweetie. Lloyd passed away," the nurse said and rubbed William's shoulder. "Were you two close?"

The elephant sat watching William with its one eye. "Kind of," William said. "He was nice."

"That's his dad. You could say something kind. That would be good for him to hear." The nurse motioned to the man collecting Lloyd's things and left.

But the man didn't wait for William to say something. He walked over to William's bed and picked up Sergei.

"Did Lloyd give this to you?" The man asked as he shook Sergei. "Did he give it to you, or did you take it?" His eyes were glassy red, his nostrils flared, and spittle pooled around his lips. "Answer me!"

THREE

"He gave it to me!" William answered. He tried to get up, get away, but the restraints kept him still. There was nowhere to go.

"When?" The man shook Sergei at William.

"Yesterday? Last night?" William wasn't sure how long he'd been out. Sometimes the sedatives knocked him out for days, but it felt like a short dream.

The timeline shocked the man. He dropped Sergei on the bed by William's leg. "Last night?"

"Yeah. I think it was. The medicine sometimes makes me sleep for a long time. But—"

"The dream wasn't that long?" the man said.

William gaped and twitched, the energy in him trying to find anywhere to escape. How did this guy know about a dream?

"Lloyd passed away three days ago," the man said, and sat on the edge of William's bed. "I'm his dad, Lloyd Senior. Mr. Mekins. And I guess you already met Sergei." Mekins pointed to the stuffed elephant.

William paused, not sure he knew what Mekins meant. Sometimes he took people too literally, but he wasn't sure what else the man could mean.

"I'm sorry about Lloyd. He was my friend. I mean, he was nice to me."

"He was a good kid," Mekins said. He looked away from William and sniffled. "I'm sorry I was angry. Lloyd's passing… Just been hard."

That made sense. William wondered if his parents would miss him. They only came around on Saturdays. That was days after his treatment. He assumed they didn't want to see him worn down, covered in puke, or in the haze of sedation. Of those three, which was the biggest deterrent?

"I– I understand." But William didn't. He hadn't ever lost someone, but he had heard people say this when someone did something they couldn't take back and then apologized for it.

"Did you meet Sergei?" Mekins pointed to the stuffed elephant.

"Yes, Lloyd gave him to me."

"No. I mean, did you *meet* him? I'm guessing you were sleeping?"

William thought about the dream. The impossible dream where he ran from monsters with a one-eyed elephant. How did Mekins know about that dream?

"I was Sergei's helper before my son." The older man stood and took a deep breath. "I passed him to Lloyd when he was five. That's the right age to still be a kid in that world. Time moves different over there."

William looked around hoping a nurse would come in and stop this weird conversation. None did. Instead, he breathed slowly to keep calm and got ready to scream if Mr. Mekins went nuts and attacked him.

"Yeah, it's a lot to take in." Mekins nodded and returned to Lloyd's side of the room. "I believe you."

"About what?" William asked.

"Lloyd gave you Sergei. Lloyd thought you could help him. I guess Sergei needs help from someone like you."

"Like me?" William wasn't sure what that meant. He'd heard the doctors and his parents refer to his *strangeness,* but that didn't feel like what Mekins was talking about.

"Someone stuck here. Someone who knows the value of freedom."

A question squirmed out of William's brain and hit his lips before it could be pulled back. Such questions could land him in the institution his parents talked about. The place they told him he never wanted to go. That's why he was strapped down to this bed. That's why he was flipped upside down, to avoid the institute. But the question came and Mekins heard it.

"Was that a dream?" William asked.

Mekins shook his head. "You get there through dreams. Your body stays here, but you're there as much as you're here."

A pulse of energy spiked through William, making his hand twitch and fingers flick. Sharp pain sprung up his wrist from the back of his hand. He rolled his wrist to see. It was blackened with the bruise from where he hit his hand on the wall in the dream.

Mekins saw him look. "Accident in the other place?"

"Hit a wall…" William examined the bruise as best he could with the restraints.

"Be careful there. My pop always told me what happened there, didn't stay there. You bring it back with you." Mekins finished packing Lloyd's belongings in a large suitcase. He zipped it with a sigh. "You get out of here, find us. You'll have questions. We have some answers."

"Where will you be?"

"Sergei will direct you. He knows how to get around both worlds pretty good." Mekins gently shook William's hand, patted Sergei on the head, said a silent goodbye and left.

The nurse came in as Mekins left and noticed Wiliam's hand.

"What happened here?" the nurse asked. William didn't recognize her. She checked the restraints, tightening them one notch beyond painful. "Struggling against these don't do you no good." Her tone turned stern. "I know you want to be a good boy. You want to be still, but hurting yourself like this," she shook her head as if to say *tsk, tsk, tsk*, "it tells us you're not getting better."

"No," William said. "No, ma'am," he corrected, "I wasn't struggling. I hit my hand on a wall in my dream—"

"Don't be talking crazy. You were struggling. Admit it." She walked to the medication tray. There was a cup there with fresh sleeping medicine. It was the stuff that made him puke. He didn't want it, but if she offered he'd take it. Once he refused and an orderly held his head back and his mouth open as they poured the medicine in. After it was in his throat, they held his nose and mouth shut until he swallowed. His mom watched it happened and cried as his dad told her it was for William's own good.

A new explanation formed quickly in William's mind. "I must have hit my hand on the bed side." He tapped his hand on the metal bed frame. The cold metal stung the bruise.

She picked up the cup of medicine and faced him. The plastic cup was frosted clear. The medicine inside was a thick dark green liquid that felt like drinking syrupy jello that hadn't set yet. William knew it tasted like the worm's slime in his dream. As she stepped toward him, the medicine didn't move in the cup. It clung to the sides as it would cling to his throat in a choking coating.

"I hit my hand on the bed. It was an accident. I…" He saw the cup coming to his mouth. "I startled."

"This will help you calm down."

His fingers flicked and flailed, but nothing else could move after the latest tightening. William didn't want to calm down. He didn't want to puke from drinking that crap. Most of all, he didn't want to sleep. What if Sergei had left him behind, and when he woke up in that dream, he was being dissolved by the worm thing? William felt the weight of the impossibly gargantuan worm on his chest. He heard the fizzing as acid dissolved his flesh down to the bone. A dark thought popped, making him calm, making him wonder, *Dissolving won't hurt as much as the headaches, and I'll be done.*

He didn't want to be done. He wanted to be free. He wanted to run off to adventure and out of this place. So he drank without complaint. He swallowed the thick syrup with a smile and thank you.

"See, its already helping." The nurse smiled and patted his bald head. "We're here to help you, Willy, but only if you let us." She nodded. "We're a team. Like the Cowboys. And they just won the Super Bowl."

William didn't watch Super Bowl VI with his dad. He had just arrived in this hospital. Dad rented a TV for a party and told him all about all the fun they had watching the game. How they missed him, and Uncle Benny asked where he was, and dad said Willy was on a trip because that was easier for people to understand. Dad said to tell anyone who asked where he had been, that he was on a trip. That explanation would be easier for them. As his eyes grew heavy, William was ready for a trip. Ready to go somewhere the nurses couldn't. Where his parents couldn't go. Where he was…

FOUR

"Will!" Sergei screamed in his face with arms ready to catch him.

William's senses surged to full awareness. His feet were still running. He was running.

"Are you back?" Sergei grabbed his arm in one powerful hand.

"Yeah." His feet regained their speed and William ran. "How long was I out?"

"You weren't out." Sergei kept pace. "Time's different here. How long were you there?"

"An hour?" William guessed and glanced back. The black worm was still there, now sliding up the wall as it pulsed quickly toward them.

"That's only seconds here." Sergei pointed ahead. "Turn left!"

William did, and the stone hallway continued. There was a light up ahead. He hoped it would be a field, or a mountain, something outside. For the past few months he'd only seen hospital walls, exam rooms, and the occasional view out Lloyd's window. Being strapped to a bed didn't provide much chance to see the world but now, who knew what was ahead. The wonder made him smile and run faster. When the hall ended, it opened into another room. Yet, disappointment didn't swell or even crash on him, it evaporated as William felt the strength in his legs. There was no atrophy like the doctors told him to expect from being kept still. All he had was power and speed, and a smile from ear to ear as he pumped his arms in a full sprint. He hadn't run like this since he was chasing George in tag last summer. That day was hot. Here it was cool. Almost cold. This air didn't have the tangy smog of New York, it was fresh. It tasted like a mountain, like what a bird tastes when it flies, like—

"Watch out!" Sergei grabbed William and ripped him from the edge. The opening was a drop. Maybe once there was a room here, but now it was a massive pit so deep all they saw was darkness.

"Whoa!" William peered down. "Thanks." He didn't want this to be a dream anymore. He wanted this to be real, and he didn't want it to end when that worm got here. Now he knew why the worm crawled to the ceiling: it was preparing for the drop.

Down in the pit, broken stones protruded and cracked to make handholds.

"We can climb down," William said.

"Sure, you don't want to fly?" Sergei asked.

"Can we do that here?"

"No." Sergei chuckled. "No more than we can climb down that."

William thought he could do it with these strong arms, but Sergei was huge and maybe not a climber. The elephant didn't even get close to the edge, much less look out.

"Are you afraid of heights?" William asked, confused that this giant would fear anything.

"Not a fear. More like extreme dislike," Sergei clarified.

William looked up from the pit. A blue dome glowed as if it was made of a midday sky. William didn't think it was real. His thoughts were quickly distracted by the vines hanging from the ceiling. "Think those could hold our weight?"

Sergei stuck his head out to see. "Yeah." He retracted into the hallway. The worm was twenty feet away now. It would be on them in moments. "Knotwood. It's used to weave ships."

Weave ships? William thought. "Okay. We swing across." He pointed to a door on the other side of the pit. "Just like Tarzan."

"Did Tarzan live?" Sergei asked. He nervously flicked his thick hands and arms in preparation for what was about to come. "I mean, you wouldn't suggest it if you didn't know he lived right?" Sergei blew out a long sigh and began to bounce, pausing to stretch his torso with rippling pops.

"Tarzan's not real." William smiled and ran, jumped from the edge and grabbed the first vine. It swung, and he with it. He leapt to the next vine. Below him was darkness, but he didn't look. The vines were swinging too quickly, the wind blowing through his long brown hair, hair that he had here. Each vine seemed to jump into his hand as he swung so fast, so far, he screamed in joy as he flew.

"Don't get cocky!" Sergei shouted from behind him. He was moving through the vines too, but not enjoying it nearly as much.

William jumped from the last vine, landed in the doorway across the room, and rolled to his feet. He marveled at how his body here knew just what to do. It was an athletic body formed from years of adventures. He didn't wonder if it was his body, or Lloyd's, or something else. William only enjoyed it.

Sergei followed and the two turned back to see the worm.

It was flying on four large wings toward them.

"I thought it couldn't fly!" William pointed to the worm.

"I said *we* can't fly. It's a guard, of course it can fly!" Sergei shouted back.

"How would I know that?!"

The two ran down the new hallway into an open room. This room was circular, four baseball fields in diameter, at least two houses tall. Massive pillars held up a domed glass ceiling. Outside the sky was black, but not the black of night, the black of outer space with stars bright, close, and draped in the green mist of a nearby space cloud. The white marble interior had a glossy sheen of neon green from the sky above that made William's mind burn with questions. Where was he? How did all this work? Why here? But he didn't ask the question he never wanted answered: when would this end? When would he wake bound to the hospital bed?

"Oh my god," William gasped.

"Sightsee later." Sergei grabbed him. "We're in the central chamber. This is where all the guards will converge. We need to get out of here."

But William couldn't move. His eyes traced the manic swirls of green. He'd never heard of nebulas in school, but if he did, he'd know that was what he was looking at. In 18-years, the Hubble Telescope would show stunning images of nebulas, but they would never compare to experiencing it up close. The energy radiating from it vibrated in William's teeth and smelled like a campfire mixed with lavender. Stars flickered between the clouds. One of them could have been the sun he knew from home, but he doubted it. This place was as strange to him as he was to his doctors, and William loved it. This place was home, not the hospital. The hospital was the dream. And he couldn't get caught here. Couldn't let the guards lock him up here. However he knew they were not interested in arresting him, only devouring him.

"Right," William said. "Where to?"

Around the room, marble corridors opened into other halls. Each corridor was marked with a symbol in the center. There were twenty-five doors. William counted them as he ran, following Sergei toward a corridor with a spiral carved in the center.

"This way. This is what we came here for. No sense turning back now." Sergei ran, his trunk flailing behind him, his loose white shirt inflating with the wind from his powerful legs, but William kept pace.

"Locking doors?"

"Yes," Sergei answered as they entered the spiral corridor. It quickly changed from white marble to a light charcoal stone. Dust kicked up behind them in a cloud, making William wonder if the floor was actual charcoal. The path descended, but before they lost sight of the round room behind them, William saw three guards converge and look for them.

Sergei and William breathed quietly and kept their running as silent as possible, but a dust cloud would eventually find its way to those giant worm creatures.

William whispered, "Where are we going?"

"Center of the Lazarus Spiral. If we live, I'll explain it to you."

"Aren't you a stuffed animal? Can you die?" William asked.

Sergei chuckled quietly. "Will, we can all die. This place is as real as the other. Just different worlds."

"Can you leave here?"

"Yes. There are places here where you can go anywhere. Just say where you want to go and you'll go."

William thought about that. Wondering if it was limited to his dreaming self. And he asked the obvious question, "Then why didn't you use one of those places to get where you're trying to go? Like, why break in if you could just ask to go there and then be there?"

Sergei shrugged. "You got me. I said anywhere, but really I meant most places. Places like this, they're sealed against those passages. Too dangerous to let just anyone in here."

"So the guards are just doing their job?" William snickered. They weren't kind, but they were doing their job.

"No. I…well, Lloyd thought they'd been corrupted. He thought this place had been compromised and that's why we were sent to check the locks."

"Who sent you?" William asked as they slowed down. A wooden door was at the end of the long corridor. It was a bone color, yellowed with age. Black tar leaked from around the edges, clumping like the medicine that put him to sleep. It drooled over the door in wet streaks, bunching up and dripping over the green patina banding holding the door together. The banding could have been salvaged from a sunken ship or made from the cavity of a giant's tooth, it wreaked of rot and the pungent stench of infection.

William covered his nose and mouth without thinking. Sergei was expecting the sensory assault but still squinted and clenched his jaw to steel his resolve.

"Later. Right now, we gotta focus." Sergei checked for the guards. None were coming. In the distance, a faint sloshing could be heard, but it seemed to be far and moving farther. "Once I open this door, the guards will come." Sergei took a deep breath. "We need to get it closed as soon as possible, but I have no idea what's on the other side. Be ready for anything."

A million outcomes rushed through William's mind, which often occurred when faced with the unknown. He tried to imagine what could be on the other side, but imagination was never his strength. Analysis and seeing things others couldn't—that's where he excelled. Thus, he prepared his mind to observe everything the moment the door opened. From there, he could help Sergei, but not until then. William said, "I'm ready."

Sergei grabbed the ring hanging from the door handle. A deep pulse rushed through the floor and up William's legs. He'd never been to a concert before, never had felt the thrumming of a drum solo while standing beside a speaker, but that's what it was. A concussive rhythm that brought the sloshing sounds closer, brought them faster.

"In!" Sergei ripped the door open. It screamed against the motion as the hinges broke from unknowable years of stasis. They were still for so long, the first time they could move they screamed in agony or delight. The sound made him smile as he looked in before moving, saw what was before them, saw everything in the room in the second before Sergei grabbed him and pulled him in.

As the door slammed behind them, William knew what they had to do and wondered, for the first time, if he died here, would he die in the hospital? If they didn't act fast, he was about to find out.

FIVE

When the door opened, William saw three things.

Flapping red flags hanging from the ceiling.

Another door across a long wooden bridge over a gaping black chasm.

Ten holes in the wall across the bridge with arrow tips pointing out.

As Sergei pulled him into the room, William pushed the giant behind the door and pulled it all the way open, hiding behind it. Steel arrowheads thumped against the thick door, with a few splintering the wood but being held fast. One arrow sliced William's stomach through his shirt. The wound wasn't deep. Just enough to spill a trickle of blood.

Sergei gasped as the arrows hit the door. He looked at the tips that stuck through the wood.

William shut the door quickly and said, "Keep low." Both of them got on their bellies and crawled toward the bridge.

The charcoal stone was darker here. The room was rectangular with a slight stone lip that traced around the wall. Between the bridge and the wall was a black pit. William smiled, considering how this was the second, and probably not last, bottomless pit he'd seen in the tower. He and Sergei were laying on a small stone platform at the edge of the bridge. Above them, the ceiling was as high as the hospital was tall, with long red flags hanging down on each side of the bridge. Gold thread adorned the flags to form a spiral at their triangular ends. They flapped in a wind William couldn't feel.

"Traps?" Sergei examined one of the arrowheads through the door. He sniffed it. "Will, I believe this arrow was dipped in Sleepweed." He searched for a term that William might recognize, but couldn't find one. "A poison. I don't know how it will affect you." He shrugged. "Lloyd wasn't always affected by the toxicities of our world."

William nodded thoughtfully and crawled toward the bridge. "I feel fine." And he did, except for some tightness in his stomach, but that would be expected when you get a cut or three as he had from the arrows that broke through the door. "Let's go."

He crawled onto the bridge, keeping low and moving slow as they came to the first set of flags. The wind was still moving them. They swayed toward the bridge and back to the wall laterally.

"Give me your boot," William said.

Sergei did so without question. William held it forward where the flags were swaying. A sharp *THWIT* split the air as an arrow lanced the boot. He pulled it back quickly.

"Sorry." He handed it to Sergei.

"It wasn't my favorite boot." Sergei took the boot, pulled the arrow through, and put it back on.

"I felt the wind when I held out the boot. Its blowing from behind

the flag on the right to behind the flag on the left. It's like a trip wire."
William had seen enough James Bond movies to know about laser
trip wires. This wasn't a laser, it was wind. And he didn't have special
glasses or sprays to make them visible.

The flags flapped heaviest at the bottom. Their tops, near the
ceiling, only swayed with the motion from the bottom.

"I think we need to climb up there." He pointed to the top of the
flag.

Sergei looked up.

"Or shimmy against the wall." William motioned to the small lip
of stones that lined the wall. They were soft charcoal like the walls,
and he knew at least one would crumble under their weight. But
another thought peeked into his mind. He couldn't find it yet, but
he kept watching the bottom of the flags. They flicked and swayed,
crossing where he held out the boot a moment ago.

"Give me your boot again."

Sergei groaned as he took the boot off. "I was just trying to be nice
earlier. These are my favorite boots."

William flicked his hand to get the boot and held it out again.
Another arrow speared it. He pulled the boot back, then quickly
thrust it out and pulled it back. No arrow. He watched the flag
again, seeing the flapping was quick. He thrust the boot out again
and pulled it back. No arrow. He held the boot up as if they were
standing. Another volley of arrows launched from the far wall,
spearing the boot.

"Okay, I got an idea. Back up to the door."

Sergei did, carrying his boot, and once back to the stone entryway, he sighed and put his boot back on. There were large holes in the side now that showed his gray ankles.

"How fast do you think you can run?" William asked.

"Very fast." Sergei looked at the arrow holes in the other wall. "Run, drop, run?"

William shook his head, knowing the only way to keep a sprint was to keep going. "No. We're running straight through."

"But the arrows?" Sergei pointed to the far wall.

"We're going to need the door. Can you rip it off the hinges?"

"But the guards?"

"We just gotta move faster than them," William said.

Sergei nodded. "This idea's crazy, but I'm in." He opened the door, releasing another deep pulse, and tore it from the metal hinges in a muffled crumble as the metal gave way.

"Now!" William took the door and ran down the bridge. He kept the door held in front of him as far as he could. Arrows hit it hard, but he ran through. The wind caught his ankles as he passed the flags, but the arrows did not. He moved too fast. He didn't look back. William didn't see the guards coming in or Sergei preparing to follow. The arrows hit the door again, this time pressing farther through the wood, but William didn't stop. Another set of flags blew by. Another arrow hissed by his feet. The third set of flags were coming as another volley of arrows came, and these broke the door in half. One arrow sliced William's side, the others stayed in the door. The slice slowed him down as he stepped into the wind and caught the last arrow in his calf. He yelped and the force twisted him, spun him off the bridge.

Sergei caught him, pulled him back, and held him as they both slid under the last volley of arrows to the platform on the other side of the room.

On the bridge, the guards were being struck by arrow after arrow until they slowed, stopped, and fell from the bridge. One tried to take flight, seeing what was happening, but it had already been struck and its wings failed to hold it in the air. It tumbled into the pit with its brothers.

"More will come," Sergei said, and pulled William across the floor toward the next wooden door. This one was the same bone color held together by the same rotten tar and patina green metal.

"The arrows got me," William said, and saw one was still in his leg. "I think…" The chimes began to fill the room. "I think the poison's working." Exhaustion flooded his body and mind as he fell out of consciousness in this world, reawakening in the other.

SIX

He was still bound to the bed. The hospital gown stuck to him in dark pools of blood on his stomach. By his right leg, another dark pool was growing. William strained to move to see what was happening, but the straps held him too tight.

Night had come. William couldn't see anything out the window other than the starless sky. He longed for the green nebula. The feeling struck him as odd, having only seen it once for a moment, but the longing grew as the stars winked in the dull black sky.

The lights in his room were off. No need to waste electricity on someone like him. He couldn't reach the button to call for a nurse. The sudden urge to pee hit him, as it did for many boys at night, but again, he couldn't reach the call button. His restraints were too tight.

William knew not to scream out, not to panic; that would just alert the guards…nurses to his presence and make them think he required sedation. Loud boys need to learn to be still, calm. He prepared a calm voice, a voice that didn't say, *Help, I have to pee and I'm bleeding!*

Softly he called, "Hello, Nurse Leslie? I need to use the bathroom." He took a deep breath and tried to pull the heat in his body up, out of his groin and into a long exhale. His foot shook trying to keep the pee in. "I'm sorry. Nurse Leslie?" he called again. "I really have to go." He let his foot shiver to distract his body from the pressure building in his bladder.

A nurse came in. Not Nurse Leslie, another one. William hadn't met her before. She turned on the light; florescent flickered to life, casting his dark room in the sickly green glow all hospitals share. She glanced at him, saw the restraints, and gasped.

"What is going on in here?" she asked while looking for his chart.

"I really have to pee," William pleaded.

She undid his restraints quickly, his hands flying free and flapping as he sucked in a deep breath to avoid peeing the bed. He got up to run to the bathroom, his arms feeling so light now that he was out of the straps. When he stood, his legs buckled from under him. He fell on the floor with the loud crack of bone hitting hard tile. The nurse went to him, lifted him up, and helped him to the bathroom where William sat on the toilet and peed for the first time off his bed in weeks.

The nurse ran back to his bed to examine his chart.

While peeing, his legs and arms flicked and flailed, enjoying the freedom that one only really knows after not having it for so, so long.

"Doctor!" the nurse called and ran out of the room.

William wondered what was going on. He used the bars to help lift himself from the toilet and leaned on the sink. The water from the tap was cold and felt so good against his dry hands. A satisfied sigh slipped from him as he closed his eyes and let the cool water run over him. William didn't see the nurse bring the doctor in or hear them talking in the other room.

"Willy?" the doctor said. This was the one who did his *treatments*. The one who put the needle in his spine. "Just come on out and we'll get you taken care of, alright, son?"

But William couldn't stand. His legs didn't have any strength. "I need help walking."

The doctor came in, stopped, and pointed to William's gown. After a nod to the nurse, the doctor took William's arm.

"What happened to your stomach?" The doctor walked William to Lloyd's old bed. William's bed was being remade with clean sheets.

Knowing the truth wasn't going to work for his doctor, William went with an easy answer. "I don't know."

"You don't remember?" the doctor said, more of a correction than a question.

"Yeah. I don't remember," William agreed, and hoped that would be the end of the conversation.

"I understand." The doctor motioned for another nurse to come over. "These things can happen with your condition."

William wasn't sure what that meant, but nodded as if he did.

"Did that happen before the bathroom or while you were in there?"

William knew the only correct answer was to stay to his story. "I don't remember."

Another knowing nod from the doctor.

"We're ready, Doctor." A nurse William hadn't seen before leaned into the room.

William's bed was finished being made and he looked at it, longing to go back, to go to sleep and return to Sergei.

"Not quite yet," the doctor said. The nurse from earlier, the one who unstrapped him, brought in a wheelchair. "Let's go for a quick visit to see if we can help make sure this doesn't happen again."

The doctor pointed to William's stomach. William wanted to assure him it wouldn't. Wanted to beg that they not go to where he knew they were going. There was no time for preparations. They were going to do this without anything for the pain to come. But saying anything would mean saying everything, and instead of talking, William's foot began to bounce as he sat in the wheelchair.

"We don't need the restraints, do we?" the doctor asked. "A still body leads to a still mind." The doctor smiled, encouraging William to agree.

William tried to stop his leg, tried to demand it be still, but his mind was a maelstrom. The coming pain, the pressure in his mouth, the pressure in everything, spun through his mind. But at least he'd sleep. He'd go back to Sergei. Back to the world he wished was real.

"Can I take my elephant?" William motioned to the one-eyed stuffed animal on his side table.

"You're a big boy," the doctor scoffed. "You don't need things like that." He motioned for the nurse, the one who let him out of the restraints, to get moving. She pushed him out of the room, stopped, and another nurse took over from there.

They went down the long hallway with fluorescent lights flickering above them. William had only been to this room twice and didn't want to go back. He pushed on his legs to stop them from moving.

The doctor stood tall and strode forward without a worry as the nurse behind kept assuring William that this would help him feel better.

After a quick turn, they went into the dark room with a long table in the center. Lights over the table would give a good view of whoever was on it. William knew it was meant for him, and he didn't resist as he was helped onto the table. The nurse who pushed him now strapped his arms down and asked him to open his mouth. He did. Compliance made things easier for everyone. She began to rub his bald scalp with a cold gauze. He felt the sticky electrodes placed where she was rubbing.

"Do we have time for the methohexital?" the nurse asked.

The doctor made some kind of noise, but William wasn't sure what it meant.

"Succinylcholine?" she asked.

"That should be fine," the doctor answered.

Another nurse jabbed a needle into William's arm. The fluid burned as it blossomed under his skin. Quickly the heat spread over his body, making his arms and legs numb.

The nurse who freed him came in and tucked Sergei into his arm. William looked at her sorry eyes and smiled to her. She shook her head, tears welling, and hurried out of the room.

"Okay, Willy. We're just going to give you one more shot and put this mask on you, then you'll go to sleep and not want to hurt yourself anymore," the nurse who pushed him said.

"Yes, I didn't think you were a danger to yourself, Willy. I am sorry we didn't do this sooner. But don't worry. Most patients have a great response to this therapy."

"Am I going to sleep?" William asked. He stared into the nameless nurse's pleasant mask of a face and looked for confirmation.

She nodded and placed the oxygen mask over his face. Another needle was stabbed into his arm, but he didn't feel this one.

A moment later, he heard the doctor asking the nurse if she was ready. She told him Willy was asleep. William hated that name. But he wasn't asleep yet. He wasn't. He hadn't gone back to the tower. Why? Why?

"Then let's get this over with. This self-injury is bad. He really got himself good," the doctor said. His words began to drag out and slow down as if talking underwater. "I don't know if we can help him after all." The last word echoed into a black void where William fell, forever descending, clenching onto Sergei as he went.

His body slammed against stone as black dust puffed up around him. Sergei was still in his hands, but now the stuffy was a giant elephant man who looked very worried.

SEVEN

"I'm asleep in the other world, but they're about to do something that might wake me up," William said. The arrow was still stuck through his calf, and blood still pumped out in the pulse of his heartbeat, quick and strained. He began to climb up the wall to stand near the white door. Other guards were coming through the first door now. The arrows were still flying, still catching them, but their wings were coming out early and lifting them above the shooting range.

Sergei grabbed the next door and opened it. William saw nothing of interest inside, just another hall, and so the two entered and closed the door behind them quickly.

The corridor descended sharply, its walls of charcoal stone now a dull, dusty black. They resembled old coal—dry and brittle, crumbling into powder rather than disintegrating into dust. Unlike the finely hewn surfaces above, these walls were a haphazard assembly of blocks, stacked with no regard for uniformity or craftsmanship. Any block seemed suitable to be laid atop the next, resulting in a sloppy structure. The gaps between stones, once filled with what might have been white putty, had succumbed to time and rot, fading to a sickly yellow reminiscent of decaying teeth, all under a dusting of black flakes.

William held Sergei's shoulder and hobbled down the passage.

"Are we still going the right way?" William asked, breaking his constant wheezing. He hissed as he sucked in deep breaths to work through the pain.

Since they left their cell, there was only one place where they could have chosen a different path. After the round room, every door led to a hallway, and that to another door. Perhaps it was too many movies of mazes and labyrinths, but this path was straight and consistent. Straight and descending. Darkening with each rotten, toxic door.

"Yes. This is the path. We were given a map, but it was confiscated. I had committed it to memory before it was taken." Sergei chuckled. "Good thing us Gajanthropes have good memories. Otherwise we'd be lost in this place."

William nodded, having heard of the memory of elephants in a documentary. They never talked about such interesting things in school, and perhaps that's why he never cared much for a place where you sat and just wrote all your thoughts without saying them, exploring them, or even taking a walk to process them. How can you learn without moving? Another spear of pain lanced through him as he put too much weight on his leg.

"But I fear you are in no condition to complete our journey. Our destination is not going to be easy for someone with only one leg."

"We just need to get that arrow out." William looked down and saw the steel tip of the arrow protruding from the meaty muscle of his calf. "If we break the head, you can pull the shaft out." He looked around. "Here. Let's just do it here."

Sergei sat him down.

"Can you get a grip on the arrowhead?" William had also seen this in a documentary. It was about field injuries in the military during the Middle Ages. They would pull the arrow out back the way it came, but that led to more blood loss and, ultimately, patient death. The key was to push it through, break the head, then pull out the arrow.

Sergei grabbed the arrowhead as William pushed the arrow farther into his leg. He took deep breaths, but the pain didn't approach the headaches or the time he couldn't get anesthesia before electroshock. Slicing flesh, tearing veins, these things were temporary flares of heat in his leg and much preferred to his brain feeling like it was being juiced.

"Break it," he said, and Sergei snapped the arrow easily. With a sharp yank, William ripped the arrow from his leg. Blood spouted from the wound in high-pressure spits. Sergei tore the sleeve from his white shirt, the frills at the cuffs billowing.

William wrapped the cloth around the wound, then laced the arrow through and cranked it to tighten the bandage. "Other sleeve." William's body went limp. He swayed to the side as the blood drained from his face.

"Are you okay?" Sergei asked as he steadied William.

"Yeah. I'll—" The chimes erupted in his head, locking his mind in their overwhelming ring. This wasn't like when he was leaving the world. It was much louder, painful, the audio version of being submerged in ice water. His eyes widened to see the energy coursing through the world around him. A dense forest of glowing golden threads fizzled into view within the corridor. They hummed with power. Other threads, like loose sweater threads, flailed from Sergei like seaweed. The world vibrated as if someone plucked a guitar string and left it to resonate. William reached for the threads around Sergei but couldn't feel them.

William didn't collapse. He didn't awaken, not how he expected, but the electroshock was coursing through his body in the hospital, and here, he wondered if he was dreaming in another layer of dream. A dream within the dream. One where the world was full of musical strings that wanted to be played. But the shock passed, the threads faded, and his leg was healed.

"The chimes?" Sergei asked.

William shook his head, then nodded, then shrugged while shaking and nodding. "My leg." He put his weight on it. No pain. "I don't know. They fixed it. The shock fixed it?" Which made no sense. The wound would still be real in the hospital. Injuries don't just disappear on your body. But this wasn't his body. It was a dream body, and who knows how those work.

"Well, let's get to where we're going before you wake." Sergei cautiously let go of William, who stood without aid. The two began walking down the passage again and paused when they reached the next door. It was white like the others, but only small bits of white could be seen through the thick black tar dripping over every inch of the door. This door stunk like the time William's dad ran over a skunk in the family car.

"From here, things get pretty crazy," Sergei said before grabbing the handle. Another low pulse rumbled through the corridor, and Sergei opened the door.

The next room was upside down. And while that should have shocked William, he was letting go of expectations in this world of what was normal. He was healing faster than he should have been. He could run as fast as his giant companion. He *had* a giant companion! Guards were worms. And now, upside down was going to be right side up. Of course. He never really needed to understand why things were the way they were; he often just accepted facts as such and moved on from there.

The two stepped into the door and fell up to the ceiling which became the floor. Both landed like cats: soft, agile, silent. William scanned the room for dangers. None stood out.

The walls of this room were black stone, but harder now, the charcoal replaced with black marble. Silver veins coursed through the dull stone, but it didn't glimmer in the gas lanterns like William thought it would. Everything here looked dead. The room was square with doors on each wall. The door they came in was too high to reach now, while the other doors were at their new ground level. Each door was wooden, but only one was white and covered in the dripping tar. The other doors were simply light wood with black iron banding. A black marble altar was in the center of the room with a crimson cloth draped over it. Golden stitching of the spiral adorned this cloth just like the flags in the previous room.

"Is it a trap?" William nodded to the altar.

Sergei went to it. "Not always." He examined the cloth; he didn't touch it, but tried to look under it. "Looks fine."

William approached it. Over each door were symbols again like in the circular room. The white door had the spiral. The others had symbols William didn't recognize.

"What's the purpose of this?" William touched the altar, ready to snap his hand back if it was a trap, but no mechanism churned to life, no gears squealed in motion. Only a dry voice called from an unseen balcony above.

"Sacrifice."

William and Sergei snapped their attention to the thin man. His face was pale and long, his fingernails longer and glistening black. He appeared fragile under a thick black robe that flowed around him like a wizard. Instead of a pointy hat, the man had short black hair slicked back, grease glittering in the gas lantern light. A large wooden bead necklace hung from his neck with a stone spiral pendant dangling from the center.

"Oh, did I startle you?" He flicked his hand in a mix of disinterest and intentional insult. "Perhaps you ought not be here if someone as meek as me can startle your heart." He smiled and embraced a black column that connected his balcony to the ceiling.

"Elijah," Sergei growled. "We have no qualm with you."

"Yet you do." Elijah hid behind the column, peeking out in a faux shyness that William found irritating. "You come to disrupt things. Disturb things."

"We come to ensure the Spiral is sealed," Sergei reputed.

"And therein lies the disruption. You disrupt plans far longer set to seed than your own," Elijah mused and flicked his hand again. The gesture seemed to sicken Elijah as much as it did William, as if it were a bad habit caught from somewhere vile. This time, William noticed it wasn't just the fingernails that were black; the discoloration extended to the entire length of the man's fingers up to the second knuckle. It reminded him of frostbite, a condition he recognized from a survival documentary.

Throughout the room, there were small green eyes emerging on the balcony. They kept low and out of the lantern light. William saw one's slimy green finger, as if it was dipped in algae-coated water, cling to the edge of the balcony. It retracted on William's notice, leaving a long, wet stain as it did.

Sergei raised his trunk, took a deep inhalation, and spat on the floor. "Keep your minions to yourself or you'll be leaving with a few less."

Elijah sighed and rolled his eyes. "Sacrifice. Sacrifice, my dear Sergei. We all must do our part, and yours is to be the offering."

Sergei stiffened at that, his breath caught, and that plunged William into worry. How could someone so big, so strong, panic? But that's what was happening. Panic was setting in on Sergei and infecting William.

Then the chimes began.

"Oh no," William said and met Sergei's eyes. "Oh no, no, no."

Sergei didn't ask. He knew. This moment had just gone from bad to worse as he was about to lose William. "Push it away," he said, almost pleading. "Stay."

Heat burned in the crook of William's elbow. "They're waking me up." Fire slithered through his veins toward his heart. William clawed at his arm, tried to pull it as the head of the first minion peeked into the light.

The thing had two eyes like a person, but the mouth opened vertically like a zipper up its face. Teeth flicked in and out of the mouth like boney tongues, while a real tongue, wide and forked, unrolled from inside. Two other creatures came into the light. While their faces stretched open, William knew they were smiling. They wore black robes like Elijah, but their bodies weren't human. They were jelly, bulging and undulating at odd angles under the black clothes. When they grabbed the columns, pulling themselves from the shadows, their fingers quivered like separated jello. A finger fell off one minion as a blob of green goop, then rolled to its owner and was absorbed back into the body.

The chimes rang louder. The burning within William hit his heart and radiated over his body as he grabbed the altar cloth and fell to the ground.

William woke in the hospital before he could see what he uncovered on the altar. But when Sergei saw what was on the altar, he smiled, knowing his odds just got a lot better.

EIGHT

William shot up to see what was happening. The quick strain in his shoulders stopped him. He was back in bed, the restraints immobilizing his arms and legs.

"Whoa, son. Whoa." His dad was there, reaching for him, not touching him. Trying to calm William as he'd try to calm any animal.

His mom sat on the other side of the room, sniffling and wiping her puffy eyes. She was still sobbing. She didn't usually see him restrained. The nurses let him move freely the one time a week his parents were allowed to visit. The doctors didn't want his parents' affections interfering with his treatment.

"And this is what I mean, Mr. and Mrs. Nolton." The doctor, the same one who gave him the needles in the back, the same one who shocked him, motioned to William with concern.

The dream of Sergei and the things crawling down the walls faded. The hospital was real now. William was sweating from the fight he'd just left. Frantically he searched for the medicine to put him back to sleep. To fight those things. To help Sergei. What would happen to him if his body in the dream world was eaten? The arrow wounds came over, would the teeth marks of those zipper-mouthed monsters? But there was no medicine. Just sad faces on his parents and resigned expressions on the hospital staff.

"The self-injurious behavior is beyond our care capabilities," the doctor said. A nurse nodded as she folded blankets on the counter beside William's bed. "He, I know this is going to be hard to hear, but he dug into his stomach with his own fingernails. We think he did the same to his leg." The doctor said and nodded solemnly as if to say, *Yeah, that's right, so sad.*

William's mom burst into another volley of tears. She couldn't look at him. His dad shook his head and sat on the bed, but didn't get too close to his son's hand or leg.

"We believe William would be best served in Listmore," the doctor said.

William's fingers twitched, the dream world forgotten as the very real world crashed in on him, stealing his breath. Listmore was where he'd be thrown away. It wasn't a hospital, but a holding pen for people who couldn't be helped. Boys who couldn't sit still or girls who wouldn't stop talking vanished in Listmore. On the surface it was a farm, but William knew what it really was: a pit. A deep, dark hole where people like him could disappear and not bother the nice people of civilized society. People who raised their hands before talking. People who sat at their desk and did their work in school without having to be told to sit down, stop tapping their feet, keep their hands from flicking. People who weren't like him.

"No," William's mom said. She stood, the chair jumping from behind her legs and slamming into the wall with a crash. "No! We'll take him home. We'll take care of him!"

William's dad went to her.

"I'm sorry, Mrs. Nolton, but it isn't your choice. We know what's best for Willy." The doctor denied her female hysterics and motioned to her, pointing out how her behavior would just make Willy worse.

"He's right, Mercy." William's dad held his wife. "They know what's best."

"I can get better!" William shouted. "I can!"

"Not on your own, Willy. You should know that by now. And doing what you did to yourself yesterday…" The doctor patted William's bald head with a dull slapping sound. "You are getting worse. We're doing the best we can. You need more help."

William's mom screamed and wailed for her baby, but she was hurried out of the room by William's dad and two nurses. They patted her shoulder like the grieving mother she was.

"I can get better!" William screamed. "I can—" He thought of Sergei. The elephant was still by his foot. "I can show you I didn't do that to myself. I can prove it!"

The doctor, curiously amused, asked, "How would you do that?" Nurse Leslie brought the doctor a clipboard. She hesitated to hand it to him. Her soft brown eyes teared up at William's desperate plea.

"Just let me go to sleep." William tried to be calm, but every neuron was firing. Every nerve ending was burning, not from the medicine that woke him up, but the nightmare of Listmore.

Outside the room, his mother screamed again. Nurses said things like, "There, there," and, "He was a good boy." Speaking in past tense about a boy still very much alive. Not quite as alive as he was in the other world, but alive.

"Please. I can prove it."

The doctor signed the clipboard and handed it back to Nurse Leslie. Her lip quivered. She patted William's arm.

"Alright then," the doctor said. "Nurse, get this boy a sedative. He needs to calm down anyhow."

Red rings around his wrists and ankles began to itch. William didn't realize he was fighting the restraints so hard to get brush burn. His throat was sore from shouting, his mouth dry. The room grew quiet with only the clinging of his restraints hitting the metal bedrailing breaking the silence. William's world was growing still as he focused his mind to return to Sergei, get a little injury then wake up. That's all he needed to do and with a room full of monstrous things, that should be very easy.

"Mom!" William shouted for her, but her crying was getting quieter as his dad and the nurses whisked her away to mourn in private. "Mom!" he screamed again. "I'll show them!"

Nurse Leslie returned a moment later with the thick purple-black medicine. While her hand quivered, the cup rattling, the medicine did not move. She pushed a paper cone of water towards him. "I'm sorry, Willy. We tried our best," she said and lifted the cold water to his lips.

He drank it quickly and nodded to the medicine as if it were a chaser.

"I'll be okay," he said.

She gave him the medicine and he sucked it down his throat, laying back and trying to relax. He swallowed the chunky remnants that caught in his throat with only minimal gagging. *Don't throw up!* He screamed in his mind. The medicine needed to stay in, to put him to sleep, for his plan to work. If it didn't work, Listmore was waiting.

The doctor sat in the chair William's mom was just in. He crossed his arms and tilted his chin in an *Anytime now* expression that made William grit his teeth.

Sleep was coming. William knew this was it. He had to move quickly. Get one of those things to bite him. Time moves slower over there. Sergei said, *Time is different over here,* and just one bite, one scratch, should show the doctor he didn't do it.

The room went dark. As William fell into the void of sleep, he heard footsteps leave his hospital room. He came to in the other world on a bumpy ride.

NINE

Each sense came alive in the new world to strange sensations. First was feeling. William was bouncing like he was riding a rickety roller coaster while laying down. Next was a loud panting filling his ears, along with snarls and scratching of bone on stone surging toward him. Finally, he opened his eyes to see the back of Sergei's floppy ears.

All his senses worked together to complete the picture. He was laying across Sergei's shoulders in a fireman's carry. They were running down a black marble corridor, this one without the silver veins. It was bubbly in places and moved like pulsing blood under smooth skin. Behind them, more of the zipper-mouthed imps were chasing them. Some were on the ground, others on the walls, and a few on the ceiling like spiders rushing toward them.

"You're back!" Sergei shouted, but didn't look back.

"What happened?"

"How long do you think you were out?"

"Few seconds here?" William thought about Listmore, his parents, the doctor. Did the doctor leave before he fell asleep? Listmore echoed in his mind. The word. The sentencing. The pit. It drowned out the scratching behind them and the snapping at Sergei's ankle where one of those things had almost caught up. Why didn't his dad fight? He let him go. Dropped him in the pit. At least his mom had cried.

"Yeah, you been out a while here." Sergei shrugged and swung a sword that matched his massive frame down behind him. It caught the closest imp creature and split it in half. Green slime splattered out from under the black cloak.

"I need one of those things to bite me!" William said.

Sergei cocked his head and turned down a hallway that branched from the main path. His body, and William's legs, slammed into the wall. They both bounced off and kept moving. Behind them, the imps collided with the wall as well, spilling and tumbling off it like a wave of teeth. They kept their pursuit.

"No way! They don't want a bite. They want a meal," Sergei shouted. "We're almost there."

"No! I need them to bite me. I need to show the hospital people I'm not doing it to myself!"

"Doing what?" Sergei said through strained breath. He'd been running a long time and was wearing down.

"They're sending me away! I can't go. It's horrible!" William shook to get loose from Sergei's grip. The elephant man locked tighter around his arms and legs.

"No! You're not going anywhere. Besides, it can't be worse than here!" Sergei saw the opening he knew was there. This was the last chamber before the locks began. The place he and Lloyd were looking for, and now he and Will would find. "Stop moving!"

William fought against Sergei's grip, reaching down to hang an arm for one of the creatures to nibble. Just a bit. Just enough to show.

And if it bit off his hand, so what? It was better than the alternative. William heard kids at Listmore were strapped down to their beds for years. They grew sores and literally rotted away in their beds. The guards were indifferent to their health, their happiness. At least Nurse Leslie and her team tried to make William comfortable. White coats, white batons, angry men waited for him in Listmore. A hand was a worthy sacrifice to avoid that fate.

"Get up here!" Sergei hefted him up and locked his giant hand around William's wrists. "We're almost there! In the next room, I need you to do your observation thing. See what I don't while I fight off these things!" Sergei shrugged and put William on one shoulder, getting ready to put him on his feet. The room was coming soon. "Don't do nothing stupid like try to get bit! I need you!"

They got to the room. Sergei slid William off his shoulder and into the room like a shuffleboard puck. With a roar and steel ringing against stone, Sergei fought back the horde of imps, keeping them in the hallway.

William stood. The imps were trying to get by Sergei. Just one would do. A quick bite. A scratch even. Minor injuries to show the hospital staff. Injuries that happened while he was strapped down. Why would the doctor think he did those cuts to himself? How could he? They couldn't have thought he got free then re-cuffed himself. And he wasn't in the bathroom long. There would have been blood on the bed. How could they believe he did that to himself? Unless that's what they wanted to believe. Did the doctor want that? To ship William away to be someone else's problem? The nurses were compliant because they didn't want to be yelled at or didn't want to clean his bed again. Did they really think Listmore was best for him?

The thoughts popped in his mind like twisted bubble wrap.

William's fingers twitched and flicked. His hands flapped. He couldn't leave the questions, the ideas—they devoured him, and he spiraled down. Hopelessness whirled in him as Sergei slew the imps, keeping all of them away. Not a single bite would come. He was trapped. He was going to be thrown away.

The last imp was slashed and splattered. Sergei faced William, looking for a report, but all that was there was a scared boy paralyzed by what awaited him in another world.

Sergei saw the balcony of this room too late as an arrow lanced through his chest. It was shot from somewhere above. An unseen sniper, missed by William's paralysis. Even now William didn't move. He watched Sergei fall to one knee. Another arrow thumped into Sergei's chest.

The giant elephant man grabbed William and shielded him. Three arrows thudded into Sergei's back. William couldn't move. His body was imprisoned by his thoughts.

When Sergei's body hit the ground, William snapped back to now. He saw his fallen friend. Realized what happened. William fell to Sergei's side. The giant's body was still warm, still soft, and maybe still alive. These arrows might not have been poisoned. They might not have been enough to stop the mighty Sergei.

"Get up!" William pushed Sergei, but he didn't move. "Get up!" William screamed, angry and abandoned by yet another. "Get up!"

"Oh. Seems like Sergei's quite dead," Elijah said. "He left you just when you needed him most. How typical." Elijah stood on the balcony William didn't see. The one lined with archers that William didn't warn Sergei about. When Sergei was in the doorway, he was covered from their shots, but when he walked into the room, he walked into their ambush.

"Get up!" William cried now, tears cracking his voice and raining freely on Sergei's white shirt.

"Besides, we didn't need him. We needed *you*." Elijah sighed. "Collect him."

Two archers jumped down from the balcony. They wore long red robes with golden stitching. The gold spiral blazed on their chest. Red hoods covered their heads, with faceless white masks hiding their inhuman faces. The one that shot Sergei first still held his bow out. This one wore a black cloak with a mask unlike the others, it had a black spiral carved in the forehead. William watched this archer shoot one more arrow into Sergei and then lower his bow. The others carried William as he kept screaming for Sergei to get up. But Sergei didn't move.

TEN

The final room was a large arena. Stairs coiled down toward a central stage.

William never knew what it was like to think about nothing. There was always *something* speeding through his mind, but now only numbness vibrated within him. A thought sprung up at that moment. Is this how his brain felt when the spinal fluid was drained from around it? Did it feel nothing? Empty? Was the headache actually a scream of pain from the emptiness?

He descended the steps, each one a deep, impenetrable black, unlike any marble or stone. Beneath their hard surface, a mysterious liquid retreated from his footfall, squishing and oozing away with an eerie reluctance. The steps, though solid, harbored this strange, viscous fluid within their depths. With every step he took, the fluid was forced out, revealing glimpses of yellowed bone beneath, as if the staircase itself were alive and bleeding its secrets with each press of his feet.

Smells seized William. Flowers. Burning. Rot. Cold. It all floated together through the air in a confusing mix of comfort and danger.

"The Tower of Ascension was built upon this place as an amplification device," Elijah said. He pointed up like a tour guide.

"This structure is designed to concentrate energies, the vibrations of reality. It is perhaps a center point for this reality, perhaps all realities."

William plodded down the stairs behind Elijah. He didn't care for the tour, but the guide continued.

"What was it built upon?" Elijah asked and pointed to the bottom of the arena. It was easily seventy feet down with a glowing magma star in the center of darkness.

"I don't know," William answered.

"Of course you do not know. You are not of this world. And therein lies your value," Elijah continued as they walked. He talked about the structure's design and how it was spirals upon spirals. Some vertical, some horizontal, but all with the purpose of attuning energy.

"Are you going to kill me down here?" William interrupted.

"A fair question," Elijah answered directly and without emotion, "and yes. The last spiral I opened incinerated the man who opened it instantly." Elijah smiled at the thought.

William nodded and was able to let go of Listmore. The hospital drifted away. He was dying here. No need to live a long life of hell in that pit when he could be murdered in this pit. Two archers followed them, along with three other figures in long black cloaks. Smoke drifted from under the cloaks, and they wore white masks but without eye holes. The one on his right was the archer with the spiral, the one that killed Sergei.

"Painful?" William asked.

"Probably not," Elijah answered, and William believed him. "The last one didn't scream. Didn't do anything except vanish." The thought of a painless death was welcome. It beat the shocks and the needles, the headaches and the restraints. A death on his feet, free to move; things could be worse.

They reached the bottom of the stairs in silence a few moments later. What William thought was a dark pit was warmly lit by a fluid magma pulsing from the heart of a spiral. It was brightest in the center and stretched to the edges of the arena. William imagined this was what the Colosseum in Rome would be like. He read about it once and imagined it to be at least as grand as this, perhaps more. A place of so many battles, so much wealth and torment, it had to be nice.

"Please stand at the center of the spiral." Elijah motioned for William to move. "Dodslav, the sword please."

Sergei's killer drifted toward William. It didn't walk, it floated. Black smoke trailed from the creature as it moved in a constant haze. Dodslav carried the sword Sergei had taken from the altar. When the creature reached William, it held out the sword as if presenting it to him.

"Dodslav is one of the faithful. I was questioning his allegiance before this endeavor but trusted his faith. Loyalty is often stated, but rarely proven for many. He believes in the power of this place, and thus I believe he will help me unleash it," Elijah said as he came to Dodslav's side. "Faith is a powerful weapon. He had faith in me to deliver him here. He uses that faith in his art. Sculptures."

Dodslav remained quiet, presenting the sword to William.

"What was it you wanted to do with this place?" Elijah asked Dodslav.

"Sculpt a new universe," Dodslav answered dutifully.

"Artists." Elijah shook his head. "They are the creators and the destroyers. They break society to make it anew."

"And you?" William asked as he reached for the sword. "What do you want to do?"

"I'm not as creative as Dodslav. I just want to destroy. Cut out the cancer that's rotted through humanity. When you've seen the world as I have, you know it is time to restart."

William took the sword from Dodslav. The black-cloaked figure drifted away, getting out of striking distance quickly. While Elijah expected all the fight was taken from William, Dodslav wasn't so sure.

"Place the sword in the spiral's heart. You will be consumed by it and open the final door." Elijah motioned to the ground with a quick flick of his hand.

"The doors were already locked, weren't they?" William asked. "That's why you sent Lloyd and Sergei here. You couldn't unlock them without Lloyd, now me?" The pieces made sense. "Was it you in disguise that sent them here?" William saw a movie one time where the villain did that. He dressed up like a villager and told the hero about a treasure, and when the hero went for the treasure, the villain showed his true colors.

"No. It was one of my followers. He sent the fools on their mission and sent Sergei's warrior friend away before he and that boy arrived here so she wouldn't spoil the fun," Elijah answered. "Let us not waste time. Do you expect long conversations and idle discussions? Let's get this done and move on."

William smirked, remembering the drive-in with his dad before the hospital, before the problems at school, before the needles and chairs, before he should have been watching movies like the one coming to mind now. "No, Mr. Elijah. I expect you to die!"

William sliced out at Elijah, catching his arm in a glancing blow. No blood splattered, the blade didn't break his skin, but the blunt force knocked the frail man to the ground. Two of the archers leapt in to fight, drawing their blades with a bright sound that stirred William's memories of Robin Hood, Sinbad, and Ulysses. The archers were the Claymation monsters from those films, and he sprung to battle. Free. Moving free. Whirling and running. His body knew what to do with the dull sword, turning it into a slapping blade that clobbered one archer in the face, shattering its mask. The other archer caught the blade in its knee. A loud snap rang through the arena. The archer yelped like a hurt dog and fell to the ground, crawling away.

The three black cloaks were floating up the stairs, away from Elijah. Their fight was elsewhere.

"Come back!" Elijah scolded them. "I showed you the way here! We are almost complete!"

Dodslav, the one in the lead, stopped.

"Artists are two things that you are not," Dodslav said. William expected a laugh to follow, but it didn't. "We are hungry. And we are patient for our masterpiece's completion. You cannot rush perfection." And with that, Dodslav continued up the stairs, leaving Elijah to William's whims.

William went to the archer with the broken mask to look upon its face. It was strangely human except the wide forehead, large nose, and beading horns poking through its forehead. Its skin was black like Elijah's fingers.

"Sergei said there were places here that can take you anywhere," William said. "Can those places take my body from the other world, somewhere else?"

Elijah recoiled, defenseless and horrified at the question. "Where would you go?"

William knew Elijah had somewhere in mind. Somewhere that terrified him. And William wanted to know where that was, but first, he had to get out of the hospital.

"Do you know where it is?!" He thrust the sword toward Elijah's face. The man winced and nodded with a little whine. "Then let's go." William waved the sword to the stairs.

"I could help you open the spiral," Elijah pleaded. "Done differently than originally planned, it could—"

"I don't want power!" William screamed. The thought sickened him worse than the headaches. Powerful people always assume everyone wants power, but William wanted something more. "I want freedom. I want to live. And I want you to get off your butt and take me to that place or I'm going to beat you with this thing until you do!"

Elijah scurried to his feet and hurried toward the stairs. As he passed the archers, he spit on them, mumbling about their uselessness. William did not think about the dramatics of Elijah's performance or suspect that the man, ancient and powerful in ways William couldn't imagine, would be defeated so easily. The younger man delighted in his victory, blind from inexperience that his prisoner succumbed to capture much too easily.

As William followed Elijah upstairs, he said something Elijah puzzled over as they left the tower. Having not seen as many movies as William, Elijah was unaware of the reference and looked around for who else William could have been talking to, but no one was around.

"I have nothing to lose. They want me to go to Listmore. Well, I'm sorry, Dave, I can't do that."

ELEVEN

Doctor Hilden didn't like to check up on old patients, but he had a tingle in his spine about this one. The tingle was just below the vertebrae where he'd place the spinal needle in patients. That's what stood out to him most. They didn't do that treatment anymore. It'd been years. New advances in radiology didn't require those old ways. And why he thought about it during his coffee break made him shiver. It was medicine. It was the best they knew at the time. Why was he feeling so scared?

The phone buzzed as he waited for someone to answer on the other end. Finally someone did, with the ever-pleasant voice of a seasoned receptionist.

"Listmore Facility, how may I direct your call?"

"Hi, I'm Dr. Hilden at Cruxlan General. I'm calling to do a patient checkup. One of my kids was sent there a few years back and I…" What? He didn't know what to say. "I was just thinking about him. Wanted to see how his treatment was coming along." Then added, "To report to the parents."

"Name?"

"William Nolton."

"Please hold." The receptionist transferred him back to the beeping sound for a few rings.

"Hello, Dr. Kaiser," a man's voice answered.

"Hello, I'm Dr. Hilden at Cruxlan General. I wanted to check in on an old patient."

"Ah, yes, Amanda said you were calling about the Nolton boy," Kaiser said. "Well, he's not here anymore. Ran off."

"Ran off?" Hilton gasped. "How?" The thought of anyone leaving Listmore was stunning. They kept the patients in a perpetual torpor. No one had the energy to stand, much less run.

"Don't know. Don't care. That kid was beyond weird. He could get hurt even when it was just him in his room. Nothing in the room but padding, but he'd find a way to cut himself up, bruise, broke his arm once. We kept him in a jacket, still had issues. Then one day, poof. Gone."

Hilden felt the pain in his spine again. A headache was forming. "Any trail?"

"We don't really look. They usually turn up. Lost or in jail or in a morgue. No one's looking for him."

And then, a question fell out of Hilden that made him shiver from skull to balls. "Did he have an elephant with him?"

"Well, see, that's the damnedest thing. We took it from him. Thought it was a bad influence. But when he left, he got it. Which is weird, because we had it locked up in a possession locker. When he disappeared, we checked for his things; all he had when he arrived was that stupid elephant. But it was gone."

"So, he was just gone?" Hilden asked, now rubbing his back, trying to press away the cold trembling in his spine.

"Well, no. There was someone in his room." Kaiser stuttered the words. "And that guy, I don't know who he is, but he had frostbite something horrid on his fingers."

"Why don't you know who he is?" Hilden looked behind him. Someone was watching. Someone was listening.

"Dr. Hilden, he's not your patient. I don't know—"

"Tell me," Hilden barked, a little harder than he meant to.

Kaiser sighed. "The man doesn't talk. We think your patient did something to his throat or his tongue, we don't know."

Hilden cringed, the pain in his back now a spear of cold rippling through his ribs and knees. "Why?"

"He was your patient. They're crazy when they get here. We don't make them more crazy," Kaiser answered. "But the guy did write his name down. We tried looking him up, couldn't find him in any of our systems."

"Who is he?"

"Maybe your boy knew him? Guy said…well, wrote his name was Elijah Adams. We just been calling him Ely for short." Kaiser chuckled. "But hey, I don't know what the hell your boy did to this guy. Like I said, he was crazy. We tried to help him."

Hilden knew this wasn't true. He knew Listmore's reputation. Knew what happened to the kids he sent there, but never had he followed up like this. He assumed they were gone. Put away.

He never thought they could come back.

He never thought about them, and now he wondered, for the first time, if kids like William ever thought about him.

INVENTORY NOTE: ITEM 23

Item Number: 23

Components:

- Stuffed elephant missing an eye

Collection: Public

This one was an interesting case. A lady came to me with this stuffed elephant and said it was a family heirloom. She said it belonged to her deceased brother who died of cancer, and was returned by the boy that her brother lent it to when he died in the hospital.

After her brother died, the elephant was returned to the family by the kid from the hospital, but they've not been able to return to Sergei's world since. The boy told her Sergei died in another world, killed by a sorcerer. Supposedly the boy captured the sorcerer, but the girl said she knew who he meant, and that man was free in the world once again.

She claimed that the elephant was a gateway to another world in your sleep, and the elephant was a person in this other world. The person's name was Sergei and he needed help. I told her I don't help toys, I just collect them, but she begged me to take it. She said she'd heard of my reputation and thought I, of all people, (her words) could help Sergei.

Unfortunately, I'm not about to trigger the Resolution of a toy just to *help* something I don't know. This is just like the boy in 14; I'm not here to help these toys. They are here to help me.

Once Dodslav returns and takes these things from me, I will never think of them again. I don't care what he does with them as long as Drew is returned. A deal is a deal.

Sorry, Sergei, but your problems aren't mine.

42

REVISITED

ONE

"Don't touch it!" Lucy screamed at her mom, but quickly regained her composure. "It's a collector's item."

Lucy and her mom stood on their front porch. Both stared at their unexpected visitor. A small doll, three feet tall with stringy black hair, dirty overalls, and dead blue marble eyes, sat on the porch rocker. Its chains squeaked as the motionless doll swayed in the evening's gentle breeze. It stared into the night beyond the porch light, unblinking, patiently sitting sentinel for whatever was in the dark.

Lucy looked out where she was watching. Nothing was out there. Nothing she could see.

The plastic bag full of books from Neil's house crinkled as she moved. This was the doll from the table in Neil's workshop. When this terror laid on the table, a paper beside it said 42. She took out the inventory book for 40 forward and looked up the doll's entry in the warm porch light.

Trudy, Lucy's mom, instinctively stepped away from the doll. "But it's just a doll." She shook her head to dismiss the unease clumping together in her gut. "You used to have one of these when you were a little girl. A *Baby-B-Real.*" Trudy knew this wasn't like the one Lucy had. This doll didn't want its diaper changed or to play school. The doll's dead eyes burned with purpose as it stared into the night. She couldn't look at the eyes any longer and turned toward something safer, or she thought: the journal.

Lucy calmly pivoted away from her mom, shielding the book. "No, Mom. It's not." Lucy ran her finger through the red journal entry for item number 42, *Ely's Doll*. Only the heading was prepared, with no description except three words scribbled quickly: *Do Not Touch*. Lucy grabbed the blanket her best friend Nadia always wrapped up with on cool nights. Nadia wouldn't need it any time soon, she was still in the hospital.

Lucy shook away the tears that were waiting to be let loose and focused on the task at hand. She wrapped the doll in a sloppy swaddle, then took it to the house and set her *collector's item* on the couch. "New hobby. Just can't do the gaming thing anymore. Not without…" Lucy trailed off.

Her e-sports stream died with her cameraman and friend, Sam. The thing from the yard sale, the thing she brought into their lives, the thing in her plastic bag with the books, took Sam and almost took Nadia. First the ship and King Dark, now this doll. Another thing she'd brought on her family and friends. Who's next to die, to suffer from her choices?

As if to answer, her mom asked, "You were expecting this thing?" Trudy cocked her head from the edge of the living room and glared at the dead blue eyes, the eternally happy smile, and the stained overalls. "Is that…" She trailed off. "Grease?" But grease didn't look like crimson-brown slashes and splatters. "Just put it somewhere I don't have to see it, okay?"

Lucy nodded.

"Are you okay?" Trudy turned her attention to Lucy, happy to see her daughter safe after all that had happened this week. Lucy was fine on the outside. On the inside, Trudy knew therapy was in their immediate future. "I don't know what happened, but when you're ready to tell me, I'll listen."

Lucy put on a brittle smile, the edges of it quivered as if it might shatter at any moment and take everything Lucy had left with it. "I'm okay."

"Do you want to talk?" Trudy asked.

Lucy shook her head and went from the living room to the kitchen. She could still see the doll across the open first floor. Lucy put the plastic bag from the hospital on the counter. Neil's journals were inside. The ship and VHS tape were inside.

"Are these for your new hobby?" Trudy reached for the journals.

"Can I keep this to myself for now?" Lucy asked gently as she grabbed the bag of journals. "I just… I don't want to talk about anything right now. Just need to decompress, you know?"

After a moment of silence, Trudy left it alone. She trusted her daughter and knew, when she was ready, she'd come to her, just like the other night. Strange things happened; Lucy came to her. That's the way it should be. Trudy gave her daughter a hug. "I'm going to go up and read for a while. If you need anything, you know where to find me."

Lucy nodded, accepted the hug and kiss, then waited at the kitchen counter for her mom to go upstairs. Lucy's fingers tapped the nervous tune of nightmare memories, each beat replaying a moment. One, her mutilated friend Sam standing in her kitchen. Two, Nadia protecting Lucy. Three, Sam—now King Dark—turning Nadia into one of his mindless minions. Four, the police station, the gunshots, the way Nadia collapsed in a boneless, lifeless heap after Lucy trapped King Dark back in his prison. Five, the hospital, finding out Sam was dead, Nadia in intensive care, wailing cries from Sam's parents as the news tore into them.

Trudy's bedroom door quietly closed and broke Lucy's finger rhythm. She moved to the chair across from the doll. The nervous tapping continued in a drumbeat of anxiety and exhaustion on the recliner across from the couch. Sleep eluded her for the past three nights, and now it looked like she had one more sleepless night to go.

"Why are you here?" Lucy whispered.

"Are you Wendy?" the doll answered with her own question. Her mouth didn't move with the syllables, it just opened and the words poured out. Lucy recognized the doll was limited in motion due to its design. She was only a plastic doll, and even possessed dolls are only the sum of their parts. Plastic. Fabric. Evil.

"No," Lucy answered and opened her mouth to correct the name, but held back.

A shadow of disappointment flickered over the doll's face. It was quickly discarded. "You have work to do," the doll answered as she fixed Lucy with her blue plastic eyes. "Busy, busy, little missy," she whispered, each syllable dripping with ominous mockery.

Lucy didn't think the last comment was at her and asked, "What work?" Her tone was calm acceptance. There was no denying this thing that showed up on her doorstep, no questioning *Why me?* or how to avoid this task. She left one horror story and stumbled into another. This doll was the one in Neil's workshop. It followed her home, and all this would end with Lucy. No one else was getting involved. There was no moving on, no processing what had happened, just riding the wave of this new nightmare.

"Two tasks. The first takes us back to where I found you. The second is less pleasant. We will discuss that on the way to Neil's house." The doll slowly blinked. She closed her plastic mouth with a click.

Trudy's door was still closed. She was giving her daughter the space she requested. Lucy knew that space didn't extend to going with a possessed doll to a dead man's house, but moving on meant moving through. This door was still open, and if she didn't close it now, it would follow her until she did.

Lucy nodded and pushed herself out of the chair. "Then let's get it over with."

TWO

The storm from last night had returned. Torrential rain assaulted Lucy and the doll in angry waves. Lucy wore a yellow raincoat to keep dry. The doll sat in the basket on the front of Lucy's bike wearing a long black trash bag. Rain beaded and drooled down the plastic bag in rivers.

Before they left, the doll had requested eye holes be cut out of the trash bag so it could see where they were going. This comforted Lucy. Even haunted dolls needed to see with their eyes. She wondered how else the doll was like her. Was it mortal like her? Breakable like her? Sam didn't die after King Dark took over his body; the bullets from Officer Littleton's gun did the killing, but only after Lucy trapped Dark in the ship again. If these toys could be imprisoned, could they die?

Her gamer nature took over as she inventoried what her opponent could do. The doll's abilities. The doll's intentions. Even the doll's gaming style, because this *was* a game. Lucy could feel it was and she had to play.

"I hate sneaking out," Lucy shouted over the storm. Thunder grumbled a throaty growl. It was the only thing she could hear over the downpour. "I can't believe I'm doing this." A flashlight taped to

Lucy's handlebars bounced in the rain as she raced to Neil's house.

The street was getting blurry, but Lucy wasn't sure if that was the rain or her exhaustion. Most people were locked up in their homes this late; no cars on the road, and few would have seen her in the murky storm. She pedaled against the storm as it pressed her back home with harsh sheets of icy rain.

Before they left home, the doll glanced up to Trudy's room and said, "I can be very persuasive. You'd be surprised what I could do before she even screamed."

That was the final push out the door. It was unnecessary. Lucy was all out of fear after the past few days. There was only the drive to be done. A deep need to walk away from this world she'd stumbled into because of a damn yard sale. Or, at least that's what she thought. A seed of curiosity had been planted and was beginning to flower. She didn't realize it yet, but she needed to understand this doll, King Dark, and the other toys remaining in Neil's house. Lucy assumed the doll delighted in threatening her mom, perhaps it fed off terrorizing others, but the doll wasn't expecting such a willing accomplice.

"Did you want to hurt my mom, or were you just trying to convince me?" Lucy shouted over the storm into where the doll's ear would be under the trash bag.

"I don't like hurting people. Sometimes it is necessary. I have a purpose to fulfill, and more often than not, your kind gets in the way," the doll said. "Motivation and leverage are often useful tools."

Lucy shook her head, but took note of the words *your kind*. Strange language to use for a ghost trapped in a doll. Wasn't she once human? Lucy's eyes began to sting. She wiped them out but noticed she was sweating. The cool fall night would have kept her temperature down, but there was a heat blowing over her as she pedaled, as if riding into a desert wind. She shook away the feeling and pressed on into the storm, into the night.

***

When they arrived at Neil's house, Lucy stopped a few driveways up and checked to see if anyone was looking. The neighborhood's lights were off, and no spying eyes peered from any windows. She turned off her flashlight.

At night this street looked more isolated than she remembered from her trips here, both during the yard sale and when she returned afterward. The streetlights flickered and faded while the moon was blotted out with silver-lined clouds. Rain kept pouring but was easing up now.

"Are the shades still down?" Lucy remembered leaving the workroom light on, but now Neil's house was dark.

"Yes."

Lucy's heart pounded as they biked off the street and onto Neil's muddy lawn. The darkness around them swallowed all traces of light, leaving the night shrouded in a thick black blanket. Every few feet, Lucy glanced over her shoulder, expecting to find someone following her, but no one was there. She felt their eyes and stopped a few times to listen, to stare into the dark, but she never saw anyone. Gradually, from behind the house, a flickering yellow light emerged from the rainy night. It was the light over Neil's back door. The one she and Nadia found earlier.

Lucy dismounted her bike and walked it toward the light with one hand out to feel for the house. Her bike hit something soft; it squished. She fell over it with a splash, squelch, and an eruption of stench.

"Nasty!" Lucy rolled out of the rotted mound of trash and into a slick of mud.

The doll didn't say anything.

"So freakin' nasty." Lucy got up and tried to flick off the filth dripping down the back of her jeans, crawling into the sleeves of her jacket.

"Are you coming?" the doll said. Dim light fell into the back yard, showing Lucy her bike in the garbage pile. Neil's back door was open, with a black trash-bag ghost standing inside. Rain ran off the trash bag in steady streams, pooling around her bare plastic feet. Through the bag holes, the doll's blue eyes glittered as they watched Lucy.

She hadn't seen the doll move on its own yet. The fact that it could wasn't a surprise—how else did it get to her house? But did it move like a kid? Did it just float like a ghost?

"Where now?" Lucy kept still.

"This way." But the doll didn't move. It didn't gesture or nod, the two eye holes stayed fixed on Lucy.

"Lead on." Lucy stepped into the slash of light from the back door.

The doll maintained its inhuman stillness. No nervous sway. No breathing. It was inanimate, as a toy should be, but the intensity in the eyes told a different story. Pent-up energy thrummed inside the doll, ready to strike if Lucy didn't obey.

Lucy motioned into the house. "You want to show me where to go?"

"Basement. It is the door beside where you found me. Go down and bring out the following items." The doll gave Lucy a list of toys to look for in the basement.

"Should I be writing this down?"

"You won't forget."

"Aren't you coming?" Lucy asked.

"No," the doll answered, and marked the conversation complete with silence.

Lucy nodded and stepped past the doll, trying to keep herself far from the three-foot nightmare. The doll stared at her as she passed. Its head didn't move, but blue marble eyes sparkled from the shadows within the trash bag holes. What thoughts lurked behind those eyes? Was the doll thinking anything? Her eyes weren't blank. They were full of intent and, Lucy thought, malice.

Lucy clicked her flashlight on and walked toward the living room. She turned left at the stairs and continued past the workshop. The light was on. She glanced in and saw it was the same as when she left yesterday except no doll on the table.

The next door on her right was the basement door according to the doll. It was white with four panels, just like any other basement door. Nothing special. No doorway to damnation or mystical portal. She didn't think of it as any different than most doors until she touched the doorknob.

THREE

It was cold, but that wasn't why Lucy ripped her hand away from the stainless-steel knob. It was the vibration. The thrumming vibration rippled through her bones, shocking her. Not electric, something deeper, something that passed by her muscles and nerves, digging into marrow. She quaked from the energy as it tried to get out of her with thousands of millepede legs burrowing through her skin.

"What was that?" She staggered from the door and shook her body to try and get the feeling out of her, but it wouldn't leave. It quieted, going to sleep inside her, but she knew it was still there, a restless slumber ready to spring back to life at any moment.

Lucy glanced down the hallway expecting to see the doll watching her, peeking around the corner with blank fiendish eyes, but nothing was there.

"It's just a door." Internal screams of *RUN!* and *NOPE!* threatened to override all other thoughts except one. One thing drove her forward. "I can't let the doll hurt Mom," she whispered, and looked to see if anyone heard her lie. Lucy blushed as she recognized the real reason she was going forward: curiosity. Fear of what the doll implied it would do to her mom, fear of what could be down there, all of it shrank behind the curiosity of where this door led. It didn't just go downstairs; it went toward the answers she wanted but hadn't demanded yet.

Where did King Dark come from? Who would have such a thing? What else is there?

Lucy yanked the door open. The scraping legs inside her returned and rushed to her skin. She shook her hands to get rid of the feeling, but it wouldn't leave. She went downstairs to get answers, to see where the door led.

The basement lights stuttered to life with a chorus of sharp clicks and a faint hum, the fluorescent tubes chasing away the shadows. Steel steps led down to a plush crimson carpet that drank in the dim light. Each step Lucy took was unnervingly silent, but the basement itself was alive with a steady, mechanical hum—surprisingly well-maintained and orderly, contrary to the cacophony of breakdown she had expected from countless horror films. How much longer can a house without an owner run? How long had it been since Neil died? She hadn't thought about that yet.

Lucy's foot sank into the fluffy red carpet, making her stumble off the last step. Beyond the stairs, the basement opened out into a series of bookshelves. Each shelf was filled with trinkets, but not in the cluttered way of a hoarder; they were in the perfect order you would expect from an obsessed collector. Toys were everywhere, each behind a neat white paper tent with a black number written on it. Lucy instantly recognized these as the ID numbers from Neil's journals. Many of the toys she recognized from the yard sale, but some were missing. Lucy chuckled and wondered what happened with those *lucky buyers.*

One toy was not on a shelf. In the center of the basement, on a table away from everything else, was a dollhouse. There was no white paper tent. No number. A dull smell drifted from the table like the night air before a blizzard. Not the pretty blizzards from the movies, but the kind that trapped kids with psychotic parents and froze people to death in icicle tombs; the kind that spawned monsters. Lucy reached to feel the cold. It came from the dollhouse's basement. From a spiral pattern dug into the wood floor painted to look like concrete.

Lucy wanted to lift the dollhouse and see if the spiral dug into the table, but the doll's warning echoed in her mind like a foghorn. *Do not touch anything.* But Lucy needed to touch the dollhouse. She needed to feel the cold, to feel if it was coming from the spiral… That thought made her laugh.

"How many horror movies have Nadia and I watched?" She shook her head, thinking of her best friend. "Not another horror movie. I just survived one horror story. Now I'm in another one. I'm not getting into a third." Lucy turned from the table. "Two nightmares a night is my max." A laugh slipped from her. If she wasn't careful down here, there would be more nightmares, and one of them would do her in. The last one she escaped with Nadia's help. Now, Lucy was alone.

As the doll described, there was a shelf near the stairs with rubber gloves, rubber tubs, and thick leather welder's gloves. As instructed, Lucy put on the rubber gloves, then pulled the welder's gloves over them. She took a rubber tub and went to the item numbers the doll had told her to collect.

9: a stuffed bear with a felt heart on its stomach.

21: a plastic golf set for a toddler.

12: a small racecar.

18: a baby mobile.

23: a stuffed elephant with a missing eye.

40: a golden genie lamp.

Together, all of them fit into one large tub, just like the doll said they would. Lucy silently collected each item but found herself frequently stopping and wondering about each one's story. She knew they were in Neil's journals, but something about this place resonated in her. "I should have brought the books," she whispered, but the words didn't have the feeling she expected. She knew she'd be back if she survived the night.

Lucy put the rubber tub down on the floor with a muffled plastic *clink* as the toys shifted inside. She secured the lid with two quick snaps and then put the welder's gloves back and threw the rubber gloves in a small trash can by the stairs.

A cold gust swirled through the basement. It could have been an open vent, perhaps a window down here, but Lucy knew where it came from.

"Did you say something?" she whispered to the doll house, but it didn't respond. Another breeze rustled the hair by her ear. A voice on the wind whispered, *No evidence.*

Lucy smiled back as she reached into the trash and took the rubber gloves and shoved them into her pocket.

"Thanks," she whispered back to the house. Another gust came to her with a hissing sound that could have said, *See you soon,* but it was just a breeze and it quickly vanished. Without the breeze, Lucy felt for the first time how hot the basement was. Hot, dry, puzzling as Lucy looked for a window or the heater coming to life, but nothing had changed. Was it ever cold? Did she imagine that? Perhaps a chill was still clinging to her from the rain.

She lifted the rubber tub and carried it upstairs, carefully wiping down each surface she touched to erase all signs that she was ever here. The only sign left behind was the vibration in her bones, digging deeper, making itself at home.

FOUR

As the doll saw Lucy come out from the hallway, she said, "We need running water."

The storm stopped while Lucy was in the house, and the doll had already removed her trash bag raincoat. Remnants of the storm pooled around the doll's feet. Dark blue stains crept up the fabric of her pants, a testament to their soaking, but wet clothing didn't bother the doll. With her bare plastic feet in the water, she again exuded an eerie stillness. There she waited for Lucy, her fixed gaze directed toward the doorway. Her indifference to her sodden state underscored the stark absence of human desire to escape the elements, to find warmth.

"Body of water or bathtub running water?" Lucy asked.

The doll's mouth dropped open with mechanical abruptness. "Body of water. Somewhere secluded." Her voice was like Lucy's mom's. A middle-aged woman, tired, and unlike her mom, depleted of anything but the passion to do what's next. Her mouth then closed, not with the natural ease of human lips, but in a quick click. As she spoke, the absolute stillness of her mouth and throat, devoid of the subtle movements that accompany human speech, sent a shiver down Lucy's spine. In the dim light, one could almost mistake the doll for a child, if not for the glaringly obvious plastic face. Yet, even these could be momentarily overlooked in the shadows. But not the stillness. That was ever-present, an unnerving calm. She didn't have the lively, spontaneous movements of a child. Instead, she remained perpetually still, akin to a predator in the wild—ever watchful, ever ready, biding its time for the perfect moment to strike.

"I know a place. This time of night, no one goes there." Lucy set the rubber bin on the kitchen table. The doll wasn't going to move first, it was waiting for Lucy to pass. The notes in Neil's journal came to mind: *Don't touch it.* Could it touch her? Is that why the doll made Lucy walk close to it? Or was it just intimidation like a bully being too close for comfort?

Swallowing, a click in her throat broke the silence. Lucy grabbed a blanket from the couch and swaddled the doll, careful to avoid touching her. The stillness was broken, but the doll did not move.

Lucy put the doll in her bike basket and bungie-corded her down like before. "Be right back." In Neil's house, she paused before picking up the container in the kitchen. Everything here was so normal. The basement was the only thing weird, and even that wasn't too different than her dad's basement filled with old junk. Neil's basement was orderly and organized, but her dad would say the same thing about his own basement. Did Neil's neighbor know about his collection? The true nature of his collection? Lucy picked up the container and took it outside, wondering how well anyone really knew anyone. After strapping the container to the back of her bike, she went to the doormat, lifted it, and took the key.

Lucy mounted her bike, slipped the key into her pocket, and peddled out of the back yard, avoiding the trash mound this time. She glanced back to Neil's house, thinking about the many things left in the basement. What were their stories? It was all in the journals at her house. The only thing without a story was this doll and the dollhouse. The doll's lack of story was because she killed Neil before he could write it down, but what of the dollhouse? *See you soon,* whispered again in Lucy's mind. She nodded as she pedaled away.

FIVE

The first place Lucy thought of when running water was needed was Patticon River. A bridge crossed over the river, and Lucy's family ate lunch at the little picnic area beside the bridge once in a while. No one was allowed on the premises after nightfall because, supposedly, some kid got hurt there years ago.

Lucy knew her town was full of ghost stories like this. Small towns like their spooky tales. But those were just stories. Lucy had a real monster on her bike, with very real, very deadly intentions.

In this town, nowhere was too far from the edge of town. A bike with a focused rider could get from one side of town to the other in twenty minutes. Lucy was focused, and the roads at 10:00 pm were dead. She thought about her mom as she stomped on the pedals to go faster. Had her mom noticed she was gone? Was she worried? Lucy wanted to be done with this first part of the night, but dreaded the next.

Two quick turns and a back trail later, Lucy was at Patticon Bridge over the Patticon River. It was more like a very large stream than a river, but it had enough current to create undertow. That's why kids never went into the deep end of the stream. They'd get sucked under easily. Once, Lucy heard that the current was strong enough to pull crabs down from the Bay, but she didn't believe that.

"Stop!" the doll said.

Lucy squeezed her brake, the tires screeched, the loose-stone road growled around her. Dust drifted forward onto the bridge, but Lucy stopped a few feet away.

"I will stay here. You must dump the container," the doll said. "Touch. Nothing."

Lucy dismounted, kicked down her stand, and took the container to the bridge. Having never been here in the night, she was surprised at how loud the Patticon River was. She'd been told it was small, the shores used as a splash pond for kids, but here it was screaming. Looking over the bridge, she couldn't see the water, but she could hear it. She could feel the cold breeze blowing up from it. The trees swayed in the wind, making them roar like a cheering crowd. They seemed to be urging her on, encouraging her to do what she had come here for. She smiled up at them, unsure why.

Two loud clicks—the handles of the container opening—broke the constant cheering of the trees. Silence devoured the cheering as the toys inside, the things that looked like toys but held something more within, breathed the river's air. Perhaps they knew what was to come and accepted it quietly. Maybe they wanted to be done as much as she did, but Lucy hesitated. Was it the right thing to do? Whispers grew in her mind. Dark thoughts festered. Infected ideas leaked from deep within her, suggesting the fate of these toys was a good idea for her too. If she joined them, if she accepted the fall from this bridge, she'd be done with everything: the doll, the journals, these damn toys.

"Wait…" Lucy looked to the doll. "What?"

The doll didn't say anything. It only looked at Lucy with its blank stare from her bike basket.

"Where?" Lucy looked to the trees. They were shaking quietly in the wind. The urge to follow the toys had evaporated and her focus returned. Where she was came back to her. Why she was there resurfaced and smothered thoughts of jumping. She needed to throw the toys over the bridge and be done with them. Joining the toys in their fall quickly fled from Lucy's mind, but she called it back. Examined it with a curious eye toward why she thought it in the first place. She'd never thought of suicide before, but it had slipped in so easily. And again, it seemed the easiest way forward. No need to complete the night. The trees cheered again, waving harder as Lucy turned to them, trying to hear their message clearly.

"Finish this!" the doll called from the edge of the bridge. "We have more work to do."

That snapped Lucy back to the task at hand. The trees weren't waving after all, they simply swayed in the wind. Their cheering was rustling leaves from the wind and no more.

As instructed, Lucy poured the toys from the container into the river. She counted the splashes and dismissed what could have been a thud. Standing in the center of the bridge, it was unlikely that a toy would have hit the shore.

Some of the toys hit the water at the same time. There wasn't a thud, Lucy told herself, and returned to her bike with the container.

"There." Lucy climbed onto her bike. "Now where?"

"Home."

"Yours or mine?" Lucy asked with genuine curiosity. Where would such a thing live between murdering people? The dollhouse flashed in her mind. Now, with some distance, Lucy remembered the mark in the dollhouse basement. A spiral scratched into its floor.

The river's wind returned with a blow that made the trees giggle. A soft, light, playful giggle. Lucy jerked around to see the trees. They swayed in the wind. Inviting her, in their hypnotic motion, back onto the bridge.

"Yours. It is time for the second part of the night." The doll woke Lucy to the moment. There was no giggling, just the wind. No invitations, only the commands of the monster strapped to her bike.

Lucy didn't protest. There was no point. She walked her bike forward to turn around.

The doll shouted, "Stay off the bridge!"

Lucy froze. The doll's voice echoed around her in the night. Instead of pedaling, she drifted back using her feet to walk the bike away from the bridge.

"Sorry," Lucy said, and tried her best to actually sound sorry, but she heard the fear. Immediate, piercing fear. As Lucy pedaled away from Patticon Bridge, hope kindled in her heart as an idea of how to stop this doll started to light up in her mind. Earlier she wondered if these toys could die, and now she had her answer. Only the fear of death would have struck such an immediate and intense shout. Lucy smiled as she pedaled home.

SIX

The doll did not have to threaten Lucy's mom again. What was required of Lucy was restated calmly, clearly, and above all, concisely.

"Find my next owner."

Neil's death wasn't a coincidence or accident or even bad timing. The doll killed him. Lucy didn't ask how, but curiosity came with a shiver. How did the doll do it? The doll could move, Lucy knew that from when it moved from her bike to Neil's back door. She didn't see it move, didn't hear bones creak or plastic click as it moved. How else could it move? Teleportation? Did she jump like a spider? Could she walk like any other toddler? The possibilities coiled in her mind while she searched for a new owner in the only place she knew: the haunted toy collector subreddit.

Nadia found this subreddit when they were trying to understand that toy Lucy got from the yard sale. That toy was still on the kitchen counter. The spaceship imprisoning King Dark. Lucy could see it in the reflection of the window behind the computer monitor. But that wasn't all she could see.

The desk was in the living room and faced out the window, which was great for a daytime view, but now the view wasn't as pleasant. The lights were off in the house, and only the dim glow of the computer screen lit the room. In the window's reflection, the doll silently watched Lucy from the couch. It glared unblinking, unmoving, unwavering. Lucy felt a pulse of heat coming off the doll like a dry summer wind. She thought it was the furnace, but as the stare grew in intensity, so did the heat.

Online, the subreddit was abuzz about @basement_rizer34 who had just passed away, and the news that his collection would be sold at a yard sale. Lucy assumed @basement_rizer34 was Neil. Other collectors were discussing the magnitude of the collection which she'd seen firsthand. There were comments about how everyone wished they could have Neil's collection and what people would do to get some of it. All these users were opportunities for Lucy. She could tell them she had something from Neil's collection and make a trade. Many were local, according to their profiles, but there were also people from around the world.

Lucy jotted down a few names on a notepad beside the computer. @bracker_breaking83 was asking if the others were sure he had died. @my_toyz_slay112 confirmed the yard sale and said he was chased away by some crazy lady with an umbrella. He said the *Death Doll* was at Neil's door before the yard sale opened. @bracker_breaking83 didn't respond.

"I found a few names," Lucy said. The heat from the doll cooled, but it didn't respond.

She clicked on the first interested user, @party_dave_w22, and started a direct message.

"Hey, I have a piece of @basement_rizer34's collection. Got it," Lucy shrugged, "at the yard sale. Interested?" She hovered over the send button. What if he said yes? What if he took the doll and the doll killed him like it killed Neil? If Lucy gave someone a bomb and then walked away, she was still culpable for the explosion, right? Did she survive the monster story if she became the monster?

Trudy's door was open; she was still reading. If Lucy was quiet, she could hear her mom flipping the pages of her latest book. The thought of getting her mom to help flashed through her mind, but was quickly extinguished when Lucy saw the doll staring at her in the window. Her mom would believe her, would help her, but the doll made it clear. This was Lucy's job. No one else. No one else was going to get hurt because of something Lucy did.

She hit send.

"Why me?" Lucy broke the silence between them.

In the window, the doll sat motionless. The night outside carved her features into whispers of form, her face reduced to a ghostly sliver of plastic barely visible in the gloom. Yet, her eyes were a stark contrast, glossy and unnervingly clear. They caught the glimmer of light from the monitor and reflected it back in eyes that should blink, should have some emotion, but were devoid of anything that could be mistaken for life.

"Your friend was too scared when you found me at the house. She would not be up to the task, and I must complete my work."

"You're wrong about her." Lucy bristled. Nadia was made of steel deep inside and she showed it when she protected Lucy. "You could do this on your own. You don't need me."

"You can walk, yet you choose to ride a bike." The doll spoke as if stating fact. "When you see us, we see you."

Lucy paused at that. She had heard something similar, but where?

The memory itched at the base of her spine but couldn't come forward. *When you see them, they see you…*

"Tick tock. Busy busy missy needs to finish," the doll said, and clicked its mouth closed.

Lucy wrote to the next user, then the next, finding each message easier to send. She worked her way through each person who posted interest in Neil's collection, only stopping when she saw a direct message from @bracker_breaking83.

The message was only four words, but those words hitched her breath: "*Did she get him?*"

Lucy turned to the doll. "I've messaged a few people." She swallowed hard to show concern. "Not easy, knowing what you'll do."

The doll's mouth fell open in a quick drop. "You have options."

Lucy cocked her head.

"You can choose not to do this," the doll said. Its mouth didn't move, the words came from the dark hole down her gullet. "I can choose to go up to your mother's room and stick needles in her gums, above her teeth, so the steel digs along the nerve. She'd scream, but she wouldn't fight. She'd be too busy clenching everything in her body from the pain."

Lucy's mind went to her last dentist appointment. She felt a metal prick into her gums. It was a novocaine injection but unlike the real dentist visit, this one was without numbing. The instrument angled and maneuvered, feigning a search for a vein while intentionally digging into bone. Her mind manufactured the feeling, but a very real shudder coursed through her body.

"I do not believe you need such motivation to perform your role."

The doll's mouth closed, having said the final word on the matter.

"I've already sent the messages. No need for all that talk," Lucy said. As a female e-sports streamer, she had heard her share of trash talk from 12-year-old boys who thought stringing swear words together was part art, part dramatic performance. And that's what this was. Trash talk meant to mess with her head. Meant to keep her focus where the doll wanted it.

Lucy returned to the keyboard. "Going to get a few more and see who can meet tonight," she said to stop the conversation with the doll. Lucy clicked on @bracker_breaking83 name, loaded the profile, and sent him a message.

"*What do you know about the doll?*"

The response was instant. "*She is death.*"

"*I have her. How can I stop her?*"

bracker_breaking83 was typing their response when Lucy checked the window to make sure the doll was still on the couch. She was.

A strange compulsion demanded Lucy's attention, and before she knew it, "Do you need anything? Like a drink?" The words felt strange but necessary, even after the threats. Why did Lucy care? This wasn't a friend, wasn't even an invited guest, but the need to be a host was overwhelming. Lucy turned to the doll and waited for a response.

"A light would be nice."

Lucy, still wondering why she'd asked, went to the light switches on the wall and flicked one up. The warm light from the floor lamp behind the couch chased away the darkness. While the doll didn't move, the room felt less tense. Its eyes were still blankly staring toward where Lucy was sitting. Lucy felt relieved, not from the tension, but from being a bad host. Her mom would have offered drinks. She always did, but why?

"Don't like the dark?" Lucy replayed the doll's request in her mind. A haunted doll that doesn't like the dark? She'd never seen that in any horror movie. Then the eye holes in the trash bag made more sense. It wasn't just to see; it was to have something other than dark.

"Don't like what's in it."

Lucy sat back at the desk. There was a link to another Reddit conversation in bracker_breaking83's reply. She clicked on it. The title of the conversation was *Notes on Death Doll.*

"If you need more light, let me know," Lucy said as she read the accounts of people who heard of, encountered, or survived the doll she now knew as Viola. Her name was in the thread.

Many of the commenters told their stories of encountering the doll and losing most of their collection. The stories were very similar to her own: the doll came into their life, usually through a trade, not showing up on their front porch. It demanded they get rid of their collection within twenty-four hours or she'd kill them. There were references to Viola talking about a *sacred mission*, but none questioned her further. For each of the stories, she'd told them to take parts of their collection—never the whole, always select parts—to a body of moving water and dump the objects to be distributed. In all the stories, Viola never went near the water.

Lucy remembered the bridge, the doll's harsh call to stop as she approached the bridge to turn around. The dark wasn't the only thing Viola didn't like. Lucy's inventory of information about the doll was growing. Weaknesses: dark and water. These added to the existing weaknesses of arrogance, assuming Lucy was stupid, and not understanding that curiosity motivated better than fear.

Back in the conversation with bracker_breaking83, Lucy typed, "*Have you ever encountered her?*"

"*Yes.*"

A moment later, another response. "*Neil got her from me. I think he knew what she was when he saw her. He took her so I could live. How did you get her?*"

"*She came to me. I wasn't a collector, but found her in Neil's house after the yard sale. Now I need to do what Neil didn't.*"

"*Did you dispose of his collection?*"

"*Not all of it. Just some. Dumped in the Patticon River.*"

"*Good luck. I'm sorry she's come to you.*"

Lucy nodded as a new message popped up from a different user. Someone was interested in her offer.

"I think we have a buyer," Lucy said. She clicked on the message and saw it was someone local.

But a new idea was forming: if the other haunted toys could be distributed to others in water, could the doll? Was it possible to dump Viola over the bridge like the other toys and be done with her?

Lucy typed a quick reply to the interested buyer. "*Sorry, someone else got it.*" She clicked send. Her eyes jumped from the screen to the doll's reflection in the window. How long was a reasonable time to wait for a response when she knew no response was coming? In the gap, Lucy tried to figure out how to get the doll where she needed to go. Where Lucy could end this night with a clean conscience.

"Really?" Lucy forced disgust into her voice, careful not to push it too hard. "He wants to meet at Patticon Bridge. We just came from there." Lucy scoffed. "He says he can meet tonight, in an hour." Lucy inventoried what she'd need: the weights in her dad's office, the case she took from Neil's house, some rope. "I just need to grab something before we go."

"Why?" Viola asked. She was motionless on the couch. "Can we not leave now?"

"You said we had to trade in cash. I need to get some from my dad's office in case I need to make change." The lie came to Lucy so quickly she smiled at how well it fit both the situation and her conscience. Lying, sneaking out; these things had become easier and easier since she encountered her first haunted toy. Now they felt as natural as being a good host.

"Ready to move on to your next collector?" Lucy asked as the plan to get rid of Viola played in her mind. A simple solution. So why was she the first to think of it?

SEVEN

"I need to stop somewhere before we go," Lucy said. "I need to tell someone where we're going in case this guy is a creeper."

"You do not think I could handle such a person?" Viola asked as she rode in the container from Neil's house. Lucy strapped her into the container, but left the lid off so Viola could see the stars. Heat poured out from her in a constant stream. Lucy wiped the sweat from her brow and saw the first emotion Viola had shown all night: curiosity. The doll's eyes shifted slightly, as if wanting to ask a question but thinking better of it.

"It's a quick stop, and I'm sure you could, but what if something goes wrong?" Lucy pedaled faster toward the hospital. It wasn't too far from Patticon River, but even if it was, Nadia needed to know what was happening. She'd understand after what had happened with King Dark. Going to her mom was too dangerous. Dad was out of town. Who else could she trust? Not that Nadia was in any condition to help; last time Lucy saw her, her entire face was covered in bandages except for one eye and her mouth.

As they passed the hospital, Lucy circled around to the side of the building. Nadia was out of intensive care and was on the first floor. Her room had a window. Streetlights lined the road and spotted the grounds around the hospital. Lucy wasn't trying to hide. Part of her wanted to get caught, questioned, and maybe delay what was going to happen. This stop wasn't only to let Nadia know what was going on, it was to say goodbye. A knot in Lucy's throat told her the journey to stop Viola was a one-way trip.

Peeking in each window, knowing no one would be awake at 3:00am, Lucy searched for Nadia's room. It was hard to tell them apart with the lights out, but the *Get Well Soon* balloon that she brought earlier stood out. It was in the shape of a teddy bear and held a giant red heart. No other rooms had that balloon.

The window was slightly open, but Lucy didn't want to disturb Nadia. She slipped a note under the windowsill. Lucy smiled, whispered, "Thank you," and pedaled on to tonight's final destination: Patticon Bridge.

***

When the note hit the floor, Nadia opened her eye. It didn't focus, but she was getting used to her body not working how she expected it to. Gritting her teeth, she slowly disentangled from the tubes and cords tethering her to the bed. She grunted and got her legs moving, happy to have them back under her control even if they still burned from King Dark's possession. The machines connected to her squeaked as she groaned with each step toward the note.

As Nadia reached for the note, her knees released an arthritic pop. She stopped and held the window to keep from falling. When the pain passed, she sighed and stooped down to get the note again. Her bones felt tight while her skin felt loose. In between, her muscles were quivering jello and nothing worked as easy as it should. Her hands couldn't grab, her legs couldn't hold her, and the air tasted like vinegar. Would her body ever go back to how it was before King Dark took control? She told herself it would, but knew wishing had no place in stories like hers. Fairy tales were for wishes. Nightmares were for brutal reality.

When she finally got to the note, Nadia pulled herself up with the windowsill and staggered back to bed. The small yellow notepad paper was from Lucy. She was going to Patticon Bridge, the haunted bridge. The doll from Neil's followed her home and was making her go there. Nadia didn't like the finality in the note's last words.

I'm sorry I dragged you into this. Tell my mom what happened. I love you guys. —Lucy

Nadia looked at the old lady sitting in the chair across from her. The old lady was another patient at the hospital who kept coming to visit Nadia. She would sit in the chair, chewing her lips with toothless gums, and wait for the nurses to come. They never came for her. Nadia tried talking to her once, but the lady never answered. Others stopped in to see Nadia, they never said anything. Only the old lady stayed. She sat in the chair and waited.

Out the window, Lucy was pedaling away. Outside her hospital room, the nurses were distracted preparing for shift change. Nadia slowly walked to her door. The old lady's lips smacked as she licked them. She nodded. Nadia knew Patticon Bridge, knew the stories, knew Lucy was going to need help.

Nadia made her way towards the window, the rhythmic beep of the monitors accompanying each step. Meanwhile, the old lady rose from her chair with a determined gleam in her eye. She navigated her way into Nadia's bed, drawing the covers up to her chin and nestling into the warmth left behind. Sighing with the delight of rediscovering an old comfort, she watched Nadia disconnect herself from the IV tubes and life-sustaining equipment that had been her constant companions. The old lady watched as Nadia swung her legs over the windowsill, venturing into the unknown beyond.

The machines beeped and screamed. Nurses charged into Nadia's room a moment later, finding it empty.

EIGHT

The ride to Patticon River wasn't long after the hospital, but to Lucy, it seemed forever. She analyzed her plans, trying to see where things could go wrong. Just like in her games, she considered the terrain, the other players, their intentions, their gaming style.

Viola wasn't a murder hobo, someone who just ran around killing everyone. Nor was Viola a glass cannon, someone all attack with no defense. She wasn't a camper or sniper. Viola, Lucy thought, was a tactician like her. And those were the most dangerous players. They observed, they planned, they played the scenarios, just like Lucy was doing now.

"What's your story?" Lucy asked as she huffed along the road to Patticon.

"Why?"

"I don't meet many murderous dolls, and I'm curious about your backstory. I like the backstory stuff in movies."

"Why?"

Lucy paused her pedaling while she considered the question. "I don't know. I guess I just like to know where things came from." The bike slowed and she picked up the pace again.

"Will it ease your mind on what you are about to do?" Viola asked.

"Maybe."

"I keep the doors between worlds closed so things that do not belong do not enter." Viola silently turned her head in a smooth motion. "There are many doors here. I prevent any more from opening."

"And the collectors you're killing are opening doors?"

"I do not kill if they comply," Viola answered quickly. "They choose death over divestment. It is their choice."

Lucy didn't buy that. It was like saying someone held you down and made you do drugs. At the end of the day, we're all responsible for our own choices and actions. Viola could spare their lives, but she chose not to.

As the two left the streetlights for the dirt path and trees outside town, Lucy replayed her plan and searched for holes, counters, and ultimately wondered if Viola had her own plan. Did she trust Lucy? Did she know something was up? In any game there are players, and usually everyone playing knows who else is playing. This was not an online battle royal, it was deadly with no respawns, but it was a game nonetheless. And Lucy was certain her opponent was strategizing as much as she was, if not more.

***

Lucy stopped a few feet from the bridge.

"The man said to meet halfway on the bridge. I know you –"

"No," Viola answered quiet but sharp.

"You want this to happen or not? He said meet on the bridge, and he's going to think something's up if I get too pushy."

Viola was silent, her mouth closed in the container. Heat baked off her in nervous tension. Lucy had left the lid off for the ride, so Viola didn't have any issues with the dark. The plan, discussed with Viola, was to put the lid on after she saw the new collector. But there was no collector, and the lid would have made the container buoyant. Lucy was happy to leave it off; Viola would sink easier that way.

"He was already skittish," Lucy said from the script she'd been practicing in her head. "You want this or not?"

"Stay in the center of the bridge," Viola whispered.

"No problem." Lucy walked her bike onto the bridge and kept to the center. The trees waved and swayed as they did earlier in the night. A cold breeze swept up from the river again, bringing sweet fall smells like cider and s'mores. She checked her phone—it was 4:00 am, no campfires likely at this hour.

"Don't listen to the trees," Viola said.

Lucy didn't realize she was listening to their song until Viola said something. Now she couldn't hear the tune, couldn't remember it. The memory of the song was like grabbing smoke. She knew it was there, knew it was something, telling her to do something, but now she couldn't grasp what. Now there was only the wind in the leaves; a few drifted down to her with a sudden clapping of branches. Cheering was the right word. Encouraging. Singing. Clapping. Dancing. For her.

"Focus on the work to be done." Viola broke Lucy's concentration on the trees.

The bike bounced over the bridge's wooden planks with a rhythmic thudding that could have put Lucy to sleep if she weren't jacked up on adrenaline for what was about to happen.

"I guess I'm just tired," Lucy said, and worried that she might be too tired to do what needed to be done. When was the last time she slept? Would she ever be able to sleep again?

She shook her head, popping her neck, whispering to herself: *Focus.* After a deep breath, she dismounted her bike and walked it the rest of the way to the center of the bridge. This was where she threw the other toys into the river.

Lucy unhooked the container. She slipped on the leather work gloves she brought from her dad's office. "No offense, I'm just not trying to have any more surprises tonight." Lucy flashed a fake smile to Viola. The doll didn't react.

"Is the buyer here?"

"I see headlights," Lucy lied. The container was off her bike and on the bridge now. In her mind, Lucy rehearsed what came next: lift, dump, splash, done. It was hard to focus with the trees, the wind, the constant thrum of energy in her mind.

"Why can't I see the headlights?"

Lucy froze at the question, recovered quickly, and answered, "They're up the road a bit. Coming closer." The time to move was now. Viola was getting suspicious, but her face showed only the emotionless calculation that Lucy had seen all night.

"You don't have to kill him," Lucy said in one last attempt to convince her to stop. One last time for Viola to wave off, to stop Lucy from doing what she was going to do.

"We all have decisions to make. This collector can choose to live. Or choose his collection. I cannot change who I am no more than you can."

Lucy's resolve hardened. "But I can stop myself from becoming a monster." In one smooth motion, she lifted the container and threw the doll off Patticon Bridge. Viola's mouth stayed closed. Her overalls fluttered in the wind as she fell from Lucy's view. The doll, mute and without protest, vanished into the darkness.

Lucy clenched the container, bracing for the splash, the final grim note to seal the night.

But the splash never came.

NINE

Lucy listened. The wind was howling, but the toys from earlier made loud splashes and they were much smaller than Viola. A splash should have been coming, but all Lucy heard was the rustling of bushes under the bridge.

The wind stopped, but the grass kept swishing. An animal was running toward her with an uneven gate. It didn't move with the steps of a deer or a dog coming out of leaves, but a lopsided hobbling.

"Viola?" Lucy asked but knew. No splash. She missed the river just like that one toy earlier.

"You know my name?" Viola's distorted figure lurched toward the bridge. She moved across the ground on all fours like a crab, her stomach curved up toward the sky. Her limbs twisted and bent with too many elbows, propelling her onward and closer to Lucy. Viola's head swiveled atop her neck until it was staring Lucy straight in the face. "What else might you know?" Claw-like plastic hands grasped onto the boards of the bridge, pulling herself toward her prey.

"No one's coming."

"Unfortunate," Viola said. "But perhaps it is best that I deal with you now. I assumed you were an innocent caught in these events as a bird passing through a spider's web." Viola climbed across two boards, quickly closing the distance between her and Lucy's bike. "I see now I was wrong. Blinded by hope in your kind to see you were not the bird, but the spider."

"I won't let you kill someone else." Lucy pulled the weights she brought from her dad's office out of her bike's basket. They were meant for the original toss, but now she was glad she didn't waste them.

"Did he put you up to this?" Viola asked. Seething rage boiled off her like a bonfire.

Lucy shook her head, confused at the question. "Neil?"

Viola squinted. "Who were you talking to in the basement?"

"No one." Lucy stepped back. "Myself." She remembered, but thought of the dollhouse, the voice on the wind saying things, but that wasn't real. Just her imagination. "You have to stop! You can't keep killing people! They can change!"

Viola pointed at Lucy with a quick motion as if swinging something at her, but Lucy felt nothing, saw nothing. The doll, in shock, didn't waste a moment and sprung at her prey. "You cannot stop me from fulfilling my duty." Lucy swung the weights to knock Viola away but missed. The doll's crab body landed on Lucy and pushed her down to the wooden bridge.

Lucy's head bounced off the boards, sending white stars popping in her eyes, but they cleared quickly. Viola's tiny hands pressed into Lucy's windpipe, strangling her without wrapping around her neck. The doll's legs encircled Lucy's torso as it pressed harder into her throat. Lucy swung one of the weights, smashing it into Viola's face, and the doll tumbled off her. A loud crack echoed through the trees as Lucy rolled over and tried to breathe. No air came through her throat, it was too thick for her to draw in. The world spun as she stumbled to the bridge railing.

Viola's body twisted, unwinding from the crab form back into that of a three-foot doll. Her black hair hung in her face, caught in the shards of a cracked cheek and shattered blue eye. The doll floundered like a toddler fumbling through steps. It ran jerky, falling toward Lucy. One fist struck the side of Lucy's knee, the other her ankle. Lucy buckled under the movement and caught herself on the railing before collapsing. A yelp of pain escaped her as Viola struck the same spots on her other leg.

The doll climbed Lucy's jeans and dug a fist into her ribs. The snap echoed into the trees above. A wheezing scream burst out of Lucy as she fell. Viola's arms curled around Lucy's neck and latched again into her windpipe.

Still holding the weight, Lucy swung it into Viola's leg and cracked the plastic knee. The leg snapped inside her overalls and hung limp. Viola's leverage shifted; Lucy took advantage of the moment, slamming her own head into the wooden bridge railing. Viola was between Lucy's head and the rail. Another snap thundered through the trees, but this one was the bridge railing, not Lucy's ribs or neck.

Another plan formed in Lucy's mind. She slammed her head into the railing again, throwing Viola against the wooden rails. Another snap, then a crack; one of the rails splashed into the river below. Lucy couldn't pull in air through her throat anymore, but kept slamming herself into the rails. She tried to scream, but nothing came out as she smashed through the wooden plank railing and dove, holding onto Viola as she went. The doll burned like holding the sun. Angry rage, seething hatred boiled from her and blistered Lucy's hands as they both fell into the river's darkness below.

The freezing water loosened Lucy's throat on impact as she screamed at the millions of needles skewering every nerve ending. Her arms were clenched around Viola, who went limp on impact with the water. The weights in Lucy's hand dragged them both to the river's black depths. This was the center of the river, the deepest part, and the pull of the undertow ripped Lucy downstream quickly.

A cloud of mud billowed up around her. Viola's lifeless eyes were wide, her mouth hung open, as she scraped across the bottom of the river. Lucy pushed one weight into Viola's throat and anchored her to the muddy basin. The other weight was shoved under the overalls. The doll didn't move.

Lucy let go of the weights; at least, she thought she did. Her hands, her whole body, couldn't feel anything. In her mind, she shouted, *Swim!* and hoped her body would know what to do. Her arms were numb, her legs just flopped around out of her control. *Swim!* The current had her, tumbling her through the dark.

SMASH!

She hit a rock. Another cloud burst around her eyes, but she couldn't see through it. The moon was getting closer. Then, bursting through the surface, she gasped for breath. Her throat burned as she sucked in the freezing air.

Swim! And her body responded, taking her to shore past the little picnic area under the bridge. Her fingers couldn't pull her body through the pebbles and mud on the shore, but they found a branch and wrapped onto it. The branch pulled Lucy from the water as she shivered and convulsed. Hot blood was steaming from her forehead and pooling under her face.

Lucy shivered, each nerve trembling with an unexpected chill that seemed to permeate the night. She couldn't recall the air ever feeling this frigid, wondering if perhaps Viola's warmth had masked the true bite of the evening. Now, left alone on the shore, the cold enveloped her, growing more intense by the moment, sending uncontrollable shivers through her body.

"Rough night?"

Then Lucy saw it wasn't a tree she was holding onto. It was a little girl in overalls.

TEN

Lucy couldn't talk. Her throat was swollen shut from the strangulation and drowning. There were a lot of questions in her mind, but they were stomped down by pain, confusion, and shock. She looked to the water, but there was no sign of Viola emerging. The silver moon shined unbroken over the still river.

"Expecting someone?" The girl giggled.

Lucy recoiled at the girl's wet overalls. She tried to scream, but her body tensed and nothing came out. Pushing away, back to the water, the girl reached again for Lucy. Her golden pigtails caught the moonlight in a shimmering halo that danced around her face. When she smiled, her two front teeth were missing, and that's when Lucy relaxed. This wasn't Viola, this was just some kid. Lucy thought of her as *Pigtails* because those long blonde braids wouldn't stop moving around the girl. She was some elementary school kid out way after their bedtime. Pigtails stuck her tongue through the hole in her teeth and Lucy laughed, but again, nothing came out of her throat.

"Come on, let's get you out of that cold water." Pigtails helped Lucy climb out of the mud to the grassy picnic area. Lucy tried to lift herself onto a bench, but her legs wouldn't stop shivering to support her. She sat on the ground and wept gasping, breathless tears as the weight of Sam, Nadia, King Dark, and Viola came crashing over her.

"Now, now," Pigtails said as she sat with Lucy. "Things can get better. Let's go for a little walk and that'll make everything alright." She looped her arm under Lucy's and lifted her to her feet with ease. For a kid, she was incredibly strong and cold. Her touch was colder than the water Lucy just escaped. Where Viola was hot, a heater in this cool night, this girl was an ice box. However they were different in other ways too. Viola was emotionless, this girl was empathetic and kind. One was a ghost, one was alive. One wanted to kill her. The other, to help her.

Lucy took a tentative step while Pigtails held her up. After another step, Lucy's legs were regaining their strength, but she still couldn't feel them.

"See. Here we go."

The tears kept coming, unable to stop now that they had started. Whatever dam that held back the sorrow for her past life, the life before the yard sale, had broken. The old Lucy, the one worried about subscribers and streaming, was dead. These tears were for her. The world was blurry. Moonlight rippled in Lucy's eyes.

"I—" Lucy tried to talk, but her throat cut the words into a strained gasp. "I—"

"No, don't talk. That's not going to help. A walk will help." Pigtails let go, but Lucy's legs held, and she kept walking. "You look like you're real sad."

Lucy nodded. Her feet kept moving up the hill. The grass was slick under her, but she had no problem keeping her balance as she followed Pigtails to the bridge.

"You know," Pigtails bounced up the hill farther, just far enough that Lucy walked faster to keep up. The spritely girl was always a few steps ahead. "You could just stay here. That will make you feel better."

Lucy kept walking but wanted to stop. She wanted to understand what the girl meant. *Rest here a while?* But that wasn't what she said, she said *stay here*. The trees were singing again, clapping at Lucy's arrival as she stepped on the bridge. More questions came to Lucy's mind: *What am I doing? Where am I? Why am I on the bridge?* But her body didn't question, it just walked forward and past her bike on the bridge.

"This is a good place," Pigtails said. "Isn't that right?" She turned to the trees, who cheered and screamed their encouragement for Lucy to walk to the railing, climb up on it, and let the horrors of the last few days go as she plunged into the water. And so Lucy did. The climb was easier than it should have been with a bleeding scalp and exhausted body, but she had no problem following the trees' encouragement. Their directive.

This is a good place to stay, Lucy thought as she closed her eyes and turned her face to the moon.

"Lucy!" Nadia screamed, and ripped Lucy down from the railing.

"How—" Lucy grunted through her strangled throat. She collapsed on the bridge, her body unable to hold her weight. Nadia fell under her.

Pigtails was gone, and the trees only shook in the wind, disappointed, jeering as Lucy looked at them.

Nadia was kneeling beside her, still wearing her hospital gown. The sight reminded Lucy of the last time she saw Sam before he was taken over by King Dark. He made a joke, always joking, and then he was a monster. Bandages covered Nadia's face except for her mouth and one bloodshot eye.

Lucy laid on the bridge boards. She wailed in exhaustion, fear, and the deep need for her nightmares to be over. The trees went silent.

"When you see them, they see you. Remember?" Nadia said as she pulled Lucy into her arms. The connection came to Lucy now. That was in Neil's journal. He talked about seeing ghosts and said it started after he began collecting haunted toys. "This is Suicide Bridge, the haunted bridge. I knew they'd see you." Nadia cried as she squeezed Lucy in her weak grasp. "They see us now."

Off the bridge, Nadia saw a little girl with pigtails. The girl nodded, giggled, and ran off into the night.

"They've been coming to me. In my room," Nadia said.

Lucy shook her head and screamed into the night, but her throat wouldn't let more than a husky siren escape.

"Come on. It's not safe here." Nadia held onto Lucy, trying to pull her up, but Nadia's frail body couldn't manage the strength. She exhausted and collapsed. "We need to go," she panted. "I can't get you up. Need your help." Nadia's heart raced like she had run a marathon when all she did was walk a mile and try to lift her friend. Her transformation left her body weak, but senses sharp to the spirits gathering under the bridge. "They're coming. We have to go."

Lucy crawled to her feet, swayed, steadied, and helped Nadia up. Even with exhausted muscles, Nadia was like lifting paper, and that snapped Lucy back to focus. She had to get Nadia back to the hospital. They left Lucy's bike, unable to pedal it nor able to get Nadia on it. As they walked into the night, Lucy glanced back to the bridge and saw Pigtails waving, inviting her back. Others were joining the girl on the bridge, slowly walking and waving and smiling for Lucy to come again. Nadia pushed her forward. When they stepped off the bridge, everyone was gone.

Both girls held each other up as they stumbled back to the hospital. Lucy needed medical attention, and Nadia needed to get back to her bed. Both of them had deep wounds to heal, only a few of them physical.

Lucy considered Nadia's words earlier, *When you see them, they see you.* This was her life now. The tears continued as she mourned her old life, the normal life she left at the yard sale. Now she was in a new world of monstrous dolls, malicious spirits, and madman collectors. The Lucy that could have been was gone, and now the new Lucy, the one surrounded by the supernatural, was here. How haunted was the world? Was anywhere safe from the things that now saw her?

More tears came because she knew crying was necessary, but other feelings were budding. Deep in her, this new life sparked a smile, not of joy but curiosity. How far did this rabbit hole go, and what would they find in the deepest recesses of this new world? There were others like Neil. Others like Viola and, according to her, things much worse. The pieces were becoming clear, and it was a two-player game. Her and Nadia were in this together, and their only hope was to play.

Her best friend's arms were still loose flesh from King Dark's effects, and the bandages were thick over her face. Neither of them would ever be the same. For Lucy and everyone around her, that yard sale was true to the sign. It was life changing.

ELEVEN

At the hospital, the girls collapsed from exhaustion. Lucy saw the medical staff rush toward her and then fell into the sleep that had been building for days. The world went dark.

She awoke with a warm hand in her own. It was her mom.

"Hi." Lucy's throat only let out a squeak of the word.

Trudy squeezed her hand. "Hi," and she started crying. "Are you okay?"

Lucy shook her head and cried. Her mom hugged her, carefully weaving through the tubes and wires. Everything wanted to come out—the doll, the bridge, the toys—but Lucy just cried and held onto her mom so nothing else could take her away. A moment later, a nurse came in to check Lucy's vitals. Trudy wouldn't let go.

"Is Nadia okay?" Lucy asked through the razor blades of pain in her throat.

Her mom nodded. "She's out of the hospital. Doing a lot better. We were so worried about you! Your dad is on his way home. He's catching flights to get here as soon as possible." More crying, more squeezing.

Mother and daughter remained curled together until the doctor came to see Lucy. He explained that the shock and mental strain Lucy had faced over the past 24 hours manifested in a psychological break, ultimately leading to her and Nadia ending up back at the hospital. Lucy was put on suicide watch after the doctors heard her story when she first arrived.

Lucy didn't protest any of this. It was much easier than the truth. She had awoken the spiritual world to her presence, and now was hunted by ghosts, demons, and monsters. That would be a one-way ticket to institutionalization, and she had other plans. She saw a new world now, and that world had rules. Fortunately for her, Neil was great at documentation, and soon she'd know the rules too.

***

Nadia came to visit the next day. The bandages were off, but she wore a white veil over her face. Nadia's brown flowing hair was replaced by a scraggly blonde wig. Lucy assumed all Nadia's hair had fallen out. She was stick-thin, having lost her curves to whatever Dark did to her body.

"Feeling better?" Nadia asked.

Lucy nodded. "You?"

Nadia shrugged. "I'm not sure how this is going to go." She motioned to her face. "Doctors say they can fix it some." Nadia looked away. "Could be worse."

Lucy knew that meant Sam.

"I'm sorry." Lucy shook her head, "I didn't know—"

"How could you?"

"I brought it to us."

"You couldn't have known. But now you do. And I got the journals from your mom, There's a lot of shit in there, Lucy. This is a very screwed up world."

Lucy reached for Nadia, pulling her face to hers. Nadia jerked away from the touch and looked Lucy in the eyes. Through the veil, Lucy saw one of her eyes was jaundice yellow with a red iris instead of Nadia's golden-brown eyes.

"And it won't leave us alone," Lucy said, but hoped it was more of a question. The bridge wasn't a fluke. She was drawn there. It was the first place she thought of, and she knew the stories. That's why she thought of it. Patticon Bridge—Suicide Bridge—where kids go and sit in their cars with the lights off and listen for the kids who died there. The ghosts had never appeared the many times Sam, Nadia, and she had been there before. But now, things were different.

"Neil talked about someone that might be able to help us." Nadia strained to remember the name through all the data she'd been consuming in those journals. "Sister Wendy. She's someone Neil talked about, but was kind of afraid of. He said she was the one who told him about this world."

Lucy nodded and remembered what Viola asked when they first met. *Are you Wendy?* Perhaps the doll was looking for Sister Wendy too. Another victim? "Then we know where to start," Lucy said.

Both girls looked out the window at the world, their new world. They barely survived the past few days. What hope did they have in this new world without some help? Lucy knew the answer: none.

"I get out tomorrow if everything's good. We'll need to tell my mom what's going on," Lucy said.

"Tell me what?" Trudy came in with flowers and a box of candy.

Nadia glanced at Lucy, and both girls nodded.

"You might want to sit down, Mom."

INVENTORY NOTE: 42

Item: 42

Components:

- The Death Doll, Viola (destroyed)

Collection: Destroyed

I shouldn't be adding entries here, but I feel like Neil would want this recorded. I've taken over his journals, his inventory, and having read these notes, I feel compelled to continue his work.

The doll, Viola, was destroyed. I buried her in the Patticon River.

I think she was trying to do good, but threatening people, killing them, that's not helping. Working with them to make the right choices, understanding them, that's how to show people a different way. Did Viola know what Neil was trying to do? Did she read these journals? Did she know his torment?

My mom took Nadia and I back to Neil's house to get the books he talks about in here. Sister Wendy's journal fills in so many of the blanks of these entries. If we could decipher the diagrams and equations in it, I think we'd have even more answers. I wish I knew where to find her, but there is no mention of that. Neil probably knew someone would find these one day and didn't want the new owner going into that world.

And I don't want to. Nadia and I want to do what Neil couldn't. We want to let this all go. Not leave it, not ignore it, but face it. Help those bound to these toys through what Neil called Resolution. We're going to help break the binding that holds these souls here. And when we're done, we're going to free Neil's brother.

Neil got bad advice. He got caught in this dark place. Dark things love dark places. Viola was right in that respect. Nadia and I are bringing the light. Shining it into those dark places to help anyone lost find their way home.

Drew, Neil's brother, will find his way home. Neil too. I don't believe a man who specialized in existence after death would be gone so easily. The brothers will be together again, Dodslav will be stopped, and at the end, Nadia and I will live our lives with our light.

No toy left behind. No soul left bound.

ONE

Smooth, plastic, dead. Nadia ran her fingers over the mask she'd been given to cover her scars. It wasn't cold or warm, it felt like nothing. And Nadia knew that feeling all too well.

She'd stopped wearing the mask and now wore a veil. The mask got sweaty and it stank to high hell; she knew anyone who didn't shrink from the sight of her would do so from the smell of it. Those foam inserts that were supposed to make her more comfortable were sponges for the oily slick that came out of her face now, not sweat but something thicker. Her doctors said it was from the burns, a type of mucus mixing with sweat, but she knew it was the rancor bile of King Dark flushing out of her system.

Nadia stood in her closet because she couldn't see herself in there. Out in her room was the computer screen, her lamp, the window… She never knew how many reflective surfaces she had. In every one of them, her melted face glared back at her in constant surprise, like maybe this time another face would be there. Her old face. Her pretty face.

Someone knocked at her door. The noise triggered her to pull the veil down. She stepped out of the closet and put the mask on her desk.

"Come in."

Lucy entered. She had changed, too, since that night. Her eyes were darker. She bleached her hair to be almost white, which clashed with her pale complexion. But she was still beautiful, even more so now with the air of mysticism surrounding her. Nadia could feel it. Sometimes she could see it as a greenish miasma drifting around Lucy's slight frame. That was another change since King Dark. Her eye, the one that had turned yellow, could see things that weren't there. She hoped it would fade, but knew, like the other changes to her body, this was forever.

"Hey," Lucy said. Her soft voice invited Nadia to look at her, to come get a hug, but Nadia only looked away. "My mom got some of that mango soda stuff you like. We wanted you to come over and help us go through some of the stuff from Neil's basement."

Nadia nodded. "Thanks, but I have a few things to get done around here." She went to her desk chair, sat, and started her computer.

"I brought a soda." Lucy pulled a bottle of Mellow Mango Sparkle from her jeans pocket. The neon orange glow of the liquid inside shone through Nadia's dark veil. She wondered how the makers of the drink got it so bright without making it radioactive.

"No thanks."

"My mom said I can't come back without you," Lucy said as she plopped down on Nadia's bed and sighed. "Your mom agreed." Lucy popped the soda cap with a fizz. The sweet smell of candied mango burst into the room and made Nadia's nostril flare. Only one could move, the other was too weak from the tissue damage she'd endured while possessed. But the single nostril smell was enough to get her attention. "And your brother's the next one to come in and try to get you out of this room."

Nadia didn't want to see her brother or deal with his irritating persistence in nagging her to leave her room. This room was her hideout. She knew what Lucy was doing, what her mom was trying to do: they wanted to help her get out. To not lock herself away. Jordan, her brother, wouldn't be as easy about things as Lucy. He was worried sick about her. She heard him throwing up last night and asking if Nadia was going to come out. He'd begged her earlier in the day, but if she left, she'd be seen.

Her mask was facing the wall and she reached for it.

"You won't need that. We're not going out. Just to my basement," Lucy said. "If you want it, that's fine, but you're always messing with it, so I figure maybe you don't want it."

Nadia hesitated, wondering if she should bring it anyway just in case her veil blew up or got caught on something. Lucy hadn't seen the real her since that night. She'd only seen bandages and the mask and not the horror show underneath.

"Just in case." Nadia said and picked up the mask.

Lucy held out the soda and offered to exchange it for the mask. Nadia, took the soda as Lucy too the mask. As Lucy walked out of her room, Nadia took a quick sip and straightened her veil before Lucy turned to see if she was following.

The two girls went downstairs and out the back door to Lucy's house. It was the first time Nadia had left her room since she got home from the hospital. That was two weeks ago.

TWO

They went into Lucy's house through the back door and immediately went downstairs. Lucy's mom, Trudy, made sure that the path was clear and without any surprises that might make Nadia feel uncomfortable. While the girls made their way down, Trudy and her husband stayed upstairs and waited for Lucy to close the basement door before they returned to their normal weekend activities.

No one would have ever mistaken Lucy's basement for being well-organized—her dad's collection of old technology junk ensured that—but some tidiness had been brought to one corner. This was the area Trudy set up for Lucy and her to investigate the toy collector's items. Once Trudy found out about what had happened, the *real* story, she insisted they approach this new world thoughtfully and with caution.

Trudy had set up a workshop area for the girls to study the toy collector's journals as well as helped them remove all the old toys from 1211 Gordon Avenue and bring them to their basement. All toys were labeled, contained, and organized. They did not sit out for anyone to touch; they remained in sealed plastic containers, with leather gloves on the work bench for the ladies to handle the toys only when absolutely necessary.

As Lucy and Nadia emerged from the last pile of junk before their work corner, Nadia's eyes fixed on one of the smaller containers. It was labeled *29* and inside the clear plastic, she could see King Dark's Scorpion ship. He was sitting inside the cockpit with his eternal scowl, the same scowl he burned into her face. Within the plastic containers, Nadia could see the thick green vapor that leaked off all these cursed things. It was like toxic gas lingering over these toys, ready to poison any who drew too close.

"I figure we could start learning more about these things from Neil's notes," Lucy said, and pointed to the four notebooks stacked on the workbench. Their red leather binding was brittle and smeared with inky fingerprints. Nadia wondered if those were from Neil or Lucy. When Lucy came over to Nadia's house, these notebooks were all her best friend could talk about. Lucy never wanted to talk about Sam or what happened with King Dark or about the night on Suicide Bridge. Nadia always wanted to talk about it. She needed to understand. She needed to know why she lived, and Sam died. Why Officer Littleton survived, and his scars weren't as bad as hers.

"Okay," Nadia said.

"Here." Lucy handed her one of the notebooks. "We're looking for how to help free the spirits in these things. If you see something, like a story about someone we could help, we'll research it more."

The notebook in Nadia's hands was 11 – 20. Checking her fingers, Nadia was thankful that her hand had returned to normal. King Dark had fused her fingers together in a fleshy claw, but after a few days in the hospital, she was able to rip them apart, and when they healed, the scars between her fingers were barely noticeable.

Both girls read in silence, happy just being together. Nadia kept checking her veil. Lucy did her best to focus on her book and not Nadia's constant preoccupation with the thin black cloth that hung from the headband over her blonde wig.

As she read, Nadia's mind kept drifting to item 29 and wondering if King Dark knew she was near. Could he feel her presence? As she continued to read, another item took her attention, and she found herself no longer staring at item 29 but now, after re-reading the entry three times, staring at a tiny box marked 14. The red ten-sided die inside had the green vapor flowing off it just like the others, but unlike the others, this item didn't have a monster lurking inside…it had a far worse creature: hope.

THREE

Friends fall into three buckets. There are friends who will stop you from doing something crazy. There are friends who will encourage it. And there are friends who will do the crazy thing with you. Lucy was the third kind, and so Nadia didn't tell her what she was thinking. Instead, she patiently waited.

Not long after the idea formed, Nadia committed to her plan. The only question now was when she could act on it.

As if on cue, Lucy closed her book with a pop as she sprung up to her feet. "Gotta pee. Need anything?"

Nadia shook her head.

"Want another soda?"

Nadia's Mellow Mango Sparkle was still full, only a sip taken. There was no way she'd drink it with Lucy sitting right there. What if her veil didn't settle right after the sip, and Lucy saw the real her? The smell was sweet, and the fizzing carbonation called to her, but Nadia knew better than to satisfy that craving.

"No, thank you," she said.

"Okay, well, I'll be right back." Lucy hurried upstairs.

Nadia grabbed the soda and took a deep swig as Lucy's feet hammered up the stairs. She re-read item 14's entry, having stayed on the page for too long now, and looked again to the ten-sided die.

Lucy was walking around upstairs, talking to her mom in muffled voices.

Instead of trying to hear, Nadia went to the container holding item 14 and opened it. The green vapor drifting around the die reached for her, then receded back into the box. The stairs were still empty, voices still talking upstairs. Nadia reached into the box, the green vapor lashing toward her fingers, trying to grab her, but it didn't need to reach. She wanted it more than it wanted her.

Nadia's surroundings transformed into a thick, green fluid, resembling wet paint oozing down a canvas. This emerald cascade gradually unveiled a room bathed in the glow of a solitary light hanging from the ceiling. Its purple bulb cast an eerie luminescence, revealing a table beneath it. At the center of the table stood a meticulously crafted stone castle tower, behind which a teenage boy was seated, seemingly waiting for her. An empty chair beside him invited her to join.

As the green fluid retreated, pooling into mottled globs on the floor, the room's details sharpened into focus. The walls were adorned with a detailed map depicting the labyrinthine paths of a cave, a whimsical poster with a dragon curled around the words *World's Okay-est Dungeon Master*, and a chalkboard. On the chalkboard, four names were neatly listed.

"Come. Sit." The boy gestured to the empty seat across from him. He wore a tight black hoodie with loose jeans. The hood was down, and while the purple light made his face appear sharp and shadowed,

Nadia felt kind eyes in those pools of darkness, and wondered if his hair was blonde or white, but couldn't tell in the intense purple.

Nadia straightened her veil but didn't move.

"No need for that here," the boy said and smiled. His perfect teeth glittered in the light. "I'm not here to judge you."

"You are here for another chance," Nadia said as she approached the table. There was nowhere else to go in the room. No door. No window. The green goop on the floor squelched as she stepped through it.

The boy nodded. "I'm Daryl." He motioned to the chair again. "And I can give you another chance at a moment in your life."

Nadia sat in the open chair. The castle tower in the center of the table had a hole in the top and a door at the bottom facing her. She'd seen things like this when playing Dungeons & Dragons with Sam. The memory pained her.

"I read about you," she said, and put the ten-sided die on the table. "I'm sorry for your loss."

Daryl leaned back in his chair and tilted his head. "I've never heard that before. Most of those who come through here want to get right to business." He watched Nadia smooth her veil again. "Thank you." His lips tightened. "Loss can take more from us than we realize."

Nadia nodded.

"Do you know how this works?" He pointed to the tower.

Nadia shrugged.

"Put the d10, that die, in here." He pointed to the hole in the tower's top. "Whatever comes out is what you roll for your second chance, but you won't see it until you are done."

"Done what?"

"Living the moment. You choose a moment to redo and roll. Your outcome will depend on your roll. Higher the number, better the outcome." Daryl's fingers drummed excitedly on the table. He waved to the tower with an eager smile and an inviting glimmer in his shadowy eyes. "Whenever you're ready."

"But what happens after I put the die in there?"

"You go to the moment. Whatever happens happens, and at the instant before the moment becomes history, you'll come back here to decide to keep that fate, re-roll for another chance, or abandon this place and return to whence you came."

"So, the worst-case scenario is I go back to how things were?" Nadia's voice rose as she asked. This seemed too good to be true. In the end, she could only have a better outcome if she re-rolled enough times.

Daryl nodded. "But you can't know what you rolled until you come back."

"But wait. So, if I change the past, does that create like a splinter in reality or something?" Nadia thought of the sci-fi books she'd read, the time travel movies, and all the stories she'd ever heard about changing the past. Often it led to a mess in the present.

"No. That's all way too complicated. Whatever you decide will be what happened for everyone. You will know there was a change, but only you. The forces that organize reality don't have time or patience for lots of chaos." Daryl snickered a laugh.

She wasn't the first person to ask, but Nadia's imagination caught on the words, *the forces that organize reality.*

"Think of the moment and it will be locked in." Daryl tapped the tower. "Cast your die or abandon before you begin."

The moment when she sprang into action against King Dark in Lucy's kitchen came to her mind. She was in the middle of a panic attack and didn't have her wits. If she rolled better, maybe she could control herself and react to the situation better. Lucy's kitchen appeared clearly in her mind, the mugs on the counter, throwing them at Dark, his stare that devoured her mind, the pain of him melting her face, melting her will to resist becoming a clone of him.

Vomit surged and dribbled out the corner of her mouth. She grabbed her face to hold it in, pressing the black veil into the stream running through the scar rivulets on her face.

"You have it?" Daryl grimaced as if he could see the pain in her mind. "Cast your roll or abandon?"

Nadia placed the die in the tower and let it go. Hollow clacking filled her ears as the green sludge rushed to the purple walls, crashing up like breaking waves. The green overtook the room and painted the world in the shape of Lucy's kitchen. Green faded to the white cabinets and counter tops. Outside, the rain was pouring, with rumbles of thunder and flashes of lightning. Daryl was gone, and Nadia didn't remember anything about the boy, the purple room, or the d10. All she knew was a monster stood across the kitchen island counter. King Dark smiled as Nadia began screaming.

FOUR

Nadia picked up the first mug and threw it at King Dark's melted face, aiming for the pus-yellow bulging eye. Her screaming filled the world around her. Tunnel vision shrank the kitchen to only be that yellow eye. It darted around and locked onto her. Nadia's arm went weak as she released the mug.

The mug flew wide of Dark's yellow eye, but the tea from earlier splashed into his eyes. He winced as the cool liquid dowsed his face. Behind him, the mug hit the window and shattered both the mug and the window. Rain and wind blew in and drenched his back and the floor.

Nadia couldn't stop screaming. Everything was frozen, even her lungs. As the scream lost all her air, it became a high-pitched wheeze.

King Dark snarled and moved around the island to grab her, but slipped on the rain flooding in through the window. His face hit the counter as he lost his footing. Nadia's screaming stopped as Lucy clenched her arm and ripped her toward the back door. Movement came easy to her legs, and escape was clear in her mind as the girls raced out into the back yard.

"We gotta get to the police station!" Lucy screamed as she ran to the gate dividing the back yard and the front.

"That's too far!" Nadia was already winded. She wasn't a runner like Lucy and knew she couldn't make it all the way to the police station at this pace. If they slowed down, King Dark—Sam—would catch them. "We'll call the police from my house!" Nadia pointed to her back door. Their yards were connected, and it was a straight, short run from Lucy's house to Nadia's.

"Okay!" Lucy said.

The two ran to Nadia's house and unlocked the doors with her security app. Once inside, they closed the door and dialed 911 on Lucy's cell phone. Nadia used her phone to turn on the lights in her house, and then texted her mom to come home immediately.

"911, state your emergency," the operator said over speakerphone.

"We need police!" Lucy panted but took deep breaths to try and get control of her panic. "There's been—"

The last word was choked off as Lucy gurgled through a strangled throat. Nadia turned, saw Lucy dangling from King Dark's mangled claw hand. His lips curled in a gnarled smile. Behind him, the front door was open. Nadia's guts sank as she replayed the moment when she unlocked the back door. In her hurry, she hit *unlock all.*

"No!" Nadia screamed and ran at Dark. Her anxiety was crushed under the guilt of making it so easy for him to get inside. "No!" She raised her fist to punch that bloated yellow eye, but he was too fast. He grabbed her, choked her, and stared deep into her mind.

Her skin started to crawl, then itch, then burn as King Dark began the imprinting process. His eye pressed further into her face, igniting the muscles in her cheeks and melting her skin as her own eye ballooned and hardened with pressure, straining to avoid popping.

Then the burning flooded her mind, scorching everything that made her Nadia to make room for King Dark's will. She'd be him.

Lucy was discarded to the ground, the transformation finishing as she screamed in agony.

The walls melted in green goop and Nadia laughed victoriously as her thoughts became King Dark's thoughts.

FIVE

Nadia was still laughing when she lifted her face out of the green goop that pooled around her. She was crumpled on the floor, her veil soaked in whatever was around her.

"Do you wish to re-roll, accept that fate, or abandon?" Daryl asked gently.

Her laugh was choked out in revulsion as she realized why she was laughing. He won. He took her again, and this time he had Lucy too. Nadia realized where she was. No King Dark. No transformation other than what he had already done to her. She climbed to her feet, still quaking from the fear of what had happened. The memory was a raw nerve exposed through a cragged tooth. It vibrated in her mind.

"Re-roll." She choked out the words. The die was at the bottom of the tower, its red form the only thing not purple in this room, a white 5 shown face up. Nadia grabbed her face under the veil, felt the sagging scars from the first time Dark melted her. "Wait…" Her fingers drifted from her cheek to the d10. "Do you know what my original number was? The first time I lived the event?"

Daryl nodded. "But I can't tell you until you abandon the die. And when you do that, you will never be able to use it again. Do you want to abandon now?"

There were worse outcomes than her being scarred. In that fate, King Dark would have conquered the world. And that was a 5 out of 10. What would a two be? A one?

"No." Nadia had a fifty percent chance of a better outcome. She was taking it. "Re-roll." She scooped up the red die and dropped it back into the hole. It clattered down the tower's insides, and again the goop on the floor became Lucy's kitchen, and King Dark was once again smiling at her from across the island.

SIX

Nadia's screams filled the kitchen. The mug from this morning was in her hand before she knew it, but her brain was too tied up panicking and didn't tell her fingers to grip the mug. As she wound back to throw it, the ceramic mug slipped out of her hand and hit the corner behind her. Shards exploded from the cup, and one hit Lucy in the eye. She yelped and grabbed her face.

The shock of the cut snapped Lucy to action. She grabbed Nadia's arm and pulled her to the stairs. Broken mug parts were scattered over the floor of the kitchen and King Dark was barefoot. He could run toward them, but that would slash his feet up. Nadia's body woke up and followed Lucy upstairs to her room.

Lucy shut her door, locked it, and turned to the window. "We can climb out here," she whispered.

Nadia saw the slash under Lucy's eye. It gushed blood as all face wounds did. A few stitches and she'd be fine.

"Sorry I screwed that up down there." Nadia shook her head and went to Lucy's window. Outside, rain and a constant growl of thunder filled the night. When the window opened, the rain didn't come in. Heavy winds drove the rain away from the window.

Lucy opened a long box under the window and pulled out a rope ladder. Her dad had it installed when he went through his big security phase. It was meant for escaping Lucy's second-floor room in case of a fire, but this emergency was a perfect fit. The ladder reached the ground.

BANG!

Lucy's door shook from Dark smashing his claw hand into it.

"You first." Nadia motioned for Lucy to go. Guilt from the mug incident drowned out her anxiety.

BANG!

The door shuddered, hinge screws pulled loose from the door frame. Lucy nodded and climbed out the window. She hurried down. Another smash into the door made splinters burst from the hinges. Nadia saw Lucy's feet hit the ground, heard the splash in the mud, and then climbed onto the ladder. The door exploded inward, sending screws and moulding flying through Lucy's room. Shock at seeing King Dark burst through the door made Nadia's foot slip from the ladder, then her hand, and she fell from the second-floor window onto the ground with a thick *SNAP*.

She screamed. Lucy screamed. Dark laughed as he stuck his melted face out the window and watched their suffering.

"Oh my God!" Lucy clutched her stomach and mouth to hold everything inside. "Your leg!" She ran to Nadia and untangled her foot from the ankle-high iron garden fencing her mom put in last spring. One of the arches caught Nadia's foot and drove through her shin, snapping the bone and leaving a jagged bloody fracture poking through her jeans.

King Dark pushed off the windowsill back into Lucy's house.

"We gotta go!" Lucy unwrapped Nadia's fleshy, worm-like shin from the garden arches and lifted her up in a fireman's carry. Girl Scouts was long ago, but some things never left your head, like how to escape a burning building.

Nadia screamed as she was hefted up, but Lucy stayed focused. She carried Nadia with a strength that surprised both of them.

"Sam's fence," Nadia gasped through the pain. "It's broken." She sucked in a hiss.

"Right." Lucy moved quickly to where her fence met Sam's. She had a privacy fence on Sam's side of the yard, but no fence between her and Nadia's yard. While Sam was the third in their trio of friends, Lucy's dad never liked the idea of a boy having easy access to his daughter's window. Not that it mattered now. Sam was twisted into King Dark by an evil toy. His interests were not of peeking through windows, but of killing worlds.

The two girls slipped around Lucy's privacy fence and over Sam's less secure split-rail fence. With Nadia on her back, Lucy ran to the street. Each bounce was a fresh wave of pain through Nadia.

Sam's back yard wasn't as open as Lucy and Nadia's. His mom was into gardening and had the yard sectioned into different growing areas. Over the past few days, the garden had gone wild, with a few crops rotting. With Sam's disappearance, his parents had no time for maintenance, and with the rot came critters and bugs. Lucy smushed through what might have been a pumpkin, sending a flurry of flies gushing up toward her. Their buzzing and panic fed from her own. Nadia clenched her teeth while she sucked in the wet rainy air to avoid eating any bugs.

The lights were off in Sam's house, but they didn't go inside. Nadia and Lucy both knew where the spare key was, but thought it would be too obvious for King Dark. He'd check there. Instead, they ran to his front yard and looked to the right.

"Police?" Lucy asked.

"Yeah!" Nadia said over the rain's constant drone. But before they could move, headlights lit up the rain around them. Lucy turned to see the car; it was her mom's. "Thank God!" Nadia's pain lapsed for a moment as relief washed over her with the rain.

"Mom!" Lucy ran to the car. It slowed. Stopped. Red brake lights and emergency flashers reflected in the rain as blinding halos.

"Lucy! Nadia!" Trudy screamed. "What's going on?!" She was out of the car now and coming around the front to open the door for them to get in.

"Police station! Please! No time to explain!" Lucy screamed as she carefully leaned Nadia against the car. Pain exploded up Nadia's leg and lingered in her stomach. She thought she was going to puke.

"Get in—" Trudy's chest exploded as a clawed hand burst through her t-shirt. Blood bloomed from the wound and sprayed over Lucy and Nadia in a hot shower. Trudy fell to her knees as King Dark ripped his hand from her back. Lucy screamed and ran for her mom, but Nadia pulled her back and pushed her into the car.

"Drive!" Nadia screamed over Lucy's sobs. "Drive or we all die!"

Inside the car filled with thick green fluid as the purple room returned.

SEVEN

"Re-roll, abandon, or keep this fate?" Daryl asked.

Nadia could feel the warmth of Trudy's blood on her face. She wiped at it, but there was nothing there. Her hands were still shaking, but not from what just happened; from what happened before. From when Dark was scraping out her will. Pain throbbed in her leg where the bone snapped.

"I remember everything from every time?" Nadia asked, still feeling the quivering nausea from when King Dark was turning her.

Daryl nodded. "You can have as many tries as you can take." He pointed to the d10. "Most people consider a high roll enough."

A white 8 stood stark against the purple light. Nadia noticed how deep the grooves that made the eight were, as if chiseled to trap the light in sharp shadows. There were only two options better than that? Better than her leg being broken so badly that it would never work again, and Lucy's mom being killed. Trudy was like a mom to Nadia too, and the expression on her face when she died, the mix of regret and apology that would be stuck on Trudy's face forever with that roll, would break Lucy. Maybe Nadia would avoid the physical scars, but seeing Trudy die would never leave her, and it would ruin Lucy forever.

"Re-roll," Nadia said quietly.

"Before you do, consider the likelihood of rolling higher." Daryl reached for her hand. "I'm not here to torture you. You shouldn't torture yourself. Take the best outcome."

"That wasn't the best outcome. Not for Lucy."

"But she's not rolling. You are."

Nadia dropped the d10 into the tower, heard the clacking, and returned once again to Lucy's kitchen. As the world formed, before she forgot the purple room, she pleaded, "Please God. Give me a ten."

EIGHT

Nadia's screams filled Lucy's kitchen. King Dark smirked his melted smile and stared at Nadia with his pulsing yellow eye. She reached for the mug, but it was gone. Lucy had already picked it up and threw it like a fastball into Dark's eye.

The mug and the eye exploded in a spray of ceramic and black gore. Nadia grabbed the other mug, rushed around the island, and smashed it into his face. Dark stumbled back as Lucy came around, grabbed a cast-iron pan from the stove top—the one her mom made eggs in this morning—and swung for the fences. It landed on his face with a crunch that dropped him to the floor. Lucy took another swing, slashing down on the back of his head as he laid face down on the kitchen floor. Black ichor drooled out from him as his body turned to TV static and flickered out of the kitchen, leaving a pool of blood as evidence of his ever being there.

"Police?" Lucy said.

"I'll call now." Nadia took out her phone and called 911.

Lucy kept the cast-iron skillet at the ready in case Dark returned. Nadia popped two anxiety pills and dry swallowed them as the operator answered.

"911, what is your emergency?"

"We need police and ambulance at…" Nadia continued, telling the operator that they were fine, but someone had attacked them, and they hit the attacker with a skillet. The operator said the police were on their way and an ambulance would be with them. Nadia's phone connection dropped as her battery died.

"Damn!" She held up the phone for Lucy to see. "I didn't charge it last night."

"We can call." Lucy took out her phone, but it was dead too. In the chaos of last night, neither of them charged their phone. "No problem." Lucy went to the landline her dad had installed for emergencies like this, but the cord for the phone was torn apart. She held up the ends for Nadia to see. "Bet Dark did this before we got here."

Lightning flashed and the power blacked out. Thunder roared in trembling waves toward them, shaking Lucy's house.

"Got a power brick?" Nadia asked.

Lucy shook her head.

"I've got a few at my house. Let's get them and we can call 911 back," Nadia said.

The two girls went to Nadia's house and saw a car coming up the street. They couldn't see who it was and thought it best to get in before anything else happened.

Nadia's house was filled with deep shadows. The only light came with lightning, a blinding light that showed nothing but colorful mirages after the flash.

"Up in my room." Nadia kept her hands outstretched and low to avoid tripping over anything. Her mind drifted to all the horror movies she'd watched with Lucy. This was how the girls in those movies got dead. They tripped. They fell. They died. Or they ran into the villain in the dark because they did something stupid like left the door open. But she knew she locked the front door, and the automatic locks default to locked when the power went out. The house was safe.

In Nadia's room, she pulled out a power brick from her desk drawer and plugged it into her phone. The brick's battery was full, and soon her phone was on with her flashlight lighting up her room. Lucy locked the door and the two waited for her phone to have enough charge to make a call.

Downstairs, Nadia heard the front door open. Her mind jumped to King Dark seeing her get the key out of the bird feeder, but the thought was quickly silenced as she heard her mother call out.

"Nadia? You home?" Keys were dropped and more footsteps squeaked in from the rain. "We're home. Jordan did great as the tree. Help him get his costume out of the car." The thought of her mom pinching her brother's cheeks as she shouted up to her made Nadia smile.

In the distance, sirens were getting closer.

"Yeah, Mom!" Nadia shouted, relief and joy dripping from her tone. "We're up here. Be down in a minute."

"What do we tell them?" Lucy asked.

"The truth. I mean, the police are coming, and Officer Littleton already heard some of the story from yesterday. I think we just tell them everything," Nadia said.

Lucy thought about that for a moment.

"On our way down!" Nadia shouted out. Her mom made a noise like she was going to shout up again, but then didn't.

"Okay. I'll follow your lead," Lucy said, and the two, flashlight in hand, went downstairs.

When they got downstairs, Nadia's parents were in the kitchen. She heard them moving around and some glasses clanging together in the sink.

"Hey, Mom," Nadia called as she walked into the kitchen. Her parents were on the floor writhing in pain as King Dark stood over them smiling, his hook hand scratching at the weeping black foam leaking from his yellow eye.

"They're unavailable." He chuckled.

Lucy yelped behind her. Nadia spun as Lucy collapsed. Wet ripping flesh broke through the agonized screams from Nadia's parents. Blood sprayed across Nadia's face. She turned to the source: it was Lucy's throat. Nadia's little brother looked up to her as he ripped Lucy's throat out with his teeth. Blood ran through the scars of Jordan's melted face as his yellow bulging eye locked onto Nadia's stare. She searched for her brother in that eye, but he was gone. All innocence, all kindness, scraped out of him with fleshy claw hands and fire.

Lucy gasped. Tears streamed from her eyes and she reached for Nadia, reached for help, but nothing could be done. The gushing blood was too much. Lucy crumbled to the floor as Jordan took another ripping bite from her neck. He sloshed the meat, making the happy food noise he always made when eating pizza. Nadia's stomach soured as she reached for her brother, for her friend, for anyone to stop this bloodbath.

King Dark chuckled a throaty laugh as Nadia screamed. Jordan echoed the laugh. Two more laughs came from her parents as the surround-sound of madness dug into Nadia's sanity.

Behind her brother, the door was open. Jordan stepped around Lucy, smiling and laughing as he walked closer. Her parents were climbing up off the floor, smiling, laughing. Nadia ran to the door, jumping over Lucy's body as the blood pooled around her. The blank stare in Lucy's open eyes hitched in Nadia's chest as she sprinted into the night toward the police sirens. The red and blue lights were coming around the corner as her family came outside, still laughing with King Dark as he turned to TV static and vanished. Nadia screamed into the storm as she ran from their laughing, melted faces and bulbous yellow eyes.

Green ink swirled up around Nadia. She slammed into a wall in the purple room, bouncing off it and hitting the floor.

NINE

Her throat was raw. Her leg screamed louder than her mouth as it throbbed with pain. Nadia rolled over, crying, choking to breathe, holding her stomach, feeling her face for Trudy's blood or Lucy's blood. Jordan's twisted laughter echoed in her mind.

"Re-roll, accept this fate, or abandon?" Daryl asked, his voice softened by pity.

Nadia didn't answer. She rolled out of the green goop to breathe. It dripped from her face, falling in clumps, silently rejoining the rest of what was on the floor. Nothing would come out of her. The tears were spent. The screams wouldn't break through her raw throat. Everything hurt, from her leg to her face. She could feel her mistakes everywhere.

"Jordan…" she whispered in a raspy stutter. "Lucy…" Nadia stayed on the floor, unable to move.

"You need to decide."

She shook her head. "I can't." Her arms couldn't lift her from the floor. They were still quaking from her first roll. "I… What, what was the number?"

"I can't say. You must see."

Nadia pushed through the green goo with her legs and crawled with her arms like a worm pressing through mud. When she got to the chair, she pulled herself up, grunting to summon the strength to make the climb. Plopping in the chair, she looked to the red d10. The number was a 2. There was a fate worse than this one. She couldn't imagine it. Her whole family. Lucy. All taken. Sam was dead. And everyone else. What could be worse?

She panted, the thought of another roll squeezing breath from her. Nadia shook her head. "Abandon." Tears flowed through her scars, and she pushed the veil to the side with her sleeve to mop them away. "Abandon."

"All of this will always be with you," Daryl said. "It is payment for the chance to change."

Nadia nodded silently.

"Before I send you back, can I ask you something?" Daryl said. He leaned into the light, but shadows still carved out his features, leaving him eyeless.

Nadia nodded again.

"You knew my story?" he asked. "Do you know theirs?" Daryl pointed to the list of names on the wall. "Did they…did they make it?"

Nadia looked to the list of names: Nathan, Emily, Carole, Lester. She didn't recognize them, but assumed they were the people mentioned in the inventory note.

"I don't know. But I will find out," Nadia said. She was unsure how she'd tell Daryl what she found since the die would never work for her again, but she'd find a way. "I'll find out." The words quivered in her throat as the memories of the other rolls fought in her mind. Each one wanted to be the one truth, but Nadia knew they weren't the truth. She knew the truth.

Daryl nodded and smiled. "I'm sure you will. May your future rolls be high, round, and happy."

"Wait." Nadia put her hand up. "What was my original roll?" She straightened her veil but felt the uneven flesh underneath. She knew the scars could be much worse, and now she bore them too, but at least she bore them alone.

"Nine," Daryl said.

The green ink flew up around Nadia and returned her to Lucy's basement. Footsteps were hurrying downstairs.

"I brought you a refill," Lucy said and froze as she saw Nadia holding the d10 out of the box.

"I'm okay," Nadia said. "But I had to know."

"Did it work?" Lucy brought her the drink.

Nadia took the chilled bottle of Mellow Mango Sparkle and took a long drink. "Not how I thought. But now it will never work for me again. So I'm immune to it, I guess."

"My mom's going to be pissed," Lucy said and shook her head.

"Is she in the kitchen?" Nadia asked.

Lucy nodded.

"Can I see her?"

"If you want."

Nadia ran upstairs and saw Trudy washing dishes. Without a word, Nadia raced to her and wrapped her in a rib-crushing hug. Trudy wasted no time in returning the intense hug, adding tears to the mix.

"I'm not sure what this is for, but I'll take it," Trudy said. She waved for Lucy to join them. She did. The three stood in the kitchen hugging until Nadia let go. She wiped her face, still feeling Trudy's blood where her kiss had just been.

Nadia held onto Lucy a moment longer, tucking her veiled face into Lucy's neck. "I—" Nadia couldn't finish and held her friend, feeling that she was safe, she was still alive.

"What happened?" Lucy squeezed Nadia.

Nadia sighed, let go of Lucy, and told them both what happened.

TEN

"You know the rules, Nadia," Trudy said, keeping her disappointment as suppressed as possible. "No using these things unless we're all together."

"I know. I'm sorry. I just had to try." Nadia twirled her soda and took another sip. She straightened her veil after, but only brushed it down once.

"Well, I see why Neil had this." Lucy pointed to the d10 that sat on the kitchen island between the three of them. "It's a do-over. And if you can stomach it, you could do over forever until you get the 10." She shook her head, remembering Nadia's experience. She wondered who could tolerate that torment. After reading Neil's journals, she thought of one person who would have suffered for so long, more suffering wouldn't have mattered.

Nadia picked up the die. Trudy winced, then let out a gasp.

"I think we need to find the people Daryl asked about. I think that's how we free Daryl and cause Resolution for this thing." She twirled the die in her fingers.

"Do you want to do that?" Trudy spoke up. "I mean, not to be rude, but this could be really useful. If things ever go sideways, we could use this to fix things."

Lucy nodded. "Yeah, it could."

"Sorry I wasted it." Nadia shook her head.

"You didn't waste it. You know a lot more now than what was in Neil's notes. And we know how powerful this one can be. We should put it somewhere special," Trudy said and rubbed Nadia's shoulder.

After a bit more talk, Nadia returned Item 14 to its box and sealed it again. The green vapor in the container flowed around it after she put it down.

"I'll find them, Daryl." Nadia grabbed her soda and went upstairs to finish it with Lucy.

Jordan was waiting upstairs when she returned to the kitchen. Seeing him made her smile and she took another sip of her soda. After lowering the soda, she didn't straighten her veil and Jordan glimpsed the smile underneath. He smiled back and reached for her hand. She took his and they went home.

INVENTORY NOTE: 14

Item Number: 14

Components:

- d10 made of resin

Collection: Private

This item was obtained in a trade with a man in Minnesota named @doorsdad821. He claimed this ten-sided die was haunted by the spirit of a former Dungeon Master who tried to save his party from a demonic force. The game took on a very real quality for this group and led to the death of the game master.

The players were released from suspicion that they murdered the boy, but the community never really let it go. This was another case of "games are bad because they are evil," but no game is necessary for people to do bad things. We don't need excuses. Just look at us. We, humans, do horrible things on the daily without remorse or even noticing. A game doesn't make us worse.

I can feel the energy of this d10. It is powerful. Perhaps this is the thing that makes Dodslav return?

According to the seller, this die allows the user to redo a moment in time. The seller said he had used it and could confirm that was indeed what it did, but the use was a horrible experience that he'd never recommend anyone suffer. Happily, I informed him that I never use the toys, and he assured me that I would be tempted one day.

After hearing the origin story, I checked in on the kids that were accused of the game master's death. They are all still alive and well as of this writing, but haunted by the events of that night. The police report cited the kids used hallucinogenic drugs and imagined the whole thing, but according to their independent reports, a monster came for them. The game master made a deal with the monster to save the friends, which led to his spirit being bound to this die. The kids stole the die and ran before the demon could claim it. I wonder what Sister Wendy would make of this?

This item is going in my private collection. There's a possibility that Dodslav goes back on our deal. In that case, I am building an arsenal to take my brother back. This redo ability could be a very handy tool in such an encounter.

Perhaps I could sell it one day. Who wouldn't pay top dollar for the chance to relive a critical moment of their life? But for now, I'll keep it in case the deal doesn't proceed as expected.

EPILOGUE

This was the final load from Neil's house. No one questioned Trudy or the girls as they loaded boxes of toys from the basement. Not that anyone was watching. Trudy expected the neighbor to ask questions, or at the very least come to see what was going on. She didn't. The old lady kept to her garden, smiling as she worked on a new lattice fence. From inside the house, the neighbor's husband was watching his wife but paid no mind to Trudy. His eyes were wide, sweat glistening on his wrinkled forehead as he twisted the curtains in his fingers. They didn't care about what was happening next door.

"Is that the last one?" Trudy asked Lucy as they passed in the kitchen. Lucy was taking out a long thin box. Nadia was organizing the car's trunk to ensure the last toys didn't slide around. They knew none of these could spill open. Who knew what that would unleash. But Trudy knew who knew: that guy Neil. Now her little girl, Lucy, knew. Her little girl dealing with possessed toys filled with malice and evil.

"Yeah, but there's something else." Lucy put her box on the floor. She motioned for her mom to follow as she went back down the metal basement stairs.

Trudy followed. The silence of the stairs brought her arm hairs to attention. She wasn't an interior designer or construction pro, but she knew the stairs should make some kind of noise. Who works to make silent stairs? People who collect secrets in their basement. They don't want anyone to hear them coming, maybe they don't want to hear themselves going to their place of shame. But this wasn't a place of shame. It was a trophy room.

Her daughter was wrapped up in these secrets now. Trudy's stomach clenched at the thought. Lucy was tangled up in this creeper Neil's mess. And what was a mess across town was soon to be a mess in her basement. It was coming to their house, her house. These shelves were empty now. Her basement would be full after this last load. Every toy was already at her house or in Trudy's car.

At the bottom stair, Trudy heard the sweetest voice carried on the wind say, *Hello*. She took a step back up the stairs. *Come see me.* The sweet tone was like sugared orange peel, sweet and delicious but with a sharp aftertaste. It lingered in her mind and soured, decayed into bitter, thick sludge. Her stomach locked up as she raised her hand to hold her lunch in her mouth.

"Lucy." Trudy waved for her little girl to come to her, but she didn't. Why didn't she? Why didn't Lucy get sick at the voice?

"No, Mom, it's okay." Lucy went to the dollhouse on the table.

Trudy gasped as her daughter got closer to the last toy in the basement. Its second floor sagged in a leering smile. The windows bulged and drooped from water damage like a cluster of insectoid eyes. A frigid breath came from the dollhouse in slow pulses, carrying with it the stink of spoiled meat and burnt books. It brought her back to the library fire years ago, where she stood and watched the fire, hoping it didn't spread into the town, to her house, to her family.

"Do not touch that." Trudy ran to her daughter, making herself a firewall between the dollhouse and Lucy.

"What do you think's the deal with this one?" Lucy pointed to the spiral burnt into the dollhouse's basement floor. "It's not in the inventory. The inventory starts at two." Lucy searched around the house, keeping her distance. "Are you number one?" she asked the house.

"Do not answer her!" Trudy shouted at the house. "Don't you dare talk to her!" The anger burst out of her with clenched fists and red face.

The dollhouse was silent.

"Maybe we should have Nadia look at this?" Lucy suggested and held her mom's arm. "You know, with her…new…" Lucy stopped there. The words *new eye* just felt weird, and Nadia hated it. Hated how it looked, how it felt, and what it saw.

Trudy didn't hear any of that. She was panting, staring at the house, wanting to smash it for ever looking at her daughter, for ever talking to her daughter. She knew it did. Why else would Lucy have talked to it? This thing was whispering to her little girl. Who knew what it was saying, what it was promising!

"We're not taking this one!" Trudy's eyes darted around the basement for a hammer, for anything she could use to smash this house. Her hands shook, vibrating from the urge to end this last toy, the toy that went too far.

"No!" Lucy shouted. "It has answers."

"How do you know?" Trudy went back to the stairs. She saw a hammer in the workshop upstairs. She would smash the dollhouse and leave it in the rubble. None of the other toys talked to her. None of them had such sweet voices that cooed and whispered into her mind like this house.

"While I was moving the toys, it told me." Lucy turned away from the dollhouse.

Trudy stomped up the stairs. Lucy followed.

"No! Mom! Don't!" Then Lucy shouted back down the stairs, "I'll stop her. Don't worry."

As Trudy came out of the basement, Nadia was standing in the living room. The midday sun cast her in shadow. She didn't move as Trudy turned into the workroom. Neither Trudy nor Lucy thought anything of the shadow being taller than Nadia and wearing a large cloak instead of the jeans and sweater she wore earlier.

"No!" Lucy followed Trudy into the workroom. "It has the answers we need, Mom!"

Nadia's shadow passed by the workshop door.

Trudy found the hammer she needed. Heavy. Big. Smashy. "Lucy, it isn't giving you answers. Things like that aren't here to help you."

"What's going on?" Nadia hurried into the workshop. Her veil floated from her face and she pulled it down quickly. "I heard you guys outside."

"Mom's trying to destroy the dollhouse," Lucy said as she reached for the hammer. Trudy pulled it away.

"Wait?" Trudy remembered the shadow passing the workshop door. The shadow in the living room. "You weren't in the living room?" Trudy clenched the hammer tighter.

Nadia shook her head. "I was outside. Ran in when I heard you two fighting."

Trudy pushed past both girls. The only place the shadow could have gone was downstairs. "Go to the car!" she shouted as she silently stomped down the steel stairs. Neither girl listened, and instead followed her down.

A black-robed figure was standing at the dollhouse. Trudy thought she heard quiet talking, a woman's voice. The sounds were too low to distinguish words, but the hiss of anger was clear.

"Who are you?!" Trudy raised the hammer.

The woman turned and faced Trudy. When their eyes met, the hammer slowly came down from the weight of the woman's presence. Stern eyes disarmed Trudy and made the girls on the stairs hold each other so they weren't blown down. The woman's long white hair spilled out of her nun's habit with wisps of bangs stuck to her sweaty forehead. She held up an ancient hand to match her ancient face. The other hand stayed down, holding her sleeve as if hiding something.

"Who are you?" the woman demanded. She stepped to the side and pivoted to face both the dollhouse and Trudy.

Trudy regained her wits and raised the hammer again. "What are you doing here?!" Her voice cracked under the woman's glare.

The woman's eyes traced the empty shelves. "Are you here to destroy or pillage?"

Trudy waved the hammer as if to say, *What do you think?*

"Then we are at common purpose." The woman put her hand down and released her sleeve. "Join us, children."

"Stay up there." Trudy stepped closer to the woman, her hand visibly shaking, but the woman's face softened.

She bowed her head. "The bravery of mothers is often overlooked." She smiled, but it didn't warm any of them. "I am Sister Wendy of the Sylvan Order. And I am here to ensure the disposal of this." She motioned to the dollhouse. "A hammer will do no good. It must be purged—"

"Resolution?" Lucy interrupted.

Sister Wendy slowly nodded.

"Are you the same Sister Wendy from the journal?" Lucy asked, thinking about the old black journal found with the inventory notebooks.

Sister Wendy nodded again, slower.

"I would ask for a moment alone with this item before we take it from here." Sister Wendy motioned to the dollhouse.

"What's this *we*?" Trudy shook her head.

"It doesn't leave without me." Sister Wendy's glare returned, intensified, and threw Trudy into quaking tremors as her will crumbled under the woman's intensity.

"It's okay," Nadia said from behind Lucy. "It's okay, Mrs.Nelson." Nadia went downstairs and touched Trudy's arm. The touch softened the fierce momma bear. "Let's just give her a moment and we'll regroup upstairs."

"Yeah, Mom. Let's." Lucy looked at the dollhouse. Sister Wendy gave it a leisurely glance and then met Lucy's eyes. "Let's let her have a moment."

Both girls pulled on Trudy's arm to come upstairs. She relented and went with them.

Downstairs they could almost hear the old lady whispering, but Nadia pulled them away from the doorframe.

"Did you look at the house?" Lucy asked Nadia. She kept her eyes off Nadia as she asked and hoped it didn't come off too direct.

"Forget the house, that lady isn't like us." Nadia shook her head and motioned for Trudy and Lucy to follow her into the living room. "There's something wrong with her. Like an infection." Nadia searched for the right explanation, juggling the words as she always did. "She looked like one of the toys was in her arm. Like a rubber snake or something, wrapped around her forearm."

"Good guy or bad guy?" Trudy asked the only question she cared about at the moment. Would Sister Wendy help them or hurt them? And there was no way she was going to hurt her girls after what they'd all been through. Trudy tapped the hammer head in the palm of her hand, feeling the weight and having the certainty it would smash an old lady's skull. She'd never thought about it before, but now that she did, she had no question.

"I think she thinks she's a good guy," Nadia said. "She's not coming off like the toys. Or that house." Nadia shivered. "Or…" Her voice dropped off as she went down the hallway. Trudy assumed the door at the end led to the garage, but Nadia stopped at a small table.

She picked up a white box the size of her fist and held it for a moment.

"What's that?" Lucy whispered.

Nadia sucked in a sharp breath. Her body reeled from the box and it fell to the floor with a dead *thud*. No bounce. No tumble. It dropped and didn't move. Nadia's chest was heaving, her hands flapping to get the feeling off her.

"What's wrong?" Trudy hurried to her and held her arms out to hug Nadia. Trudy knew not to initiate a hug when Nadia was having a panic attack, and that's what this looked like. Nadia threw herself into Trudy's arms.

"It's horrible." Nadia didn't look at the box. "It's horrible." She tried to catch her breath, motioned to the box. "Hide that before Wendy gets up here," she whispered.

Lucy grabbed the box and ran it out to their car.

"What is it?" Trudy asked.

Nadia shook her head, trying to loosen what she saw from her mind's eye. But it wouldn't leave. "We can't hide that one. They'll be looking for it."

"Who?" Wendy asked as she came out of the hallway. Trudy startled and gently shifted Nadia behind her. Over Wendy's shoulder was a black sack bulging like Krampus carrying children. Trudy knew it was the dollhouse wrapped in the tablecloth.

"No one," Trudy answered.

Sister Wendy stared at Nadia, but the girl didn't meet her gaze. "We should get home before dark."

Lucy came back in across the living room. She saw the sack over Wendy's shoulder and let out a relieved sigh.

"We are." Trudy motioned to Lucy, Nadia, and herself. "I don't know where you're going, and I don't care."

"We're sticking together," Wendy said and walked toward the kitchen door where Lucy was standing. "Until I see your intentions are true, I am not leaving you."

Trudy wanted to object but knew it wouldn't change anything. When she agreed to help the girls navigate this world, she knew it would come with dangerous people, dangerous things, haunted places. She didn't want Wendy around Lucy or Nadia, but from what Lucy told her about Sister Wendy's journal, perhaps this woman had answers that could make this all end sooner.

"Then let's get going." Trudy motioned for Wendy to lead. "That goes in the trunk, and if you don't act right, so do you."

"I have a companion who will be joining us," Wendy said as she brushed by Lucy with the black tablecloth.

"You never said anything about that," Trudy shouted as she gathered with Lucy and Nadia in the kitchen hallway. A bright pink scooter beeped cheery and loud outside as Wendy walked around the house.

Trudy followed her out and saw a spritely young woman wearing a leather jacket, jeans, and long curly black hair under a helmet. Her scooter was a two-seater with a second helmet on the other seat.

The young woman waved eagerly to Sister Wendy and shouted in a high-pitched cheerleader squeal, "Hi, Sister! You found them? That's so great. Are they joining us for dinner?"

Sister Wendy sagged at the sight of the sunny woman, which made Trudy smile. "Who's that?"

"My acolyte." Wendy rolled her eyes and took her sack to the scooter. "We'll follow you."

"Why don't they join us for dinner? I made that new birria beef stew recipe." The woman on the scooter beamed. She was a real-life Barbie doll with the eagerness to have a party burning from every inch of her bright smile.

"No." Wendy handed her acolyte the sack. "Follow them."

"I'll follow you," the young woman said to Trudy, and gave her a bright, gleaming smile.

"She should have sent that one in," Trudy said.

Lucy chuckled.

"That one's like you guys. She's a good guy." Nadia smiled at the woman's bright aura.

Trudy, Lucy, and Nadia got into the car. Lucy sat in the back seat. She turned to look out the window as they drove back home. Her eyes never left the dollhouse as it whispered to her, telling her tales of how the toys were more than haunted things, they were batteries. With enough power, they could open doors that could help Nadia go back to how she was before King Dark. That power could bring Sam back like nothing ever happened. It could restore her life and close the door to this life forever.

All she needed was a few more toys. A few more batteries. And the dollhouse would show her how to open the passage back to her old life. To a future she couldn't imagine.

THE END

AUTHOR'S NOTE

I hope you enjoyed Passages.

The title for this book came before all the stories were completed. This was the first time I completed a book two for any of my series (many were started). And while I didn't know exactly what would come out in this book, a theme quickly emerged.

Everyone here is opening doors and many of the characters are walking through. Not all of those doors go to good places. We'll see these characters again soon, but for now we're leaving Lucy, Trudy, and Nadia with Sister Wendy. If you read Neil's notes in *Life Changing Yard Sale* or you've read *Early Birds Pay Double,* you know Sister Wendy isn't the safest person to be left with, but they will have to make do.

In the next book, *Origins*, we're stepping back to where it all began. The doll house, the demon, Neil, Ely Adams, Viola, will all be back. We'll discover the origins of these characters, and even, the Lazarus Spiral itself. From there, I think we have two, maybe three, more books in the series main story line. Don't hold me to that. You never know where a story will take you and I cannot say that I've always had a handle on this tale. The fact it became a series was never part of the plan. Turns out the stories from *Life Changing Yard Sale* kept coming and as they did, more books appeared. With that said, I want to make sure we have a complete arc for the characters and the toys.

While there are 42 toys in the collection (43 if you read carefully), we will not see the stories of all 42 in the Lazarus Spiral series. There are other stories outside of the series that are starting to build up like *Early Birds Pay Double*, *16*, and *Inflection* (working title). As we continue into the spiral, more stories outside of the series will come along. I'm enjoying this world too much to let it go anytime soon.

But *Passages* doesn't just connect to *Life Changing Yard Sale*. Long term readers will recognize the world William visits from *Library of Lessons & Lies*, as well as some of the book titles in Ely Adams' study. I don't try to connect the stories, it just kind of happens but I love what I'm building. Perhaps it is from growing up reading Marvel comics where all worlds connected, all tales crossed over into the lives of other heroes and villains, but my stories seem to take on this interconnected life as well. One day I'll (maybe) produce the ultimate reading guide showing all the intersections, an annotated encyclopedia of all my tales but for now, I hope you enjoy the easter eggs.

These haunted toys have taken on an important role in my life now with no signs of letting go. In this manner, I understand Neil's obsession. Hopefully, I do not succumb to the same demons as he when it is time to part ways. But we have a long time before then, and until a haunted doll tells me otherwise, I'll keep going here.

See you in *Origins*.

Tim

2/14/2024

NEWSLETTER SIGNUP

Don't miss a turn in the Lazarus Spiral! Signup for my newsletter to get the free novella, *Early Birds Pay Double* and meet Sister Wendy, the Preacher, and the Death Doll, the night before the yard sale. Discover who else comes to Neil's house and how they fuel the murderous monster growing within Neil's neighbor, Mrs. Annabelle Morton.

Signup for the newsletter now to discover more in the Lazarus Spiral:

https://timkulp.com/newsletter-signup

LAZARUS SPIRAL BOOKS

16

Early Birds Pay Double

Life Changing Yard Sale: Lazarus Spiral Book I

Passages: Lazarus Spiral Book II

Origins: Lazarus Spiral Book III

OTHER BOOKS BY T. KULP

BLOTS

[dis]connection

Library of Lessons & Lies

Shadows, Stains, & Secrets

BY TIM'S PEN NAME CY BORGMYN

Trial of Mirror Mountain

Treasure of Crumbling Cavern

The Light of Enki

Monsters Dance to Twilight

LEAVE A REVIEW

I hope you enjoyed Passages. It would really mean a lot to me if you left a review on the store where you purchased this book. Honest reviews welcome (even if you didn't like the book). Reviews help other readers know if this book is for them.

Who do you think would enjoy this book? Let people know in your review.

Thank you!

Tim

www.ingramcontent.com/pod-product-compliance
Lightning Source LLC
Chambersburg PA
CBHW050757190726
48285CB00005B/1699